Between the Shadow and Lo

West Coast Trilogy: Book 1

Lauren Sapala

LOST
LETTERS
PRESS

Cover design by John Price.

Books by Lauren Sapala

Fiction

(West Coast Trilogy)

Between the Shadow and Lo

West Is San Francisco

Enormous Forces

Nonfiction

The INFJ Writer

Firefly Magic

The INFJ Revolution

For my Uncle John,
who taught me that the only way out is through.

Part One

September 2000 to August 2003

The mystic Gurdjieff says that we are not one, but many people inside. There is the part dressed in tattered rags. There is the glorious, robed one inside. There is the madman. Maybe, that's what hurt does. It cuts us into different people. There are some parts with their gaping holes that break off from the core, and then they roam inside us, reminding us of our own poverty.

—Ritu Kaushal, *Walking through Transitions*

Worse than not realizing the dreams of your youth, would be to have been young and never dreamed at all.

—Jean Genet

Chapter 1

I let Lo in because I thought she loved me.

Isn't that why you let each of them in sooner or later? Even if it's only a voice in your head?

I thought I was the only one she could love, because I guaranteed her existence. It was, after all, my head. So we had to trust each other. I trusted Lo to protect me from the world and she trusted me to handle the everyday stuff. Paying the bills, making sure we ate regular meals, and running every single day, even in the rain. But Lo didn't show up until the spring of 2001, and even though it didn't seem important at the time I know now that it's essential to tell what came before that.

I graduated from college in May of the year 2000. Three months later, in August, I moved to Seattle with two friends, Tom and Bret. Tom was eight years older than me and an ex-Marine. He lived in a falling-down house with a bunch of other guys not far from campus, and in the last year I had been there frequently for the parties and become close friends with him. Bret was a girl I met my sophomore year when I was still living in the dorms. I didn't know her that well but I needed a third person to help balance out the crazy idea of Tom and I picking up everything in Michigan and moving all the way out to Seattle, a city none of us had ever been to before, and where we knew only one guy, Jared. And looking back, I can see now that Tom and I knew even then that Jared couldn't really be counted on.

Right before we left Ann Arbor Tom helped me put on a big garage sale. We mostly just dumped everything on the front lawn of the house I shared with three roommates. The rest of the afternoon we watched people pick over the things my mom had left behind when she died and my dad had left behind when he moved away from us before she died. It made me feel more like an orphan than ever. When it was over we heaved all the leftovers into the dumpster in back.

Jared was Tom's best friend. He had graduated the year before me and promptly moved back to Seattle, where he was originally from. Tom worshipped him in that way that men do when they find another man who they wish could have been their brother in this life. Me, I was just in love with him. When I called Jared drunk in the middle of the night I had no idea if he was also drunk, or in love with me too. One of Jared's most distinctive traits was a vagueness that infused everything he said or did. Across 2,000 miles of telephone wire his intentions spread into a thin milky smoke that lazily dissolved into promises that might have been misunderstood, or never made in the first place.

After our friends helped the three of us load our stuff into the big rented U-Haul we posed for one last picture, me and Tom and Bret, standing in one lonely clump in front of the truck. The sun is in Tom's face, making him sort of glare into the camera, but Bret and I look all right, we look happy. I can't even remember the picture being taken. I don't remember being happy.

We drove to Seattle straight through, only stopping for gas, and also at one desolate rest stop in Idaho to call Jared from a pay phone, letting him know we would be there soon. He had promised us we could crash at his place for a few days, until the apartment we had found online was ready for us. Both Tom and I were nervous. Tom with little-boy expectancy of seeing his long-lost best friend again, me with a sickening tightness in my gut warning that even though I was crazy in love with Jared that was no guarantee that he was crazy in love with me.

I thought about him every hour of the drive, saw his face at every mile marker we passed, even though Jared wasn't the kind of guy people ever turned their heads to get a second look at. He was semi-tall, semi-skinny. Fine, light brown hair, sometimes scruffy, sometimes slicked back with a few drops of water. Blue eyes. Pretty non-descript.

But Jared had something in him that drew attention, something that sparked and caught fire and finally promised things, so many things, without him saying a word. He played the piano and harmonica, and sometimes the drums, but his one true love was guitar. He slouched over everything like it was an instrument. Shoulders hunched forward, Jack Nicholson eyebrows arched up, he slouched over coffee tables and kitchen tables and pool tables, keyboards and steering wheels and bars. He slouched over life. After a year without him now, I could only pray his shadow would again fall over me.

Along with the slouch came the smirk. Jared always looked up from under his eyebrows at me and Tom with that smirk, saying *whatever* to everything and anything asked of him. The slouch and the smirk turned him into someone else, someone like Mick Jagger or Bob Dylan. His eyes held the long dark bulging-crotch nights of rock stars. When I caught a glance of him fast and then looked away, the negative imprint of film left behind my eyes was of a man onstage.

Sometimes he wore loud sportswriter shirts and hats like Hunter S. Thompson, with sunglasses to match. The look was perfect, he *was* the part. Cynical and sardonic, the slouch and the smirk shone through. It always made him into someone else, and never was he more himself.

I had met him one night by accident, in the bathroom of a college party. We locked the door for privacy and talked about Irish horse thieves, trading bottles of beer and laughing at all the people outside trying to get in. I knew I loved him immediately. I'd tried everything to be near him since. It was simple, and brutal. I loved him more than anything, and so I would *do* anything. Anything to be near him. Anything at all.

When Bret and Tom and I got to Seattle we spent a few days at Jared's place, and a few nights at the bar with him where he introduced us to his small circle of friends, a guy named Daniel and two girls, Kim and Jana. Then we moved into our apartment just north of Seattle. A week or two later Tom got a job throwing freight at a nearby grocery store and I got a job waitressing. Bret found a position clerking at a drugstore. Soon we settled into a routine. Tom worked the graveyard shift, and Bret and I worked during the day. In the evenings we went to the bar with Jared and his friends.

Jared and I had an easy understanding wrapped up in a strait-jacket of tortuous difficulty. Both of us were alcoholics, that was the easy part. Whenever we saw each other the first priority was drinking. And because we were young, me 21 and him 24, we wanted to go to as many different bars as possible to do the drinking. The difficult part was that we loved each other, or maybe only I loved him. Maybe we hated and loved each other by turns. Possibly he didn't care at all.

I never knew what either of us felt or wanted. Outside of my own father, Jared was the most evasive person I had ever come across. When I was around Jared I only experienced two states: confusion or anguish. It felt just like home. Even at the time I knew he was eerily similar to my father, but I didn't care. I couldn't. I had no control over myself around Jared, and deeper than that, I knew I had no right to even want that control. Jared was a force that had unsettled every aspect of my life. There was no sense in arguing with the hurricane that had already blown my house off its foundation.

Bret and I knew Cassady had been fucked with from the very first time we met her. Impossible to say who or when or how many, but the truth of it—the damaged part of her—shone naked and blazing out of her eyes. While her restless mouth stayed silent, her face sucked in slightly like the faces of most survivors. A slave to a nervous tic, she relentlessly chewed the insides of her cheeks.

We met Cassady through Sid, her boyfriend. We met Sid through Jared and Jared had found him through the band he was in, the one he'd joined by answering an ad in the paper from three guys looking for someone to play keyboard. Stuck in the desert in New Mexico combing through the Seattle music rags looking for a break, Sid had answered the same ad put out by the same three guys looking for a bass player. When they took him on he packed all of his belongings and moved to Seattle. Cassady followed a couple of months later.

Sid was scuzzy. The first time we met him we were all standing in line outside a club in Pioneer Square in downtown Seattle. He'd come to meet Jared, but Jared and Daniel and Kim had cut up to the front and so Sid ended up at the back of the line with me and Bret. Sid had platinum-blond spiked hair and he wore too-big mirrored sunglasses with a leopard print shirt open at the collar, a white leather jacket, and white leather boots that matched. He moved his head and neck in a constant chicken peck motion and whistled out of gritted teeth.

Sid told us then about his girlfriend Cassady, driving at that moment through the desert, barreling forward to Seattle, to Sid and the band, to everything on the other side. I thought about what a long drive it had been from Michigan, and about how Jared and I kept getting drunk and sleeping together but he still barely even talked to me. It had never again been like that first night in the bathroom at the party. We had never discovered another topic that brought us as alive as those long-ago horse thieves. Later, at another club during after hours, I looked at Jared out of the corner of my eye. He had already lost interest in his cigarette even though he had just lit it a moment before. It sat dangling and half-remembered on the edge of his ashtray. Unfinished smoke circled his head. I shrunk into myself and thought about how much I hated being out after last call.

Two days later Cassady showed up.

She was tall and slender at first glance, but I knew she was strong just by looking at her. Her jet-black hair was cut short and it crinkled up in curls all over her head. Her eyes were ringed with heavy charcoal eye shadow, but when I looked closer—under all the black—I saw they sparkled like ocean water, with clear shades of green and gray. She wore a leopard print tank top that matched her leopard print purse. The purse looked like it had seen better days. But what I remember best was the jagged mottled bruise on her left arm. Like a flag, or a road sign that comes swimming out of the darkness, all bright white and green in the black, so bright that I couldn't see anything else.

We were at a new bar that night, an Irish pub called the Emerald Crow down by the waterfront. It was the end of November and we had been in Seattle for a little over three months. Jared, Daniel, Kim and Jana crowded around one end of our long table like birds on a phone line, while Cassady and Sid clustered together like two lonely cells at the other end. They didn't talk. Instead, they lit cigarette after cigarette off the last one burning in the ashtray. Bret and Tom and I sat in the middle, making a shaky bridge between the two groups. Finally Bret, in her good-natured way, asked Cassady if she'd ever been anywhere cool.

"I've been to Paris," Cassady answered shyly. She looked up at Bret from under all the black.

"That's what I'm talkin' about! C'mere!" Bret motioned to her to move down to our end. In the three months of living with Bret I had come to quickly find out that she could make friends with anyone. Bret had an open friendly face spattered with freckles and long reddish-blonde hair that cascaded all the way down her back. She was a natural hippie who loved everybody and never failed to make all of us laugh. If anyone could get Cassady to open up, it would be Bret.

Cassady nervously looked at Sid, but he waved her off, his expression hidden behind the sunglasses that covered the top half of his face. Only his mouth moved as he lit another cigarette. As Cassady talked we found that her voice was low, and dropped even lower at times, but we didn't have to strain to hear her. There was a deep nasal urgency to her words that was oddly sexy, oddly persistent. It wanted in. She told us about Paris and the rest of Europe she'd seen, and New Mexico, and finally Sid. And by the end, Cassady was in. We were friends now.

In her drill-beat monotone Cassady whispered to me and Bret that she had been so excited to come out tonight and meet Sid's new friends, but then on the way there he had called her a cunt. Her lower eyelids wobbled with tears. I wondered if all that black eye makeup was waterproof. Then Cassady said, in her flat even way, that she supposed she was a cunt sometimes. I thought about all the ads I'd seen for waterproof mascara. It was always some blonde happy chick running through waves and blinking her eyes and smiling to split her face open. I supposed Cassady probably cried a lot dating Sid. Did she pick her mascara after carefully reading the package in the drugstore aisle? Did she automatically hunt for "waterproof" in tiny script because she knew what was coming? Or did she believe it would be different—she wasn't running through any waves—and so she got whatever mascara she wanted, fuck it if it happened to be waterproof or not? I looked back at her. Tears spilled over her lower lashes now, making black tracks down her cheeks like footprints in the snow.

A few minutes later Sid got up to use the bathroom. Cassady watched him go with wet and pleading eyes. Bret shook her arm and tried to joke with her.

"What? Do you think he's going to cheat on you or something on the way to the bathroom? I don't know, Cassady. This place is kinda small—I think we'll notice." She winked at her and cracked a smile. Cassady sighed and absentmindedly pulled out a few strands of her black hair.

"He's done it before." she said, never letting go of his rapidly diminishing figure with her eyes. Bret raised her eyebrows and shot me a look. We grabbed the waitress as she went by and ordered another round.

After that night Cassady started hanging out with me and Bret after Tom went to work during the evenings. We all smoked pot and it was nice to have a third person to get together with, get high, and watch TV. She told us about the fights with Sid and how they beat each other up all the time. I noticed the bruise on her arm again, which had now faded to a pale yellow stain. Underneath it were two new ones, small and dark purple. Cassady didn't seem to care that she hit Sid or he hit her and she didn't seem to care if anyone saw the bruises. We never saw her cry over the fights. She only cried when she talked about Sid cheating on her, and that was all the time.

Chapter 2

Jared dumped me in January. It was a cold gray morning, raining as usual. As I watched the rain slide down his bedroom window he told me it was over. I felt half my heart die right there, in that second, like a candle going out. The other half whimpered and rolled over, waiting for its end to come. Why? I demanded, and it seemed like the only word I could say. I heard myself saying it again and again. The part of my heart that was still alive clawed a hand up one of the walls inside of me, desperate to be saved. Jared hesitated.

"If you tell me to stay with you, I will." he said.

I felt sick. I couldn't think. I wanted him more than anything, but not like that. Not by bending his will to mine. It was wrong. More than that, it was *gross*. How could he even ask that?

No, I wouldn't do it. "No," I said, and that was that. The other half of my heart let go and collapsed. It twitched once and then died.

When I found out a week later that Jared was seeing Kim I suddenly knew he'd been with her the whole time. I looked down at myself and saw that out of nowhere I had a ragged hole through the middle of me. This must be what it feels like to die by cannon ball, I thought. After that I started seeing Jared in my dreams, on television, on billboards, in the most dissimilar stranger's face. Everywhere I went, there he was, and I knew there would never be any escape.

The driving force in my life had been, up until now, my need to find the special thing that was inside of Jared. To find it and make sense of it. When Jared left, the need was still there, but he had taken away whatever special thing it was that was inside of him. And then my need grew. It got bigger and hungrier. I could feel it eating things inside of me.

I started walking for hours every morning before my shift at the restaurant. While I walked a constant stream of venom in my head kept a steady beat. My mind cooled from the sting of betrayal, my thoughts coalesced. A voice that was strong and cruel came from somewhere deep within me. When the voice split away and talked to me all by itself I started calling her Lo. I didn't question if I was making her up. Lo was real and I knew it. She'd been living in me, and waiting, for years. She'd watched me at my lowest points and saved up a thousand slights, a million minor offenses. She forgave nothing, and now she wanted revenge.

Everything Lo said sounded like something she might have taken from Charles Manson. She made arguments that smacked of lunacy but fell into a weird sort of sense. She pinned the buzzing in my head down with a poison glance as her voice needled deeper. When a man and woman joined together, she said, it always seemed to be the woman who melted away, just like a cake of soap dissolves so slowly that no one ever sees it go. No one remembers who used it last. Jared had nothing I needed, she purred. A need could never really be satisfied anyway, she promised, and every need was negotiable.

I had to choose, she said, and that was the catch. I had to choose Lo. If I surrendered to her, I had to give up everyone else. She would tolerate my friendships, but she would not tolerate divided love. She had to be my only real lover, and sometimes, my only me.

I knew Lo was mad and not just insane. Insane is reading the phone book to drink up all the people inside, or wanting to crawl inside someone else's body with them and live there on a full-time basis. Insane is talking to voices in your head and listening when the voices talked back. That was me. But going mad is different. Mad is the man with a bomb strapped to him at the post office. Mad is knowing you're insane and not caring. Mad is thinking it's better on the other side, cleaner. Things are more...even. And because Lo was mad, because she knew she was insane and didn't care, I trusted her more than I trusted myself. She wasn't operating from any ulterior motive.

And later, when Lo ordered me to stop questioning everything so much, I stopped thinking about it entirely.

I had been working as a waitress for a few months now and I hated it. After Jared dumped me I decided to quit that job. I wanted to work in a bookstore instead, for the simple reason that I really didn't like anything else but books. If I was surrounded by books all day, able to lay a hand on their clean solid warmth whenever I needed it, I might get my mind all the way back. The weird shit that was going on with Lo's voice in my head might go away all on its own.

So I applied at the two bookstores in the mall out in the suburbs. I applied at the big fancy old-fashioned brick bookstore downtown. I drove up and down Highway 99, and applied at every bookstore in every strip mall, even the Christian ones with faded plastic crucifixes hanging in the windows. No one called.

It looked like my whole Seattle plan was a bust. It was the middle of winter and Jared was gone. Bret's bright personality was dimming a little more each day. And I could tell the rain was getting Tom down. When he got really drunk his sadness slipped out. Walking over the snowflakes of broken heart carpeting our living room floor was like stepping on broken glass, a thousand tiny cuts that burned my feet like hot coals. I was the one who had dragged all of us here. The only one getting out unscathed was Jared, who had retreated slowly and steadfastly, since the first moment the three of us had arrived at his door.

And then, one bookstore called.

The store was tiny. Nestled in an itty-bitty corner of a strip mall on Highway 99, it sat in between a Safeway and a sports bar. When I got there for my interview things didn't look good from the start. The manager was a big woman with dark brooding eyebrows. She looked like she chopped and carried firewood daily. She also looked pissed. Like this day was just another shitty diaper slipped on underfoot. She introduced herself as Val and took me by the elbow, ushering me outside.

The interview was short. We sat next door at a scuffed plastic table in the Safeway deli. Old people sat at all the other scuffed plastic tables around us, drinking coffee and winding down the time. In between the static buzz of the store intercom Val asked me questions. I smiled a lot and tried to look like the perfect fit. She didn't seem impressed with my answers. She didn't seem to like me either. After 15 minutes my sharp perfect-fit smile wilted and my face started to itch. I felt greasy. I started to feel stupid. I stared at the old guy next to us sitting in front of an untouched cup of coffee. He was picking his nose and had hair coming out of his ears. The ear hair waggled every time he got a really good pick in.

When I got home I stared at the wall, hating myself. I thought about what I was going to drink that night.

20 minutes later the phone rang. It was Val. When she offered me the job I could hear it in her voice that she didn't sound so

happy about it. It looked like someone else had just quit and now she had to make do with my greasy face and stupid answers. Whatever the reason, I didn't care. I hung up the phone and cracked open a beer to celebrate. I had a job. I was not a loser. I just had to figure out the rest of my life. The beer in my hand looked to be a good beginning and I drank it down.

I loved the bookstore. I was around books all day, it was mostly quiet, and the people I worked with were weird and kind of nice. I worked the late shift with another girl and the two of us closed the store together every night. That was how Sadie came to be one of my best friends.

Sadie was the smallest girl I had ever seen. She looked like maybe she was 14, except she had a labret through her bottom lip and lots of other piercings and tattoos. She was cleanly and perfectly beautiful, with coal-black hair cut like a boy's, translucent white skin that showed delicate blue veins at her temples, and a mischievous face like a wicked elf. I just knew she was the type of girl who deejayed her own late-night pirate radio show on the side, or maybe built masterpiece guitars from driftwood she collected on the beaches of New Zealand.

But I couldn't even talk around Sadie at first. I was sure if I did something strange would come out, like how I'd moved across the country not just because I was in love with a guy but because I actually wanted to crawl inside his body with him, because he had something I desperately needed but I couldn't say what that thing was, because I didn't even know. Or how a voice that called herself Lo had shown up recently and decided to move permanently into my head with me.

But then one night I was working the cash register when the tape ran out and I needed Sadie's help. Changing the tape was an incredibly simple task. But I just couldn't get the hang of it even though I'd tried about a million times in the two months that I'd been there. I could never get the holes in the tape to line up with the spokes in the register. Every time, I ended up ripping off length after length of crumpled paper, feeling like I was going to cry. This time was no exception. I started to silently panic. And then I heard Sadie's sarcastic little voice behind me.

"Need help?"

Sadie had caught me in a moment when my incompetent slob nature was leaking out of me like it would a crazily tied package, something oily in one corner and something greasy and shit-brown smeared on top—no return address. My face went red and my armpits started to prickle. Mutely, I shambled to the side as Sadie nimbly, perfectly, and all-at-once jumped to the register. With a quick sure sound of reeling paper and one final snap shut, the task was accomplished.

For the rest of the night Sadie hung out with me at the register and told me her story. She was from California but moved to Seattle in high school. She was 21, loved punk, was punk, lived punk, and had one brother, Jet, who was her best friend. She talked to me in one long fluid outburst, punctuated by crazy sideways leprechaun looks and mad punching hand motions. She also told me she smelled poop everywhere and poop always found her. Then she told me funny poop stories until it was time to close the store.

After Jared left my insides felt sticky and raw. Bits of sharp bone had broken off in my heart. It felt like every note of pain I'd ever absorbed was now being vomited out of every one of my cells. It reminded me of driving over those slanted spikes at the entrance to parking garages—easy glide going in, but if you mistakenly backed up they would knife everything to shreds on the way out. The outline of myself had blurred and grown dim. I shivered and shimmered into the background of the world as my rate of progress toward complete invisibility took on speed.

But in the next few days as we worked shelving books together, Sadie told me more stories, and I started to feel better.

She told me that her dad was crazy and never wore shoes, not even in public. Her mom was banned from the state of Nevada because of an "episode" she'd been involved in years ago, but no one really knew what happened, not even her mom because she'd been too drunk at the time. She talked about how she and her brother Jet had grown up in the desert east of LA and how Jet didn't believe in the concept of shame and how he'd broken in through the bedroom window of one of her ex-boyfriends to get some of her stuff back, and then strolled out the front door. But first he stopped in the living room on his way out to chat with the guy's parents about what a douche bag their son was.

I got the idea that Sadie and Jet were alive, like I'd never heard of people being alive before. They had balls. They would rather have their guts dragged out of them than hand them over willingly with less pain. The line between me and the rest of the world hiccupped and my descent toward the invisible, what I thought was the inevitable, began to retreat shade by shade. Like film slowly running backwards.

But still, as Sadie and I traded stories, I didn't talk about Jared. And I never talked about Lo, not to anyone. Her name was a talisman. If I said it out loud it wouldn't be magic anymore, it would just be a name.

Chapter 3

In the spring of 2001 Jared bought a house on Beacon Hill and Cassady and Sid moved into it. I knew Kim stayed there every night because Sid had quickly grown tired of her and Cassady told me all about it. Tom still saw Jared all the time too, a fact that gutted me whenever I thought about it. I felt like I was the only one who wasn't seeing Jared anymore and the truth of that killed me.

Cassady called one night, and when Bret answered the phone and handed it to me with a worried look I already knew it was another fight. Cass sounded woozy and weird and then abruptly hung up. High on tequila myself at that point, I grabbed a kitchen knife and shoved it down into my boot. Then I bolted out the door as Bret yelled after me to be careful.

When I got to Jared's every light in the place was on. The front door was thrown wide open and I could hear Sid and Cass shouting. When I stepped inside I saw blood on the floor. Cassady and Sid stood two inches from each other. They reeled back and struck at each other like two cobras and then I saw blood around Cassady's mouth. It looked like lipstick, except it was too runny. Sid hit her in the face again, and then blood started spewing out of her nose. When I went for Sid he got my arm, slammed me on the ground, and then punched me square in the chest. Coughing and choking, I rolled over and spotted the phone on the floor next to me. I grabbed it and dialed 911.

The cops showed up and took a report and then they took Sid away. Since no one else was home, I cleaned Cassady up and wrote a note to Jared explaining all the blood and pinned it to his bedroom door. After he got out of jail the next day Sid went back to Jared's. Cassady moved in with us.

Cassady's nose was broken. There was a trial and everyone went except for Jared and Kim. I watched as our small group of friends filed into the courtroom and chose sides one way or the other, like the families of the bride and groom at a wedding. From my Cassady pew I saw Tom walk in, clumsy in his good clothes, and look back and forth between the two sides. Then he sat down on Sid's. When he looked up at me I looked away and didn't look back during the rest of the proceedings.

Sid got off with anger management classes. Cassady got counseling for chicks with boyfriends who gave them broken noses. Then she went back to New Mexico to get the rest of her stuff. Tom and I weren't talking much, but we put on a big steak dinner for her anyway before she left. Cassady said she'd be back in July and Bret marked the day on the calendar after dinner, a big red circle that showed when we'd begin scouting the horizon for sign of her sails.

Tom was still working nights so I barely saw him at home, but things were tense between us after the trial. Not only was Tom still friends with Sid, but he also hung out all the time with Jared and Kim too. My face locked shut like a deadbolt whenever he mentioned any of them to me but he didn't get it. I started to think the blood trail that leaked from my heart and followed me all over the house was invisible.

I knew it wasn't fair of me to want Tom to stop talking to Jared but I wanted it all the same. And even though I knew Jared was mostly friends with Tom because Tom was bigger and stronger and braver than he was, I also knew I would never tell Tom that. When Jared got drunk and picked fights with the dumb jocks he hated, it was Tom who was there at the end to fight the guy, even though he hated fighting more than anything. He would do it for Jared. He would do anything for Jared, and somewhere inside Jared knew that. Somewhere inside Jared felt kind of shitty about it too but he used it anyway. But if I told Tom that, it would break his heart, just like mine was broken now.

When I came home one day Tom was packing his few things into boxes scattered all over his room. "Hey Lo..." he said as he saw me walk past. I stopped and looked at him and winced a little at the nickname he and Bret had taken to calling me. There was no way he could have guessed what it had turned into. I stepped gingerly into the doorway of his room.

"What's this?"

Tom tossed his alarm clock into the box nearest to him and wiped his hands down the front of his pants.

"I'm moving out. Goin' to Jared's new house."

I slowly nodded my head and concentrated on a pair of Tom's sneakers lying on the floor. I couldn't look at him.

"That's cool. You'll have fun there...with him." I couldn't say his name.

"Yeah!" Tom perked up. "It will be fun—Jared's my best friend you know."

I looked from the sneakers to his face and then stared back at the sneakers again.

"Yeah, I know."

I went into my room and shut the door, leaving Tom to pack the rest of his boxes by himself.

∼

I first met Tom during my junior year of college in 1999 when he lived in the same house as Jared. Because Jared's room was huge, everyone used it to drink and play cards. That cold early-spring night in Michigan the black March wind blew in through soft-bellied screens and cooled our heated cheeks. The guys were drinking beer and I had a jug of cheap red wine. I hated cards and had gone off alone, finding myself in a strange room, Tom's room. He was sitting in a chair in the middle of it all by himself, drinking a beer.

"Have you seen the movie Devil's Advocate?" he had asked suddenly. I studied his face that could have been carved out of rock. It looked like pieces of broken mountain formed the marble overhang of his forehead. Eagle brows jutted out like cliffs. Then I saw he was still staring at me. He asked his question again.

"The movie—Devil's Advocate. With Pacino. Have you seen it?"

I slowly shook my head. "No, I hate movies."

He nodded as if that were completely normal.

"Well, here's the thing...in the movie Pacino plays the Devil and..."

And he told me everything, about God and the Devil, and then about himself as I sunk down onto the floor. I sipped my wine and went on wondering what this strange man could possibly be. For the rest of that year and then into the next—the year 2000—when I convinced him to come with me to Seattle to find Jared, I never stopped wondering.

Made of granite, Tom never got hurt. When a sharp knife fell on his upper thigh and sliced into him at the Ann Arbor deli where he worked, he pulled it out without blinking. He took a shot of whiskey and went back on working. When a guy at a stop-light got into it with Jared one drunken night, Tom put his fist through the guy's car window and then calmly apologized and kept walking. When Tom needed stitches he slapped on duct tape and claimed it would heal just as fast.

He chewed on his solid meaty hands constantly, the nails barely there, gnawed into red slivers of tortured flesh at the ends of his fingers. Humming on the balls of his feet, eyes skittering under stone brows, hands in his mouth as he chewed them over, his eyes were gray-green marbles bulging out of his head. He stared off into the distance all the time, toward the horizon, watching for storms. Tom was a nervous cowboy, an Old West champion of the white magic legends in America that were sick now, and maybe dying—maybe all the way dead—knowing the time for cowboys was almost done, ready to protect whatever it was that needed protecting—especially me and Jared—chewing his bleeding stone fingers and looking for rain all the while.

He was a soldier too. Tom was a Marine. Trained as a sniper, Tom believed in his country even if he didn't trust grownups anymore. He didn't ask questions, he didn't need to know the answers. If there would be rain, there would be rain. Dutifully and constantly, Tom scouted the horizon for suspicious clouds. He didn't ask why.

Tom had shown me a picture of him in his Marine Corps unit. He was folded into the lines of soldiers split up in two or three rows, all of them buzz cut with big grins. Young guys with barely even any beard to grow, 19, 20, maybe 18, probably just out of high school, probably some of them still virgins, acne fading into pits that resembled lost tribal scars, high on the cheekbones and cut at a slant, making them look somehow mean through their innocence. In that picture I recognized Tom by the granite underneath his face, his skeleton made out of a mountain.

Chapter 4

E very day that I walked in the rain Lo dug deeper into my mind. She kept saying that what I needed was someone I could bring into me, instead of me dissolving into someone else until finally, one day, I resolved to take her advice.

I met a guy at the bar that night and when he called a few days later I agreed to meet him at his house. I showed up with a case of beer. We split the case and made small talk for hours until it was almost empty and tilted unevenly to the side. When he leaned over me to grab the last can, I leaned into him and grabbed his dick.

When we got to the bedroom and undressed I discovered the guy was covered with fur. I ran a hand down the alarming amount of fuzz on his back and let my fingers linger on the small tuft of soft hair I found at his tailbone. The man had a pelt, and he also had a smell. It pushed itself up into my nostrils like a sweating fat man overflows his airplane seat. I gagged and choked it back. It was armpit, and it was everywhere. The guy seemed to be oozing the essence of B.O. like a scared skunk sprays its musk in defense. I wondered if I'd triggered it by startling him when I grabbed his dick. His glands must have gone into overdrive and then released

23

the stench from the warm nervous pockets of his skin. I was revolted, but I was curious too. The smell was its own entity, dark and hot and slithering around the room. I moved up and down his body, surreptitiously sniffing. It really was all over him. Every square inch of the poor man's body stunk. Even his feet smelled like armpits.

But I wasn't here to have a good time. This was for Lo. She was here to taste and touch and smell, even if the smell was bad. She was here for pure experience and so far she was pleased.

During the sex my hand got caught in the guy's actual armpit. I hauled it out, expecting it to be dripping and steaming like some lost article pulled out of a swamp, but it looked okay. Looks aside, it stunk to high heaven. I sniffed it after the guy fell asleep and then buried it under a pillow and tried to breathe through my mouth.

After Cassady had gone back to New Mexico in May Bret and I started hitting the bar a lot more, and the bar we went to most of the time was the Emerald Crow. Even though we had started going there with Jared and his friends it felt like our place now. We showed up one night in early June excited to see the live music they had lined up and happy that summer had finally arrived. Sitting in the front row, I noticed during the show that the drummer kept catching my eye. He smiled at me through the flash of his drumsticks and the tangled frenzy of his arms beating against the drums. When the show was over he immediately came and sat down at our table.

He said his name was Ki and the name seemed to match his surfer look. His face was easy and open, with a wide loose smile and a large friendly nose that bobbed happily like it would on a bear in the circus. His blond hair hung to his shoulders and was extraordinarily sleek and shiny, as if it had just been ripped off of a purebred Golden Retriever. But what I was really interested in was the way he twitched.

The twitch hit Ki every few seconds. It was like his face—his eyes especially—underwent some sort of mini-explosion. And when it did, for a split second I forgot everything he was trying to lay on me, and I only saw him. The twitch was an interruption and every time it interrupted, I wondered. In that moment of seeing, with particles of wonder rustling down over my head, through my hair and into my eyes, I saw certain cracks in the world. In the pause of the interruption I saw how make-believe everything was, and how there was also a crack running right down the middle of me.

The twitch disappeared when Ki was drumming. It was only when he climbed down off the stage—*TWITCH-KA-BOOM*—that it came back, like a case of determined hiccups.

A couple of hours later I took off with Ki and we went to his place where we sat outside on the grass and drank some more. He told me all about his band, how he wanted to be a musician and nothing else. But I was losing my grip. I was too drunk and Lo was taking over. Ki's spark didn't register on her radar. She didn't care about his stories even if I wanted to hear them. Then I went limp. I let go of my life again, letting Lo take what pieces she would.

When I woke up the next morning I turned and saw Ki sleeping beside me. I remembered most of the night before, my memories trailing off into an annoying vague grayness instead of shooting straight into a black hole. The blinding morning sun also lent them a new solidity, as if time had been encased into hard and dependable plastic memories. Memories that could never be destroyed or broken, forcing me to cart them around forever.

I pondered my options. He was going to wake up soon. I could feel him already moving agitatedly under the surface of his dreams, preparing to leap out of sleep like a runner's leg muscles flicker before the shot goes off. His eyelids fluttered and tested themselves against the fabric of unconsciousness as he sighed into his next breath. I wanted to dig my heels in and stretch out the time. I found him repulsive.

But waking up after a drunk was when Lo saw the world as it really was, rotting away. Breathing in the stink of it fueled a wild horniness in her to have her way with it. She turned to Ki and gave him a good hard push. He was going to wake up soon anyway, she said.

Ki rolled toward me and pulled off his shorts without opening his eyes. I looked down. Out of everything I remembered from the night before, I couldn't believe I hadn't remembered that. I'd never seen a bigger penis on anyone—in person, on an animal, or in the movies. It was simply monstrous. I felt like I should have thought it was deadly, or at least dangerous, but it only appeared over-grown and stupid.

I looked back up at Ki and saw that he still had his eyes closed, but now his lips were coming toward me. I sighed and changed positions to get away from his mouth. As I laid back and got comfortable I recognized the position as the one I was usually in at the gynecologist's office, right before they warned me it was going to be cold and shoved up the speculum. Lo peeked around from her hideout and smacked her lips. Didn't I love Hemingway? she asked as she reminded me of the book I had just read. He was a hunter of lion meat, too, she said. And then, her incisors glittering like fangs, she dived in.

I ran into Ki sometimes after that night, always at the Emerald Crow. The memory of his monster penis faded, but the thing I never forgot was his twitch. I watched him play with his band many more times and always saw the twitch disappear whenever he was drumming. Then one night I saw the secret of it all at once. I'd assumed the twitch vacated the premises when he was at the drums, but it was the exact opposite. He *was* twitching, but it was impossible to see because every show—every song—was all one long twitch for him.

The twitch was the sign of the thing that lived inside him. But the thing wasn't him. It was an outsider that took him over when he drummed. The twitch was the glint of light through a chink in the wall. It was the flash and play of shadows behind the keyhole. It was only a sign, not the thing itself. The thing itself was the one beating the drums.

~

Cassady came back to Seattle in July of 2001. She promptly moved into Tom's old room and the rest of that summer a steady flow of visitors passed through our apartment, some of them old friends of mine and Bret's from Michigan and some of them old friends of Cassady's from the desert on their way someplace else.

All in all, when I had my first episode of alcoholic nervous breakdown, there were more than eight people staying in an apartment designed for a maximum of three. I counted seven other heads on the morning after my mental collapse.

The night before had started out badly. Cassady and I had been at the Crow matching each other on shots of Jameson before we got sick of the bright lights and the frat boy crowd and decided to go to Satan's Door, a club hidden up an alley not too far away. It was easy to find coke there and the martinis were gigantic.

Satan's Door consisted entirely of two key features—the club's perfect parallels of red and blue, and the fact that it was little more than one giant corridor. The whole place felt like a tunnel. After descending a grimy stairwell we entered the first two rooms. These were the blue rooms, small and dim and where people lolled and talked and got blue with no one they knew when they were tripping or rolling or high on coke with an urgent need to intimately socialize. After the blue rooms we passed through the dance floor to the bar in back, both bathed in flickering red light. These were the hot rooms. The dance floor was where the dancers and club butterflies crashed together, tore each other apart and beat the air around them with ripped and bloody wings. The bar in back was designed for mating, dating, scamming or flirting, for making whatever flavor of love to strangers needed at the time.

Standing in line I spotted Jared, Kim, and Jana waiting in front of us. Tom stood awkwardly behind them and stared at the ground. He'd obviously seen me before I saw him. My throat suddenly constricted.

When we got inside I cut my way straight to the red bar in the back and ordered a martini. Gin. Beefeater. Very dry—exceedingly dry—very cold. Up with an olive. When it came I drank it straight down and ordered another. As the bartender turned away to shake the gin I pitched forward and caught myself on the bar by my elbows. Then all of a sudden, there was an explosion inside my eyes, and half my sight was gone. Half the world was black, half lost. The edges of the lost half dripped black into the half that was still there. In the jagged crescent moon of sight that still remained I saw Kim. I pulled myself off the bar and staggered. The black half wanted me too, I could feel it pulling, but I had to finish things here first.

Then Lo made herself known to me. Her voice pierced and held the crashing torrent of that long lonely drunk river in my head. Sounding almost kind, she told me I was fully capable of breaking Kim's jaw. Gently, she methodically listed all the reasons she deserved it. As playfully as a feather on the breeze, she reached out a finger and traced the swell of bone under Kim's left ear and then held my eyes with her own. There could be no hesitation, Lo said. She lifted a disciplined index finger up toward me. I agreed, nodding my head to show her I understood.

I turned to go but Lo held my wrist a moment longer. She reminded me that if I touched Kim inside the club, bouncers would pull me off her in a matter of seconds. I know—before I can sock her in the jaw, I repeated. Before we are finished with her, Lo hissed. She shook my wrist slightly and the rest of me shook then too. She warned that I'd almost floated to the bottom. My mind was approaching extreme toxicity. In fact, we were probably going to lose consciousness in the next 15 minutes. I had to act fast.

Cloaked in black shadows, under red dimpled lights that flashed through the darkness, Jared and Kim didn't notice me next to them until it was almost too late. I saw in the quick widening throb of their eyes, like a panicked pulse beat, that I'd already startled them almost into full-blown fear. They hadn't expected me. My hearing was getting worse by the second. A foamy sea roar filled half my head. Over the crash and bloom of the waves I threw my voice to Kim like a rope and asked if I could have a word with her outside. I was trying not to shout. I knew they couldn't hear the ocean next to us, and I could feel my eyes burning, flashing with the red in the room. Sea storm and red blood light, and Lo's warm whisper in my ears, stole my voice and cut off my air. All of it was in my eyes and I knew I'd betrayed Lo's purpose from the outset. Kim shrank back terrified. She saw my eyes—they all saw my eyes and they were scared. I didn't have pity for any them. I was scared too and I was standing inside of it. But all of that fear fed into Lo, and only made her stronger.

Then, I was the one who got taken out.

It was the gin.

The world shimmered in and out of the black—a new kind of veil that was coming down all around me—and as I had not yet learned to walk within it, my legs gave way.

I had never known the veil before that summer. It seemed to be something that Lo brought with her into my life, although she never talked about it. The way it worked was like this: After coming out of a blackout I had two sets of memories. The veil was the wall that divided them. The first set of memories was made up of actual stuff that had happened to me. Those memories began in normal life and spanned the early part of the night, each one preserved perfectly in its own file, labeled and lined up cleanly in my head, waiting for me to open it again someday. Like almost all memories had been for me for most of my life.

It was hard to say exactly when the second set of memories began. But they were always made up of only the small slice of the outside world I was allowed to see from under the veil before it descended completely. The veil fell to just above the lower half of my eyes, as if I was pretending to be asleep and peeking out from under my eyelids. But when the veil came down my eyes were physically wide open. There was no material wall. The suffocating velvet of that thick black theater curtain existed only in my mind.

But that doesn't mean it wasn't real.

Once the veil was down, it never lifted. Not until the booze ran its course through me and I was back to sober the next morning.

The morning after Lo convinced me I should try breaking Kim's jaw, the fragmentary second set of memories shone through like an invidious stain. I knew what I'd done. I sensed every sick twist and turn of the story even if I couldn't remember the particulars after my legs collapsed under me. I sat on one of the two sagging chairs in our living room and watched all the random people staying in our apartment file in and out of the kitchen to look for breakfast. My eyes were almost swollen shut but I could still see the flash of neon on red brick at Satan's Door.

I felt like I'd been hit by a train. My face was ready to split open like a ripe watermelon. My eyes were bloodshot, the whites around the screaming capillaries tinged with yellow. My tongue was white and my head was spinning. I smelled like a fat and pasty middle-aged alcoholic man.

Cassady sat next to me and in between introducing me to her

friends—a band of transients who had arrived the night before and who she had promised a place to stay for the week—she told me everything she remembered and, like a kindergartener clumsily pasting together a paper chain, I matched scene to scene until I had the entire awful story in front of me.

I had lunged at Kim. I had fallen, then screamed, and then gibbered madly, laughing and crying, until Cassady got me out of there. She saw Jared, Kim, and Tom driving away as she apologized to the bouncers on the way out. Tom looked back at her once, and then looked away. Then she had loaded me into the car and driven me home. I had screamed almost the entire way.

My brain lumbered brokenly around in my head. Bloated and defeated, it twitched pathetically, threw itself at the walls and then slid half dead back down the sides of my skull. I decided to let my hands make the decisions. I reached for the phone and dialed a guy I knew from back in Michigan who now lived in Portland. I made plans to drive down to see him the very next weekend.

Chapter 5

At the end of August our lease was up. We had been in Seattle for one year, and now that we knew our way around, Bret and Cassady and I decided it was time to find an apartment closer to downtown.

After combing the papers, I found an apartment with three bedrooms for rent in the Central District. The Central District was also known as the CD and it was ghetto. Oddly wedged in between the yuppie condos on Capitol Hill and rich Madison Beach on the other side, the CD was made up of rundown houses with balding lawns that had cement stoops worn smooth as soap from people sitting, killing time on them every day. Stoop sitters are either old people who are set outside by a relative because they're too old to move off the stoop or people chained to the stoop by the thing they can't stop doing that won't let them move anywhere else. Like junkies. And alkies. I'd been an on-and-off stoop sitter for the past three years and I liked our new neighborhood.

The apartment was on the bottom floor of a house and the house was sinking into the ground. After we moved in I stopped throwing loose change on my dresser because it just slid off the other side. I also noticed that the slant pushed me into a slight jog going from the kitchen to my bedroom. The whole place was downhill. It was easy to get caught by the slant and pushed downhill with it. Easy to start running at that slight jog and not slow down again back to normal.

To get my balance back I applied myself to dating the guy in Portland, Bobby, with the discipline of a karate black belt. I called him regularly—at least once every three days I counted—and drove to Portland every other weekend. I let Bobby take me to movies (I hated movies), and to bars (where I carefully watched how much I drank), and on walks around the city (making myself hold his hand until the last possible second I could stand it and then dropping it like a hot worm and wiping my hand on the back of my shirt when he looked somewhere else). We had cozy conversations over breakfast, lunch, and dinner. We had sex in the quiet and empty sun-washed afternoons in his Portland studio. I ended up hating Bobby all the same.

I hated him for being weak and genuine, and because he wanted a wife. I hated him for being sweet and generous in life, when to me, the world tasted like old blood and the mush of millions of crushed soggy bones. I hated myself for hating him, but I hated him the most for wanting to be with me.

It seemed like he was going into the ring with the bull and a few sugar cubes, thinking the bull can be soothed or tricked, thinking that could ever be enough. By now, I knew that to win one has to nurture a vendetta against the bull. Getting out alive means that you always finish a kill. My vendetta, inchoate as it was, was still floating to the surface. It lined the inside of me like wallpaper. Gluing me and Lo together, it was becoming a cocoon, spun from the silk of a long red flag.

Whenever I showed up on Bobby's doorstep in Portland I was usually wired on cough syrup, which is what I drank on my off-drinking days to kill the edge. Days with Bobby counted as off-drinking days because I couldn't drink as much as I wanted, and not drinking as much as I wanted counted as the edge. The Robitussin kept me safe in a bubble. It measured and encapsulated everything into sane little compartments so that I was able to take things out of the world and into my bubble one at a time, examining each one at leisure. When I was sober the world attacked me and threw everything at once. I couldn't distinguish the flaming spears from the food drops.

Bobby was well aware of my constant brooding depression. But the meaner I was, the more cheerfully innovative he became. After sex one Saturday afternoon I decided I was tired of Bobby and his smiles and his dimples, his cheerful curly hair. Dressing hurriedly, I said I was leaving to head back to Seattle, instead of staying the entire weekend. The dimples faded.

"But why?" he asked. "Aren't you having fun?"

Fun. What a bizarre thing to say. I swallowed hard and heard a dry click in my throat. The late September heat pressed down on us. I exhaled the air in my lungs with a dry rattle that left a stale taste in my mouth. I could really go for a beer.

"I have...some stuff...uh, some things I have to...it's just...it's time to go, that's all."

I knew how bad it sounded. I didn't care.

Bobby was quiet. He watched me pack the few things I'd brought and then he started telling me jokes. First there were chickens crossing the road and then animals going into bars. Then the jokes became riddles, and when I saw the sun setting from one of the tall windows in the studio I knew the afternoon had slipped away without me noticing, and I hadn't packed anything at all. And so, this time, I stayed.

After we moved into the little house on a slant, I went out every morning I wasn't hungover to continue my walks with Lo. One day I started running and then I ran every day after that. I jogged up to Capitol Hill and then down to the waterfront.

Downtown Seattle was my favorite place to run. Underneath the slate-gray Seattle skies, running into the wind that came off the water, I saw loneliness spread over the city like a huge limp hand. Coming over the hills, panting hard, I looked over the water of the Sound and saw the same thing I felt inside. Everything was sad and gray. Everything was lonely without feeling it. Before any people had ever been around on planet earth, the water and the sky had still been here and still been like this. They were all alone without a voice from any person, without warmth from any hand. That was exactly how I felt inside.

Working the evening shift at the bookstore, I stared out across the parking lot, over the far trees to the distant purple dusky peak of Mount Rainier. The mountain was another presence that echoed the desolate bottom of me, only it was turned inside out and pointed at the sky instead of down into the well of my mind. I was just so fucking sad. Unutterably sad. But I couldn't get at the sadness inside of me. I couldn't put my hands on it. What the hell was I so sad about? Looking at the mountain, the bookstore faded away, the fluorescent lights faded to black, the few customers poking quietly around didn't exist. Everything died one day and I knew it. I couldn't stop knowing it. I couldn't stop feeling that knowledge and it seemed that so much of me was poured into this one feeling that there wasn't room for anything else. I couldn't feel past this sadness.

Most of the time I blamed it on Jared. His name was still an ever-present ache in my chest and the sadness seemed to match that pain. But when I lost myself in the mountain, or the water and the sky, I knew that wasn't true. I had always been this sad just as Mount Rainier had always been in the same place. In those terrifying moments I saw it, clear and real. Jared was just some guy I knew. But the sadness...that had been with me for as long as I could remember, and now it was growing. It was settling over me like a long winter in my bones. The sadness was a cold black world with no light in it anywhere, no hope. I couldn't accept that this cold black world maybe just was, or that maybe, it came from somewhere inside of me.

~

At the end of November, a few days before Bobby was due in town to spend the weekend in Seattle with me, Cassady brought home a new friend. His name was Alec and we'd met him the week before at the Avatar, the Pioneer Square after-hours club that sat just around the corner from the Emerald Crow. Alec was tall and raw-boned, and he had blue hair. He had just broken up with his boyfriend and we all agreed on his incomparable merits as a couch surfer. He was willing to watch any show on TV and he didn't eat much, if at all. Also, he always had drugs.

And so, two days before Bobby arrived, Alec moved in. He seemed perfect. He never complained, he never borrowed money, and he had recently taken up making handcrafted jewelry. Sitting around in the dark slanted cave of our living room, we chuckled together with the sitcom's laugh track and listened to the comfortable click of plastic beads under Alec's fingers.

That Friday night Bobby and I went out to the bars with Cassady and we all came home together. When we got up the next morning Cassady was gone.

It wasn't that odd for Cassady—or for any of us—to leave in the middle of the night. When she called later that afternoon and said she was up north, about a half hour from Seattle, and stranded, I wasn't surprised. She'd been seeing a dirtbag bartender who worked up there and who had decided not to give her a ride back home. In fact, he wouldn't even let her wait for one inside his house, so as Cassady came to the end of all her explanations I realized with sharp sudden clarity that she was actually standing in the rain down the street from the guy's house, where he couldn't see her or know she was still waiting for someone to come pick her up.

I grabbed my keys and Bobby followed right behind. I shot a quick glance at Alec, sitting at the end of the couch. He looked up and smiled his beatific smile at me. I could hear the measured *clack-clack-click* of the beads sliding off his fingers and onto the string of the rainbow bracelet he was making.

"Sorry we've gotta go—" I said as I took the jacket Bobby handed me.

"Don't worry," Alec interrupted me. "I'm not going anywhere. Go get Cass."

I smiled back at him.

"Go. Go!" He laughed and waved me out the door.

That was the last time I ever saw him.

We got back to the house two hours later. Cassady was soaked from the rain—and in the middle of the one millionth sentence about how the dirtbag had treated her like dirt—when we pulled up to the house and I interrupted her.

"Hey Cass. Your car's gone."

"Huh?" She shook wet hair out of her eyes. "Oh—yeah. Whatever. I told Alec he could take it when he needed to. Gave him an extra set of keys and shit. You know."

"Oh," I answered. "Cool." We climbed out of the car and then ran through the rain to the slanted porch. Cassady shielded her eyes and looked up the street. She shrugged.

"Yeah, he'll be back. Sometime soon."

But the next morning, Sunday, Cassady's car was still gone and there was no word from Alec. Bobby and I left for breakfast and when we got back we found Cassady sitting at the end of the couch, where I'd seen Alec peacefully sorting his beads only the night before. With her elbows on her knees, she hung her head and stared at the floor.

"A check cashing place called," she said without raising her head. "They wanted you to verify a check made out to Alec Anderson."

I walked quickly to my room and pulled my checkbook off the dresser. I bent it back and let the pages run under my thumb and then did it again like I was examining a flip book, trying to understand how the cartoon moves all by itself. The second time through I found it. Two out-of-sequence checks missing. With the checkbook dangling from my hand, I went back out to the living room. Cassady was still staring at the floor and Bobby was staring at Cassady. Bret had joined them and now looked at the checkbook in my hand.

"Yeah. Mine's gone altogether," she said.

Cassady looked up.

"Fuck," she said softly and then fell silent again. The rest of us stayed quiet. There was nothing else to say.

I broke up with Bobby that night. When I saw the look in his eyes when we found out Alec was a scuzz—an outright degenerate, as Bobby said—I got mad. I could see now that Bobby had thought Alec was a piece of shit all along. But I wasn't so different from Alec. I didn't steal, but I didn't feel like I had the luxury to assume I wouldn't do something similar in my lifetime. Bobby had no idea. For him, the world was divided into good people and bad people, but my lines had cracked and dissolved. I wasn't sure which side I stood on anymore and I wasn't sure there were even any sides to stand on. But I couldn't say those things out loud. I couldn't explain it to Bobby.

I already knew he wouldn't understand.

When I walked Bobby to his car in the rain he said he was going to miss me. I didn't answer. I stared through him at the curtains of rain coming down and then he kissed me. I had no feeling in my lips but I still knew how he must have felt them— cold and dead, just someone else's skin pressed against his own. He got in the car and pulled away. I knew he would turn and wave at the end of the block, but I didn't stay for that. I trudged back through the rain, into the slant, and didn't look back.

The cop who came to take the stolen vehicle report asked for a description of Alec. When we told him he had blue hair, he paused. He raised his craggy eyebrows and looked at the three of us. "Lovely," he pronounced, slowly and sarcastically. We bowed our heads simultaneously. It was clear now that Alec's degeneracy had spread to us. It was plain to the cop that we associated with a bad sort—what else could possibly be expected of people with blue hair? People who did drugs? People who hated life? The unsaid words peppered us with stings, leaving small bright welts, like a nest of paper cuts, on our faces.

They found Alec a few weeks later. He'd been holed up in a motel in Ellensburg with Cassady's car, but after a high-speed police chase that ended with Alec plowing headlong into a tree, he broke his pelvis and both hips. He had a long list of prior offenses and so they arrested him in the ICU and then when he was well enough they transferred him straight to jail. About a month later, Cassady got a check in the mail. The letter that came with the check said that Alec had to pay her back every cent for the car. The checks were never going to be for more than $15.00, but she would get them until the car was paid back or he died. Cassady lowered the letter, looking over it at me and Bret.

"I kind of hope he dies," she said slowly. Bret and I nodded. So did we.

Chapter 6

As winter settled into Seattle, Bret and Cassady and I now spent more time at the Crow than we ever spent at home. We knew all the bartenders, all the waitresses, each booth and table, and every beer they served. In the middle of the tornado of our lives, the Crow was an oasis. The same place and always the same people.

I started sleeping with one of the bartenders on a regular basis. His name was Kellen and he was a big guy, with a bald head and a gray-black beard and mustache. His blue eyes were really blue, like an electric sign, and they accented the air of finality in his gestures. When he cut his eyes away from something he was done with it. Not like me, who couldn't ever move out of the circles cramping always tighter inside my head. My thoughts dragged me around like a pack of wild horses, but Kellen looked too big and too solid to ever be dragged anywhere.

After getting drunk and sleeping together a few times Kellen told me who his dad was.

"Who?" I was lying on my stomach with my tits propped up on a pillow resting under my ribcage. I bent my wrist and examined a hangnail.

"Scan. Sean Gallagher," Kellen repeated. He rolled over to his side to face me and started rubbing my back in small circles. The balls of his fingers on my skin annoyed me.

"Who's that?" I started in with my teeth on the hangnail.

"He's the owner! That's what I'm saying—my dad's the owner of the Emerald Crow!" The blue in his eyes wiggled like a sun-spackled wave and he laughed. Kellen's teeth were ivory perfect in front, but I could see the fillings in back when he opened his mouth wide.

"Oh...well..." I didn't know what to say. "I guess I didn't know that." I looked at him blankly. I felt like something was expected of me but I didn't know what. I went back to my hangnail.

"Yeah, he's pretty cool...Sean's pretty cool..." He rolled again onto his back and lay staring up at the ceiling and smiling. I could see the glow of the thoughts over his head, like phantom fireflies. Images of his dad, soupy love and strong black threads of trust revolved like a mobile around him. Inside, I felt my things move too. It was just a flicker, a tiny almost invisible one, but it was there. The hate was creeping back in.

Two other bartenders, Nick and Billy, flanked Kellen and formed the top triangle in the pyramid that formed the Emerald Crow. These three were in turn supported by a cast of waitresses, who served the drinks they made and put up with all of their jokes. In the kitchen, the cooks were young and male and lean, punks who held a grudge when another cook used their knife. Eyes burning black into the hollows of their faces, they stood in the kitchen doorway watching Kellen, Nick and Billy, and ground their cigarettes into the floor with the heels of their black boots like they were itching to shoot somebody.

When December narrowed itself until Christmas was directly in line with its crosshairs, preparing for the end when it would gently squeeze the trigger and blow the brains out of the rest of the year, the death threat brought new energy to the rainy, dark-winter, every-night parties at the Crow. Everyone tipped better, the waitresses were friendlier, Nick and Billy poured bigger shots and stiffer drinks, and the first-few-glasses euphoria was sweeter and lasted longer. We made new friends and rejuvenated the ties with the regulars we already knew.

The bar itself was decorated with Christmas lights and silver tinsel. Red and green ornaments and glittering glass globes hung from the ceiling behind the cash registers. When Kellen's dad—Sean Gallagher the owner—showed up on Saturday nights with his Emerald Crow Band he wore a Santa hat onstage as he sang. The jukebox played happy Christmas carols and the endless cycle of songs about pain and heroin by Seattle bands whose members were really from Olympia or Renton was interrupted for once. Nirvana and Alice in Chains were replaced by "Jingle Bells," which everyone claimed to be tired of, but someone kept playing anyway.

One night, a couple of days before Christmas, Kellen and I sat at the bar. He slung an arm around me and looked wistfully at the twinkling lights. Sean Gallagher sang and strummed his guitar onstage, the white puff on the end of his Santa hat falling in his eyes as he bobbed up and down. Kellen leaned in like he was going to tell me a big secret. I felt his mustache tickle my ear.

"These are good times," he said.

I never forgot that.

Because he was right. It was a good time...for a little while.

Like others I wanted to keep my real self hidden from, I humored Kellen. And one ritual that he insisted upon—and that drove me crazy—was breakfast. He loved it. Every night I spent at Kellen's I knew I was expected to hop in his truck the next morning and be driven to the nearby diner for a big greasy spoon breakfast. And during that rainy dark winter between 2001 and 2002 my digestive system wasn't doing well at all.

The digestive system of an alcoholic is like a manic depressive toddler. It's never good, that's for sure, but there are calm periods between explosions that lull one into a false sense of security. For me, the morning after a binge began with the morning piss, dark and reeking like hot pond-water. My bowels stayed relatively quiet for a while although my stomach burned, a sign that I was definitely going to have to puke soon.

Then the physical nausea—that burning in the pit of my stomach—expanded like acid steam until it ran all through my body. With it came a sort of emotional nausea, a slowly creeping revulsion of the self. Remembering pieces of the night before was frequently enough to bring it on.

Sticking a finger down my throat never worked. Apparently I wasn't equipped with a gag reflex—which was great when I went down on a guy, but sucked when I had to be at work that morning and needed to expel the puddle of hydrochloric acid lying in the bottom of my stomach. Just because someone's a drunk doesn't mean she can just drop out of her life, at least not at first, not in the early years. When I had a particularly hungover morning I also still conducted the normal routine of going to work, I just had to manage the frantic railing of my digestive system at the same time. So I really tried to make myself puke if I could, and if I puked up anything it was a deep bright yellow, dense and phlegmy stuff that was bitter as rancid medicine.

Then, once my stomach had settled down, I was starving hungry, like I hadn't eaten in weeks. My appetite made me lax. It made me vulnerable. I always forgot what had happened last time. And that's when it always happened again.

Five minutes after eating I felt great. My body received the message that the vital arsenal of nutrients and defense materials, severely depleted the night before, had been sent back-up supplies and was now replenished. My brain, the control center, read the messages and believed the reports from down south. Things had been bad, there could have been an emergency, but the danger had passed. Now it was only a matter of restocking. For a few minutes I was totally in balance. Until everything slid the other way.

20 minutes later, usually while waiting for the check with Kellen, I started to remember what had happened last time. The fog of amnesia completely lifted when my lower intestines started jogging. Things were shifting. An abrupt falling weight in my lower abdomen rapidly transformed into a formidable load—a howling monster, long and wide—made of pure poop. It moved sluggishly at first, but then gained in speed and determination until it traversed the length of my lower intestines with the frightening abandon of a hysterical giant worm. Attempting to change my position, I desperately squeezed my butt cheeks together, inwardly shouting *HALT!!!* But then the load freaked out, bucking like a wild horse, and bolted to the gates of my anus. My anus saw the load and knew what was coming (having seen it all before) and hit the CODE RED button, sending emergency flares to my brain.

30 minutes after eating my digestive system hit ground zero. I had to SHIT and I had to SHIT NOW. And it was going to be a project. It wouldn't be enough to lock my bare butt onto the toilet seat in the slippery grip of complete desperation. I also needed handholds to clutch while I sweated and fought it out. The load of poop was a cantankerous and evil bear, clawing at my insides as it ravaged its way out. A simple bodily function became the vessel for something very near Satan.

The initial rush of hot poo—swampy and steaming—was ecstasy, but really only a short-lived alleviation of pressure. The subsequent shitbursts were horrific. The corresponding muscle spasms bathed me in streaming rivulets of perspiration. As my hair dampened and finally soaked onto my forehead and the stench rose, I started to lose hope. I seized on any direct visual object to stare at in concentration in a last ditch attempt to concentrate and calm the tide and swell of the creature that moved through me.

Eventually the ordeal ended, relaxation gradually washing through my broken body. The fumes rising from my torn and bleeding ass seemed almost friendly. I thought it might be safe to flush. As I washed my hands and rinsed the sour sweat off my face, the low vapors of amnesia drifted back in. By the time I walked back out to the table, back into the life I was in on any given morning, the spell of forgetting had begun again.

Bret and Cassady knew about ass explosions. They suffered from them the same as I did, but because I drank the most I had it the worst. Me going out for breakfast all the time with Kellen was getting to be a problem.

But then all of my problems were solved when Kellen dumped me. He ended it in the first fresh week of January, over the phone. I saw him in my mind, running a distracted hand over his bald head, mumbling that he couldn't see me anymore while he penciled in someone new for drinks on the 12th. I felt myself catch and slip somewhere inside—something that had nothing to do with Kellen but was triggered by him all the same. I drank for the next two days. On the second day, when the gray January afternoon folded itself into the cold black wings of the Seattle night and I was sufficiently drunk, Lo helped me to pull on black vinyl from head to toe and we went out into the rain. I was looking for worse than what I already had.

Chapter 7

That winter my transformation really picked up speed. It was like years ago a girl named Leah was born, and in all the years since I'd spent every minute of every day picking out things Leah would like and doing things Leah would do and saying things Leah would say. But I was picking and doing and saying the wrong things because I had no idea what the right things were for me. The Leah that existed now could have been anyone. But I wanted to know what I really had inside of me, what I had in the way of raw working materials and what could be made out of all that raw.

The winter of 2001 sliding into 2002 was like the constant rain I watched sliding down shadowed windows all over Seattle. Dark shapes glided past me, a bulk of shadow underwater casting its massive size in outline above—the shark under the boat—and me stuck like an idiot on whether or not I had enough courage to reach for it and risk overturning that boat. I never could leave anything be. I was always picking at everything. The boat might flip over, and I was scared of that, yeah, but I was also terrified that if I didn't peer over the edge—if I didn't touch the looming shadow —I would be found someday in the bottom of the boat, dead with both hands folded neatly over myself...as if I had never been reaching at all.

I'd purchased the black vinyl outfit two months before, along with boots that were black vinyl too and sported three-inch platforms. Wearing the black vinyl costume I felt powerful—and powerfully weird. The frozen smiling faces in the ads on TV, the forever happy silhouettes on peeling billboards, the people trapped between the glossy pages of magazines—these people did not dress up in black vinyl for the hell of it and then go out and determinedly drink themselves into a blackout. But then another voice whispered at the back of my mind. I only wanted to hurt someone because I was hurting so badly myself. I only hated other people because I felt so wrong and out of place. And then Lo lifted one black vinyl boot and crushed that whisper. Using the three-inch platforms, it was surprisingly easy to kill.

The evening I went out after Kellen dumped me I made my first stop our new hangout at the edge of Pioneer Square, a pool hall called Cathedral Cue. Bret and I had been drinking there a lot lately because Cassady was working as one of their promoters. She'd been out of work for two months before landing the gig at Cathedral and Bret and I had been paying her share of the rent. As a promoter, Cassady's job was to draw customers to the new club that had just opened up underneath the pool hall. It was called the Hole-in-the-Ground Lounge and not only was it located in the basement, it was the basement. The cement floor was bracketed by a tiny bar on one end and by the shadowed hulk of turntables on the other. A couple of old funky couches separated two skinny iron tables from the dance floor. There was one strobe light that flickered weakly, like it was drunk too. There were no customers.

Cassady's main job was to pass out cards at other bars. The cards entitled potential new Hole-in-the-Ground customers to a discount on cover, and Cassady got one point for each card turned in at the door. So many points added up to so many dollars on Cassady's paycheck. Although the gig seemed easy enough, Cassady wasn't so good at passing out cards. She either crawled to the highest point in the bar and dropped all of her allotted cards for the night onto the sea of people below, or she made her way to the stage and threw the whole stack into the air as enthusiastically as possible, hoping to hit the greatest range.

But no one picked up the cards Cassady threw on them and no one showed up to the Hole-in-the-Ground Lounge. The few people that did wander down were usually lost and trying to find the bathroom.

Bret and I didn't care if the Hole-in-the-Ground was a success, but we did need rent. And so every time Cassady pulled her cards-into-confetti trick, Bret and I hunted around the different slippery dark-bar floors, getting drunker from bending over so much, and gathered up all the cards we could find. I handed them out to people with a genuine interest in getting them to come to the club, but after a while, Lo couldn't help herself. She just had to screw with some of the guys.

She started telling lonely-looking men that the Hole-in-the-Ground Lounge hosted thong contests and I was a waitress there trying to drum up business by being in the contests. She met their eyes and placed a light hand on their wrists as she told them they had to come down and vote for me because if I won I'd get a huge bonus on my paycheck.

But Lo's latest con ended when I showed up one night and the owner of the Hole-in-the-Ground—a pudgy guy named Louie with a haunted sinister face—approached me. Still twitching from a quick-snorted blast of coke, he wiped at his nostrils and yelled at me that a group of guys had shown up earlier looking for a thong contest. I ran my hand down the sleeve of his suit like a stream of cool water and promised to think of something else, something that didn't involve telling any more lies to get customers in.

Cassady lost her job at the Hole-in-the-Ground pretty soon after that. Louie told her it was because business was slow. Privately, Bret and I thought we'd seen most of the meager profits go up Louie's nose. And we still stopped by the place from time to time because we'd ended up making friends with the bartender, Mr. Mann. He'd been the only other person there with us night after night, waiting for the club to be a success, waiting—like we were—to make rent. But when he wasn't making drinks for us he stood around behind the bar and read books by Charles Bukowski. When I told Mr. Mann I'd never heard of the guy he brought in half his collection the very next night and insisted on loaning it to me. Introducing me to Bukowski was the most help I'd gotten in years.

The night I wore the black vinyl suit out for the first time I decided to stop in to see Mr. Mann. When I got to the Hole-in-the-Ground I saw that, as usual, no one was there. The dance floor was empty and a familiar lone figure stood in back at the bar, hunched over a book. Mr. Mann's silhouette was just as disappointed and embittered as my mood. I couldn't wait to see what he was reading.

When Cassady and Bret got there I was already pretty high on tequila. The vinyl felt like it was cooking me. Oily drops gathered on my forehead and a pink angry heat suffused my face, blooming into my cheeks like rage-flowers. My blood climbed higher. A fire hose of wrath bucked and snaked inside me and then I turned it on Mr. Mann. In the next second I couldn't remember what it was I said that had hurt him, or what had happened. Cassady's face floated toward me through the smoke and she took me away. We drove through the rain to another bar north of Seattle, where the bartender was the dirtbag who fucked Cassady months ago and then made her stand on the corner to wait in the rain for her ride, and I still hated him for that, I hated everyone, and when I saw the guy he looked just like a target, a huge piñata seesawing in front of me. When he served me my first vodka tonic I made a face at him and...where was Cassady? She was gone now but I wasn't sure where. It seemed like we had talked, I felt the shadow of my hand waving her off. No last few pieces...everything lost...unremembered... until—*THAT'S IT*.

He cut me off.

Cassady's dirtbag bartender had CUT ME OFF.

I slunk away from the bar and sat simmering in silent rage at a table in the back for the next hour. When I looked around the room I found that Cassady had indeed left. I had no idea where she had gone but it didn't seem important now. Not as important as finding something else to drink.

Then Lo came up with a plan. She found two old guys and got them to agree to buy me some drinks. I saw Dirtbag whisper something to the bouncer and now he was watching me too, his eyes rolling around the room like a cop car's searchlight at a strip mall after dark. We had to be careful.

Lo told the old guys to buy a round and then duck around the corner and meet me at the table in back. They could hand off drinks to me under the table. I could tell they were confused, but willing to play the game for a possible piece of ass. Everything went off as planned, at first. I got the drink under the table and checked for surveillance using the mirrors that covered every wall of the bar, and then gulped as much as I could, as fast as I could, without being seen by Dirtbag or the bouncer. In this way, I got down four more drinks. The world was thankfully bleeding together again, looking like it did an hour ago, before I had to stop drinking.

But then I got carried away chugging my fifth drink and took my eyes off one of the many mirrors I was supposed to be monitoring. The glass chattered against my teeth as it was yanked out of my mouth. It was the bouncer, his searchlight eyes rolling up to the ceiling as he held my arm and propelled me to the door.

Outside I stood and rubbed my elbow where he'd pinched it in his lobster-like grip. When the door slammed shut I suddenly realized how cold it was in the middle of the Seattle night in January. I wrapped my flimsy coat around myself and flipped off the tavern's big blinking sign. The neon buzzed back at me.

I'd been 86'ed.

When you're a drunk—a serious mean drunk—you already know you don't fit in. You know the way you act is violent and inappropriate. You're used to people not wanting you around because you cause problems, but it doesn't hurt because you're already in on the secret. You already know how much you suck. But getting 86'ed means you not only crossed the line in normal land, you got sent home from the never-ending drunk's party, where they accept anyone and easy chicks get to be extra awful. Getting 86'ed forces you into the cold gray area between hard partier and bad drunk.

Worst of all, it means you can't go back to that bar unless you do the same apologetic hangdog, pathetic day-after shuffle used regularly with your friends. It's beyond humiliating to dance like that with a stranger—like the owner (copping looks down your blouse the whole time) or the bouncer that hates you (and refuses to look down that same blouse out of pure sneering contempt). Getting 86'ed is one of the first signs you get as a serious drunk that instead of you controlling it, maybe it's controlling you.

After getting 86'ed my spirits fizted out like a wet candle wick. I was too far away from downtown and Pioneer Square to get to another bar where they'd know me and scrve me before last call, and I was too drunk to try any other bar in the immediate area. I already knew they wouldn't let me in. Finding enough in my pockets for cab fare, I took it as a sign and flagged the first taxi I saw.

20 minutes later I was back downtown, and back to our little house on a slant. One minute after that I realized I had lost my

keys. Out of money and without a phone, I plunked myself down on the porch and absentmindedly watched two crackheads fight it out across the street while I thought about what to do.

Then I remembered the window to my bedroom. I never locked that window. I never locked anything. I even left that window unlocked after Alec robbed us. Stealing was pointless in my opinion, especially for someone to steal from me, who spent all my money on booze and didn't have anything else. The experience with Alec hadn't given larceny any more interesting angles, it hadn't even turned into a good story to tell later, and so I hadn't ever thought any more about it. In fact, the only time I had ever thought in depth about stealing was when I read *Crime and Punishment* and imagined Raskolnikov, that weasely rat, bashing in the skull of the old woman I pictured as Kathy Bates in black Russian rags. Of course, the crime was murder, but it seemed really that he had stolen from her. In some weird way, as he bludgeoned her, he was stealing her experience of her own death. To me, *that* was really stealing.

I knew I could count on that window being unlocked.

Even better, the air mattress I slept on was right underneath the window so I'd fall onto a soft landing pad once inside. I scrambled to the backyard, my boots clicking ferociously on the concrete. My black vinyl caught the beams of the white full moon. Like a cat burglar, my silhouette was outlined in cold detail as I stalked my way to the rear window.

I was right. It wasn't locked. I could see the little latch turned to its side in the moonlight. But since I'd never entered our backyard before, I'd never seen the gaping hole (that looked about three feet wide and God knows how deep) right underneath the same window. I planted a hand on the side of the house and peered in. It looked like something rusty and sharp had been thrown into the hole and now waited for me with its teeth bared. I moved closer to the edge. There was a glint, fast like an eye winking, and then something else moved. I backed up and replanted my boots. Then I went for it. I jumped.

I hit the wall of the house—*WUNK*—and reeled backward. The memory of the glinting winking thing in the hole below leapt into my mind as a full-blown swamp monster. I fell and missed the hole and the puddle behind it, but bashed my head and my ribs on a pile of garbage nearby. Rusty spikes poked out of the pile and stabbed at me as I peeled myself off the mess. The heel on my platform boot had gotten caught in something on the way down and now it felt like I might have a sprained ankle.

Wincing, I stood on both feet. I hurt, but the liquor acted like a hefty dose of painkillers. I brushed myself off and decided to look for another unlocked window.

After a once-around the house I came to the gloomy conclusion that Cassady and Bret took more of an interest in theft than I did. Everything was locked. Everything except for one small window into our living room that only opened five inches. I tugged and pulled and then rattled it and waited. I tried it all again. Five inches. Five inches was the max, the absolute limit.

I sat on the front porch and watched the same crackhead I'd seen earlier smoke his pipe, by himself this time, the guy he'd been fighting with was gone. I watched his lighter spark like a winter firefly across the street, tiny explosions in the dark, and me invisible to him. No sparks marking where I was this second. I shook my head. I had to keep my mind with me. I was ready to pass out, but if I concentrated I could do my most precise thinking, the crystal cold brilliance that came when all my other illusions had been shattered. It usually happened right around three or four in the morning. And in just a few seconds, the brilliant idea came.

The window wasn't going to budge. I completely accepted that was a condition that could not be changed. The only thing I could change was me. And the only detail I really needed to negotiate in order for me to fit in the window was not my size but the amount of space I took up.

I remembered reading about fakirs in India, the guys who walked over hot coals without feeling any pain or were buried alive but slowed down their heartbeats to survive without air, using the power of the mind. I remembered another story I read when I was little, about a man who trained himself to see without using his eyes. I believed in the power of the mind. When I was drunk I couldn't doubt the power of my own mind. I thought about the fakirs again and saw how it could be done. I'd simply flatten my torso and then insert my whole body into the five-inch window space, like you punch in a subway ticket and it takes you where you want to go. I would be my own ticket and if I was flat enough I'd get punched in.

Now I went over the logistics. The very bottom of the window was still high enough on the house to be at the level of my chin. There was no way I could flatten myself down to a less than five-inch width and be able to get in that window with a torso that was bent into an awkward shape. If I was going to be flat going in, I had to be absolutely flat the whole way through. The window looked out on the narrow walkway between our house and the fence bordering the neighbor's yard. The distance between the fence and the window was about four and a half feet. I was five feet, three inches. Five feet, six inches with the boots.

If I stood in the middle of the walkway with my back to the neighbor's fence—facing the window—and reached behind me with both hands to grip onto the chain link, I could swing my legs up. With both arms outstretched for added length I was sure I could make it. From there, I would flatten myself.

It was go time.

I braced my hands on the fence, closed my eyes, and swung—and missed. My boots clattered all the way down the side of the house and left skid marks. I tried again and I missed again. And again...and again. I gave up on the fifth try.

I needed leverage. I crawled up to the top of the fence, gripped the links, and then tossed my legs out behind me blind, praying that I'd reach that window. And finally, the stripper boots worked in my favor. My three-inch heel caught on the windowsill. I pushed the heel in until I had inserted almost one whole foot into the window, and then I swung my other leg up. With both boots in, I gripped the fence with slick sweaty hands that were getting slipperier by the second.

I realized instantly I was facing the wrong way. I was looking at the ground, but the plan called for me to be on my back so I could suck everything in to be as flat as an empty envelope. But since I was now a human bridge stretched between the neighbor's fence and our house, there was no going back. I would have to slide myself in from this position. As I sucked everything in and pushed all the air out of my lungs, one clear thought floated to the front of my mind.

It was the flaw in my perfect plan.

In order to slide into the window, I had to let go of the fence.

There was no way around it. I had to let go of the fence and the windowsill wasn't going to support the rest of my body hanging out there in space. In fact, if I did let go my body would immediately bend and fall to the concrete waiting below. I'd probably break both ankles. No way around it, I wasn't going to be able to let go of that fence.

My plan sucked. I didn't give a shit about Indian fakirs now. Hanging in mid-air, my arms started to tingle and go numb. I reflected that Cassady and Bret would be home soon enough. The clubs had to close sometime, even if it was when the sun came up or later. They'd let me in. I started to lift my boot out of the window, but when I lifted nothing happened. I applied more force. Nothing. I looked down the gleaming moonlit length of my starry vinyl self strung between the house and the fence like a string of taut black Christmas lights. I saw how the window had fallen an inch in its old wooden frame and now both heels—both boots—were stuck snugly underneath the glass.

Rage bloomed in the middle of me like blood in a clear fish-bowl. I screamed, shaking my hanging body between the fence and the window. The windowpane jiggled and tinkled, the chain link fence clinked in time to my screams until I went hoarse. When I finally shut up I swiveled my head from side to side. No lights had come on and the street was still deserted.

I shook myself again and sobbed. Tears dropped pathetically on the pavement below me—the only place I wanted to be. I hung between the window and the fence, a limp dishrag now instead of a bridge. I had been broken by the dazzling, truly unexpected fortification of the little house on a slant. When I stopped crying, and after I was positive both of my arms had suffered irreparable nerve damage, I shut up again. I tried pushing my boot farther in instead of trying to drag it out. Unbelievably, it worked. The window jolted upward from the push and the boot came free. I repeated the process with the other foot and suddenly I was on the pavement.

I let go of the fence, dragging my arms behind me like dead things, and scuttled back to the front porch. I huddled down in the corner and stared at the street, watching the sun rise with shuttered eyes.

Bret got home 15 minutes later and let me in. I collapsed into bed. Sometime after that, I heard Cassady come home with some other people. And then the *bleet-bleet-bleet* of my alarm pierced the sun-yellow haze filling my room, and morning assaulted me again (how many mornings could possibly be left?). I groaned and pulled myself out of bed.

The night before came back to me in horrid little gray pieces, like flecks of brain matter shot out through the back of someone's head. Fighting nausea and the flickering shadows of memory (they would be content to stay shadows until the booze wore off, it was usually right around 10 or 11am when those shadows shrieked into larger-than-life monsters, loud as a train wreck inside my head until I'd absorbed every hairline fracture of the breaks I'd caused, every ramification of what I'd done the night before, and started calling around, eyes cast down at the floor while I gripped the phone and waited through each torturous ring, ready for someone to answer on the other side, ready to be sorry for all of it, for everything, for the rotten and rotting me they all invited into their lives, and with only a few well-placed apologetic words too, oh yes, I was ready to be really sorry this time), I pulled on some clothes and headed out into the living room, and came face to face with a beautiful stranger sitting on my couch.

Wearing a cream-colored cowboy hat and matching boots, and drinking from a frosty can of Coors Light with a case of the same beside him, sat an extremely tall, extraordinarily good-looking, light-skinned black man with immaculately kept dreadlocks. He smiled warmly at me as I stared.

"Hello," he drawled in a soft and pleasantly husky, polished voice. "I'm Richard."

"I'm, uh, Leah...um, what...I mean...are you..."

"Oh!" he exclaimed. As if I had just arrived at the party and hadn't yet received my nametag.

"Why am I here, you mean? They..."

He trailed off with a dismissive wave behind him, presumably indicating Cassady's room and the other strangers sleeping in it.

"...Brought me here." He surprised me by finishing the sentence after all, and with a satisfied pursed grin, like I had taken the nametag he offered and pinned it on in just the exact right way, like I had added something to it, maybe a tiny sunshine face with shades and a big grin, giving the ol' thumbs up—everything's fine here, yesiree boy, just dandy. But I was doubtful.

"Care for a beer?" he offered. I decided to like Richard.

He tossed a cold can of Coors my way and I caught it. I opened it and drank fast, wiping my mouth feverishly, with some vague hope that this incredibly beautiful man would see me in some sort of okay light. I knew that he couldn't possibly take any real notice of me—a bleary, greasy blob of crap that reeked of last night's martinis—but I wanted him to at least see I could keep cool when I chugged a beer first thing in the morning before I headed off to work for the day.

I heard a latch click behind me (and saw again how wrong I'd been, everything was locked up tight everywhere in this house). It was Bret. She stumbled out of her room in rumpled pajamas and looked around. She looked at Richard and squinted. My mouth was still fastened around the can of beer but before I could swallow, Richard interjected smoothly with his introductions. His long honey-colored fingers grasped tenderly at Bret's pale freckled arms as she sunk into the sofa beside him, and then expertly flipped another can out of the case, plucking it gracefully out of Bret's lap and dropping it into her palm. Richard's hands were faded brown doves, and his eyes trembled and then shook with laughter as Bret and I watched those hands fly and weave and fold into each other as he told us stories about South Africa, where he said he was from, and the diamond mines, where he said he did business. I watched Bret crack open a second beer and laugh with Richard at the last thing he said. I felt like we had all been transported to a cocktail party on planet Bizarro—the guests were really gracious, super cool and all that, and all the booze was free, but boy was everyone really weird or what?

I still hadn't found out exactly how Richard had come to be in our house that morning with a case of Coors, but I assumed Cassady had brought home a group of after-hours partiers from the Avatar. Richard had been the first one up—if he'd ever even come down—and now he'd found another party in our living room, with me and Bret.

But some mornings—like this morning—I still had to go to work at the bookstore up in north Seattle. I waved to Richard and Bret on my way out, but they hardly noticed. Bret was dialing the phone, while Richard studied the menu of an all-night pizza joint down the street. They didn't look up when I left.

Chapter 8

Bret and I warned Cassady that the upstairs neighbors were getting fed up with all the people showing up at all hours, but she ignored us and kept bringing home new bums, meth heads, club rats and couch surfers every night. Drunk, high, or just plain fucked up, every single one of them shouted and screamed when they said anything at all, and they only seemed to visit our house between the hours of 3:00 and 6:00am. It wasn't long before the neighbors reported us to the landlord and he kicked us out.

The last week we were there I ran into Big Tino as I wandered through the living room on my way to take a piss one morning around 7:00am. The house was quiet and Cassady was nowhere in sight. The front door hung open, traces of faint pink dawn light blew in with the cold night air. The sun was just coming up. Tino was a fat Latino guy with sweet and troubled eyebrows—like a grownup five-year-old still worried about Mom's bruises. He sat on our couch counting a stack of money. I knew Tino and I liked him, even half-asleep I could feel his comforting worry wash over me like a big warm blanket. I watched his chubby fingers as they primly laid out rows of sharp little square bags. Big Tino was also a notorious glass dealer.

I shot an eye toward the door.

"Where's Cass?" I asked.

Tino licked his finger and placed it on the bag he had just laid down. "She'll be right back." he said, and went on whistling under his breath and laying out bags. His eyebrows knit together in his familiar worried way as his eyes ticked down, counting the rows.

We moved out three days later.

Bret and I convinced Sadie to live with us, and we moved back to north Seattle while Cassady stayed downtown. We moved on the last day of January, a wet and gray butt-end of a day. Cold, slushy and rainy. The sky had that fleshy white-gray texture that bleeds into the earth and the water until the horizon bleeds white-gray too and everything is indistinguishable.

Sadie and I shared the same work schedule at the bookstore, to save on gas. When we worked together we also worked on our constant private dialogue. It was all about questions. Who were we? Why was everyone else so different? Why were we so fucked up? Why wasn't everyone else? The only thing certain was that we offended a lot of people and a lot of others thought we were crazy. And we knew we were crazy, and sometimes out of control, especially when we drank. But we wanted to be honest and loyal, and we never wanted to make anyone else feel like shit on purpose. Not without a reason. But then, when I was alone again, I saw that Lo had a lot of reasons.

Most other people—the people we talked to and waited on at the store, the people we made out with at the bar or took home and fucked later—they weren't honest. But they weren't liars either. They were somewhere in between, make-believing their world was just like the movie playing in their head. When the lines didn't match up we were supposed to look away politely like you do when someone flubs a line in front of you, waiting and anxious for them to fit back into the scene and story, hoping they won't do something rash onstage, like have a nervous breakdown. But all these other people had no idea they were acting out anything. And they all thought they were honest, even if they so honestly were not.

Sadie and I couldn't come up with any answers. So day after day we kept shelving books. And at night, we got drunk again.

Bret had been dating a guy who lived in an old run-down deserted building near the waterfront. He called the place the Bat Cave and it was only accessible by a tunnel, drilled through the walls by long-ago workmen and then abandoned. The Bat Cave had no furniture and the only bathroom was a bucket. Bret's guy had a roommate on heroin and a hanging sheet to separate the room into two smaller ones. She was terrified of the Bat Cave but it looked like she loved him.

But then one day he was gone. He didn't just stop calling, he straight up disappeared. He abandoned his job at the Crow and no one knew anything. Bret never heard from him again. A few weeks later the mouth of the tunnel leading to the Bat Cave was boarded up, we assumed the roommate on heroin died quietly inside. Bret's heart was broken.

In the evenings after work, instead of hanging out with me and Sadie on the couch, smoking pot and talking about what hadn't gone on last night and what had, Bret trudged directly to her room and closed the door with a firm and final snick of the lock. It stayed closed the rest of the night.

And then one day Bret announced she couldn't take it anymore. She had decided to move to Chicago in the fall. Chicago was close to her friends and family, close to home. She had no home in Seattle. She wasn't upset, she was decided. Sadie threw me a zipped-up glance across the kitchen, but I kept my eyes on

Bret and nodded without saying anything. I knew better than to try to change her mind.

～

Tom and I hadn't talked much after Sid broke Cassady's nose, and on the surface I blamed him for being Sid's friend instead of ours. But I knew that wasn't true. Tom didn't take sides. Not ever. The truth was I thought Tom wanted to be friends with Jared more than he wanted to be friends with me. And I knew why too, and that made it worse. Jared wasn't crazy.

After I got my feelings hurt I stopped speaking to Tom. But he forced a truce one day when he showed up surprise-like one morning at the new apartment and Bret let him in. He stormed into my bedroom and I woke up to his hands waving frantically above me. His face worked in small convulsions and it looked like he might have been trying to cry. After living with Cassady, I'd taken to sleeping with ear plugs. When I saw him looming over me making hideous faces, I assumed he was having a heart attack. My sleep-bleared mind concluded Tom had somehow managed to get to me right before he died, for his final moments. By the time I figured out Tom wasn't having a heart attack but only trying to apologize, I'd been panicked and frozen for too long. My silence served as acceptance, our friendship was newly sealed.

And as spring rolled into summer our friendship only grew as we discovered our compatibility as drinking partners. Neither of us ever wanted to go home, at least not alone, and so we were willing to put in extra hours during after-hours, together. We spent most of our time at the Avatar, the skeezy Pioneer Square club around the corner from the Emerald Crow. Kellen and I had forged an uneasy respectful distance and so I started out most nights at the Crow again. The back of the Avatar could be viewed from the alleyway outside of the Crow, and it was easy to see what was going on up at the club when they yelled last call down at the Crow.

Looking up into the Avatar's back windows, we were really looking into the third-floor ladies bathroom. The windows were mostly blacked out with red tint, but we could still see the shadows inside. If the Avatar was packed, the ladies room was full, and we watched a multitude of shadow shapes colliding and then rapidly splitting apart again, like drunk ectoplasm. We saw the same shadows bend at the window in predictable succession, each snorting the line of coke laid out on the windowsill.

Tom and I always arrived at the Avatar past last call because we didn't go there to drink. I kept a bottle under my driver's seat for after-2:00am purposes anyway. The Avatar was where we went because there was no other place to go. Because we didn't want to go home. And that seemed to happen a lot.

The club consisted of a stage, a dance floor, a long wrap-around bar, a few tables. It was a huge cave of utilitarian space, a lot like a barn. Big and cold, empty. The chairs, the tables, the bar, everything was made out of metal, all of it worn smooth and indifferent by a thousand drunks and junkies. Every one of them existed in that space as a compromise—an agreement to wait for the next high, and an acceptance that time is necessarily killed between highs. Waiting through sullen resentment, and then resignation, and then inescapable rage at being denied that high right now, this second, in this now, this already THEN-and-THEN-and-THEN chain of moments experienced and disappearing behind us. No one knows time like the drunk and the junkie. For us there was nothing else, except the running down of that time. Those chairs were worn smooth by all of us, by the current working steadily onward beneath us.

The Avatar played the same songs over and over, garbled and indistinct, without end and with a lot of bass. There were strobe lights and cage dancers, and stray yuppies swizzle-sticking Cosmopolitans, but there were also dark pockets and club rats. The Avatar was a manifestation of Seattle's gray underworld, where it really did rain all the time.

If I'd seen some of the other regular customers at the Avatar on a crowded street in broad daylight I'd probably have run screaming from them. But walking through the gray underworld light I had no fear. They were my cohorts and my comrades, in the trenches with me and fighting for every breath. The Avatar regulars *were* me.

Most of them were cokeheads. In the spring of 2002 cocaine was everywhere in Seattle. E was on the way out and coke was in, way in. And it was easy to buy at the Avatar.

The cokeheads were easy to spot. Usually fun and slightly manic, they ticked-ticked-ticked right along. All white teeth and intense selfish eyes, waiting-waiting-waiting for you to finish your sentence so they could start one of their own. The same words repeated from last night, the same hang up, the same conversation looping like a broken machine. And when they started coming down they were crankier than a cat with sand in its eyes. The short-lived burst of charisma from a blast of coke was only enough to cover the more obvious holes in someone's character, like a patch on a bald tire.

I didn't do coke, but something in me was broken, just like it was in the cokeheads. I was an alcoholic whose poison was driving my addiction into insanity. The bouncers turned me away from the Avatar's door a few times because of the bright red flags gently unfurling in my eyes, tipping them off to what was really going on in my soul, and what would probably surface given enough time. It was the part of me that was getting more violent, more unpredictable—more Lo—every day. But I got into the club a lot too. And when I did I danced for hours, my mania steady and strong as a heartbeat. It was the only pulse I knew. The only indication of life inside me, that weird little hot and cold flame burning like a coil in the center of me, driving me on and making me move furiously, like one possessed, until the sun came up outside.

Lately I'd spotted a new renegade group of regulars at the Avatar, a grittier, meaner group. The meth heads. Back in the summer of 2002 the only meth heads I knew I met at the Avatar. I didn't know then that I'd be getting intimate with the life processes and scrabbling habits and the dead reptilian mind of the meth head in the very near future. I didn't know one of my best friends was going to have to break off loose pieces of his soul and sell them for little bits of meth. But that was Tom, and that came later. That spring and early summer the meth heads were still only objects for detached study.

The meth heads populated the fringes of the Avatar. They were ghosts, but they had substance. Like sea wraiths, they slunk and twisted and twined their way through the club. The white ones glowed with phosphorescence and the dark ones were gray as ashes. They clustered toward the back of the club, in the narrow walkway you had to hit to get to the bathroom. That back hallway was littered with ghosts—a meth head nest.

One night I met a resident meth head named Trinity. He was friendly and shouted light conversation to me over the vibrating edge of the dance floor. A flailing girl in silver sequins jostled us off the floor and we sank back into the shadows. I looked at the clock projected on the far wall, it was almost 5:00am. Then Trinity coughed twice, short and harsh, and spat two teeth into his hand. Under the strobe lights I saw glistening traces of blood and drool. I twitched before I could stop myself and recoiled. The tape measure I'd started unwinding into him reeled back with a snap. I was horrified, even through the drunk that muffled everything else. I stared at him, but didn't ask the questions I wanted to.

He laughed at me.

"It happens, darlin'. No worries. They're back teeth and no one'll see."

He drew an invisible line with his index finger over the two rows of yellowed—albeit intact—teeth in the front of his mouth. He was right. I couldn't tell he'd just lost two teeth, and neither would anyone else. Trinity pocketed the lost molars and stole away, evaporating like smoke.

But Trinity was only a small taste. What really interested me was the female meth head at work.

The Avatar was a den of vipers, a pit on earth, and a black hole in space. A vortex of human refuse and degeneracy. So obviously, the lighting wasn't great. The bar glowed faintly like a dying fire and the dance floor only used strobe lights. When Tom and I first started hanging out there, every tiny table had its own tiny candle. But then even those tiny points of light disappeared. It was just too dangerous, having fire accessible at various stopping points throughout the club. Now, the lighting was beyond low, beyond dim. It was the gray grainy duskiness falling before full night, the twilight of twilight.

Added to that was the fact that every single person at the Avatar was on something.

So between the bad lighting and being super fucked up, a moderately attractive girl appeared absolutely gorgeous and a chick halfway dead appeared moderately attractive. The female meth heads wove in and out of the crowd as they pleased because even though they were possibly half dead, they were still female. Females, Lo said, have a value they carry with them wherever they go.

Most people don't like to admit that vaginas have economic value, but they're one of our most valuable natural resources. Lo said that no matter where you are in the world, someone wants one, and no matter who you are as a woman in this life, someone needs yours. A vagina is really the first form of cold hard cash there ever was. Better than drugs that don't last and more solid than gold, vaginas allow women to move about unmolested, in a way that men can only dream of. It may not be safe for a woman to walk down a dark alley by herself at night, but she can approach anyone in a public place and link herself to them, be let in and protected by them.

As long as she knows what she's doing, and as long as she operates in terms of the cold hard currency sitting right underneath the smile and the shake. And, Lo added, as long as she's alone.

Like all women, the female meth head—running around with her vagina like a blinking pink dollar sign flashing between her legs—knew she could use it without really using it. The vagina itself can remain safely tucked away while its powers and restorative benefits are received. It sits humming between a girl's legs like a car idling at the curb, and that vibration shivers and quakes into every nerve and every vein, even up into the eyes, making them droop like an old movie star's, and through the eyelashes, making them flutter like Bambi's. Invisible unbreakable fibers of vagina work into the blood in her cheeks, making her blush like a warm glass of pink wine, and redden her lips to match the ones down below, the ones framing the center of all that power. When Lo told me to be completely still under the strobe lights and the pounding surf of the music crashing over me, and quiet way down deep inside, then I could feel my own, pulsing in the center of me and electrifying every cell. I knew all the guys could see me lit up that way from the inside out, without ever even coming close to my vagina. Or, more simply, I knew men would give me stuff if they thought I might give up some pussy. And all the chicks who were meth heads knew that, too.

That was the female meth head at the Avatar, at her finest. The sea wraith. The diaphanous mermaid weaving in and out of the crowd. Bright white skin like coral underwater, huge eyes like great big pools of black ink, and long dead-damp fingers from the sea that reached and clutched as they drowned. The mermaids only had one function, one mode, one task without end: They searched. They sniffed and hunted and looked and scratched and bled. They wanted and they wanted and they wanted, and they only ate meth.

The first female meth head I knew by name was Angela, and she was beautiful. She was white like the center of a candle flame, ethereal in the 4:00am twilight of the Avatar, and she moved like seaweed on the ocean floor. Her long black hair shone like coal, flowing from her temples away from her black almond-shaped animal eyes. She could have been Queen of the Mermaids. But then I saw Angela outside one night, standing in line waiting to get into the club. In the true orange streetlights I saw her real face. The skin on her cheekbones was falling and her cheeks folded in like crumpled paper. Her eyes were like cartoons and her body was all sharp angles and despair. She was dying in front of me—a mermaid out of water.

In those days the meth heads at the Avatar were a novelty, a new sort of wind-up person. They mindlessly took things apart and then couldn't put them back together again. They had the first symptoms of paranoid schizophrenia, but so did I. And wasn't everyone at the Avatar crazy anyway? Wasn't Lo?

Tom and I sat at the Avatar's bar and watched the other regulars and gossiped about the people we knew. We talked about everything except Jared. I shied away from the topic like a spooked horse. But I talked around it and then Tom talked around it again, and it was like he was sitting right there with us anyway.

There was always some guy looking for something at the Avatar but I didn't want any of them. I didn't want someone to tell me Lo was beautiful or charming. I already knew that she was. And I didn't want someone to find me interesting or amusing either. I already knew that I wasn't. What really turned me on was when I was judged and found unworthy. When amounts were tallied and I came up short. I wanted silence and an indifferent shrug. I wanted zero, lower than that, nothing, and no one's eyes on me. I wanted someone who would forget already that I was even there.

Since no one else could do this as perfectly as Jared it was possible for me to spend night after night, weeks rolling into months, in search of the something I could never find. Tom was looking for something way easier—an attractive girl who would sleep with him. She didn't have to unravel the bloody knots in his head. She just had to have most of her teeth and look good underneath the strobe lights at 3:00am, our most desperate hour. Neither Tom, nor I, ever found anyone matching our requirements, and so neither of us ever went home with anybody. But after a while we didn't care anymore and it seemed like those nights were just ours.

We knew no one could love us. We spent those tragic summer nights at the Avatar sitting outside at the café tables, watching the dregs of Pioneer Square ooze and scuttle by, and planned our defense against life. We agreed love didn't really exist. I'd risked everything for Jared and he didn't want me. Tom had fallen in love years before and ended up bankrupt and devastated, alone. Both of us would never do it again. Now that we knew what fucked-up messes of people we were we couldn't pretend it wasn't that way a second longer. Once you see a thing, you can't go back. Love was an invention, not a discovery.

Everyone had an empty place inside, we decided. Meeting someone new, fucking someone new, getting attention from someone new was a way to fill it. To avoid looking into the empty places, people used each other as landfill.

Sometimes Cassady or Bret joined us for after-hours, or we brought along someone we had met at the Crow who seemed like fun. But it was always easiest when it was just the two of us.

When we didn't have to worry about communicating with a third person and could fall into that invisible rhythm that hums between close friends, and some brothers and sisters. Even when I wasn't talking I was still talking to Tom. And when I was talking I didn't have to say as much, because the rest of my words were already in his head.

Chapter 9

I'd plotted my dream revenge against Jared and Kim thousands of times. My favorite idea was me setting up a video camera in my room and bringing Jared home and then fucking him in front of it. In my fantasy I mailed the tape to Kim and when she saw it her heart burst into flames.

But as time passed, my dreams of revenge faded. It was unlikely Jared would sleep with me again, ever. He knew I was insane, and he and Kim also probably thought I was pathetic. I knew they were right. I was pathetic. But they were assholes. I still wanted to slice Kim in the ribs. And then when all my plots had almost been forgotten, Lo got her chance.

Tom called one Saturday night and said he was going to a party—did I want to come? I hesitated. Who was he going with? He started spluttering excuses before he even got to his explanations.

"Okay, I know, I know—okay, well—Jared's going—but there's gonna be other people there, too. Oh! And no Kim...definitely no Kim. No Kim. Seriously. Oh! And no Jana! Just me and Jared—and Daniel. Daniel's cool though! You should come! Really. It'll be fine. Kim won't be there."

He sounded tired already.

I cracked open a beer and cradled the phone between my ear and my shoulder. I sipped off the foam from the top of the can as Tom spluttered on.

"I mean c'mon, I don't like her either, but she won't be there, right? But—well, if you don't wanna go I understand. But you should go. You should, really. It'll be fun."

Tom didn't know what he was saying. I should definitely NOT go. I told myself I wasn't allowed to be anywhere near Jared when I was drinking. It was Saturday night and I was drinking. It was a horrible idea.

I agreed to go and hung up the phone.

After finishing a few more beers I got dressed for the party. I evaluated myself in the mirror. Even though I drank constantly my figure was shaping up well. I'd been running regularly for months now. Plus, I'd been buying clothes that fit Lo's taste more than mine. I threw on a nearly transparent top and some mascara and knew I had a good chance of snagging any man I wanted. Except, of course, for Jared.

I picked Tom up at Jared's house, the house where only a year before I'd seen Sid break Cassady's nose. I pulled into the driveway and honked. Tom bounded down the steps and into the car a few moments later, cold and rainy Seattle air gusting in with him. He slammed the door shut.

"Jared's at the party already," he said by way of explanation. "We'll meet him there."

I looked at him and raised my eyebrows.

"Don't worry." He looked right back at me. "No Kim."

We got to the party and Tom was right, Jared was already there. And as promised, Kim wasn't. I'd brought a fifth of tequila and got straight to the kitchen, setting out my supplies and pouring shots, as soon as we walked in.

With a row of Cuervo set up, and five little lemon slices sitting obediently in front of each shot, I was quickly drawing attention. First a few guys approached me and then more sidled up, like wild animals drawn to the smell of cooking over a campfire. I started passing around the shots.

After a couple rounds I noticed Jared standing on the fringes, slouched against the doorway. He looked at me with that old sardonic, but not unkind, grin that used to get me hot—used to just plain get to me. I suddenly didn't care if the five guys around me thought I was it. I just wanted Jared to keep looking at me that way.

I waved the other guys off. Complaining, they dissolved back into the party in the other room, bidding me last minute, walk away come-ons. I ignored them and beckoned to Jared.

He sauntered over.

"Wanna shot?" I asked.

He shrugged. We were two seconds into the conversation and I was already panicking. Getting him drunk, giving him more and more liquor until his defenses were down, it was all I had. My big secret was that Jared—from the second I met him until even this moment—terrified me. He was indifferent and sarcastic and his derision of everything surrounding him scared me speechless. Whenever I was around him, I wanted to be spectacular. I wanted to be more than a surrounding. But I never was. Worse, I knew I never would be. Jared was the only person on the entire earth who saw me for what I really was—a nothing. I had to have him near me.

"Well? Do you...? Wanna shot?" I tried again and held my breath. I would explode if he said no. The night would be over if he walked away.

"Sure." He shrugged again as if it didn't matter. As if I didn't matter. I already knew I didn't.

I poured two shots. We drank them down, fast and together. I immediately felt better. I took comfort in the burning in my stomach. It was an old friend—one that hurt me, but only down to a certain point. I liked to know where the boundaries were, I always counted on that certain point.

I poured two more. I gulped mine and then realized Jared hadn't taken his. He was fingering the glass and looking at me.

"Have you talked to Trak lately?" he asked. I jumped on it. Trak was our friend from Ann Arbor, back in Michigan, and Jared definitely cared more about what he was up to than about me. I said I had and that Trak had told me he was moving out to Seattle but it was all up in the air at the moment. And now Jared was really listening to me, now I had information he wanted, now he was leaning closer. But Trak didn't have any money, I said. He wanted to finish school and he didn't know if he even wanted to move to Seattle anyway. I bit my lip and racked my brains. I couldn't think of anything more to say.

"That's too bad." Jared said, and he looked away.

The tequila was riding me hard now. My mind was a blank and he was ready to be done with me, ready to walk away. And I was ready to go back to what I already knew, what Jared let me know every time, that I was a nothing and a nobody. A sum lower than zero. But then Lo stepped up and said something I never would have dared. She said one thing that forced Jared to really look at me again.

"I always thought you had a thing for Trak, you know." I was as surprised as he was when it came out of my mouth.

"Huh? What? Me? What are you talking about? Why would you think that?"

I'd jolted him for sure.

"Do you think I'm gay or something?" he asked. He didn't seem mad, just flustered. I tested his face for any sign of the fear of being found out. There was nothing in his face. I proceeded cautiously.

"Well," I paused. Lo shoved me hard from behind. "Yes."

"Why?"

"Look, when we were all in Ann Arbor you guys were always drunk and when you were drunk you always seemed to jump on Trak's back, wrestle around with him, you know..."

Jared snorted. "So?" He folded his arms and tried to act casual. I took another look into his face and suddenly saw what I'd mistaken for nothing. I knew Jared wasn't really gay—I'd had sex with him too many times to know that. But when I looked back into his face and saw him become—maybe for the first time in front of me—just a little unhinged, I knew that Jared didn't know much about himself either. The truth was: He wasn't gay, but he thought maybe other people might think he was. He was scared that maybe they would think he was. It was a weakness, the first weakness I'd possibly ever seen in him. And before I had time to fully appreciate it, Lo pounced.

"So? So...I think you're gay. That's what." I retorted, giddy now from the tequila and Lo's jubilation spilling over the rim.

"Well, I'm not. I can assure you—I'm not." He finished, rather pathetically I reflected. Lo stood up and cheered. She made a 'Sock it to 'em!' sign with her fist and then gave me the all clear.

"Prove it." I stated flatly.

The command hung in the air between us. I felt like I'd just slapped someone.

We ended up in the bathroom. Jared sat on the lid of the toilet and I sat on his lap, riding him backwards. Halfway through, the door burst open and lodged against my right foot. A big doughy guy, red-faced and drunk, looked in and burped at us.

"S'cuse me," he hiccupped and lurched off down the hall. I kicked the door shut again. It banged open two seconds later.

"Whoops! Sorry bro!" Another guy stumbled off.

I kicked the door again, but it didn't even make it all the way closed before it hit the next poor jackass in the face.

"Oh, sorry—holy shit! What the fuck are you guys doing?!"

It wasn't just another drunk jackass. It was Daniel. Kim's friend, Daniel.

We were caught.

Of course, Kim found out. There was a scene, although I wasn't there to witness it. I only heard about it through Tom. There were tears, there were threats, there was screaming. There was no breakdown, from either one of them. In fact, they didn't even break up, not even for a few days.

The last few minutes with Jared haunted me. How he'd pushed me away after Daniel barged in on us. How he'd looked stricken at being found out and then wouldn't even touch me. But he had agreed to it, right? We'd gone into that bathroom together, correct? If he really wanted to be with Kim, how come he was fucking me in a strange bathroom in the middle of his friend's party? Was I really insane?

I was slipping again. But things were different now. I had Lo, and Lo could see clearly what I couldn't see at all.

Jared had conned me. Really, he'd been conning himself this whole time and I got sucked in on the periphery of it. Every story he'd told me about the person he thought he was I'd believed, and they were all stories he had drawn for himself.

But after Lo lured him into that bathroom I never saw him the same way again. Now I knew he was just a regular guy. He wanted a regular girlfriend who pouted and played games and who was a bitch with predictable familiarity. He wanted to cheat on her so they could fight and then have makeup sex. He wanted to hurt her and make her angry just to see her face change sometimes because he was bored with her and bored with himself. None of his outlaw angles were true and they never had been. Jared wasn't different. He wanted a burden on him, an easy way out, more attention from everyone, more now from right now.

Just like anyone else.

Chapter 10

As I ran through the wet, gray streets every morning I traveled back in time. I saw Seattle as it had existed millions of years ago, a cold tropical jungle trembling and dripping with constant rain. Before time began, I saw the outlines of the city already built into that jungle. Giant ferns sprouted from the Space Needle. A curtain of mist fell over it all, shadowed stone of buildings and wild green warrior trees, a veil that lightened in the summer and dragged heavy every autumn. I saw that the veil was inevitable, that it couldn't be circumvented, or avoided. It was a shadow that stalked the city. Something that couldn't be outrun, and something that would always return.

Walking through the wet, black streets at night I looked down alleyways and into dark storefronts. The whole city seemed to be abandoned, but then I reached the heart of downtown and saw all the bars with their windows filled with warm yellow light, winking out into the darkness here and there, casting a luminous glow onto the sidewalks outside. Anyone left in the city congregated in these bars because they knew they had been abandoned too. Everyone was lost. And everyone knew it would never stop raining because the sky didn't know what else to do over this city but cry. One night I smoked a cigarette in the alley next to the Crow with a strange gloomy man who told me Seattle was a waiting room. "You wait to be called by whatever it is that's gonna call you," he said. I drew sharply on my cigarette and squinted against the smoke, looking out across the street to the rainy waterfront and over the Sound. "Like most waiting rooms, it seems like everyone else there is trying to ignore you," he went on. "Tomorrow it will rain again, and the wait will be longer."

Seattle had a thousand hiding places, and so I felt right at home. Everything was private. As I passed people on the sidewalk, no one looked into my face trying to guess my thoughts. Everyone looked down at the ground or up at the gray sky, trying to guess when it would rain again. I noticed quickly that there was never a first rain in Seattle, only an every rain, and everyone huddled into themselves to keep out of it.

Before I moved to the city people warned me that everyone was generally depressed in Seattle. People in Seattle wore black, they said. People in Seattle jumped off buildings all the time. It was because of the rain that demanded so much and left no room for anything else, especially not the sun. But I found that people in Seattle were really just like all the people in the rest of the country, who were generally depressed. None of us made much of an allowance for hope.

~

The Crow was emptier on Sunday nights than on any other night of the week. The lights in the poolroom were brighter and the bathrooms were colder. The whole place was bigger. One Sunday night Bret and I found ourselves there with a funny sinister gnome of a guy named Ratt Stilskin and two other regulars, Alden, a sad slight boy with big dark eyes, and a guy named Chaz.

Chaz was the resident pool shark at the Crow. Volatile in a

lazy sort of way, everyone I knew assumed he was a cokehead with careful self-control. He had his own set of keys to the pool table, which he bounced nonstop in one hand while waiting for his opponent to take a shot. He worked as a waiter at a jazz club down the street and seemed to be just getting off work every time I ran into him, and so he was always in the same black dress shirt and pants, lending him a peculiar air of changelessness. I imagined that even after the Crow closed he probably still stalked his way around the pool table, forever racking the balls and bouncing his keys. Forever strutting into position to get exactly the right shot, intent on driving the ball home.

That evening Chaz listlessly knocked the balls together and bounced his keys while the rest of us drank, taking steady pulls at our beer without interest and without meeting each other's eyes. Ratt Stilskin and Chaz started a game as Bret and I watched, exchanging bare words with Alden. The music from the jukebox was depressing and overplayed, the waitresses grumpy. It was a bad night all around.

Finally we all decided to go to Alden's place. The five of us limped out of the dead freezer of the Crow and hailed a cab, piling into it all together without hope, not caring who got an elbow in the face. Once we got there, the party fizzled to a total flat. It was after 2:00am so we hadn't been able to buy any more beer, and Alden didn't have anything in the house. Ratt Stilskin and Bret started arguing about nuclear power plants and Alden passed out on the floor. Chaz and I sat in the corner and talked in low voices. So far I found him entertaining. He didn't patronize me. Also, I could see he had a little courage and a lot of charisma. I knew most other men at the Crow hated him and I saw it from that angle too. Chaz was cocky and he liked to strut. But while he might have been an ass, I could see he wasn't a weasel. I decided to fuck him.

I leaned forward and rested my wrists on my knees, my fingers dangling in an implied invite, and Chaz scooted toward me gradually until his knees were less than a millimeter from my own. He folded his hands in the same position, fingers down and lax, his eyes caught on mine. If Bret or Ratt Stilskin looked over they would see us huddled together secret-like, the image of monks praying or businessmen cutting a dirty deal—spinning faith between us on the down low, trusting each other for only these particular moments.

I told Chaz almost everything. How the thought of belonging —me to someone or someone else to me—started a shudder deep down in my bones. What I needed was to live my life as a drunk! I said loudly, whacking my palm with my fist. Chaz's eyelids twitched a hair's-breadth higher. Instantly, I quieted down and folded my hands back up. Life as an alcoholic was hard on my mental state, I explained. I was mostly excitable, sometimes emotional. I suffered from bouts of soul-snapping loneliness. I cut my eyes away. Heat was creeping up my thighs.

Chaz hadn't looked anywhere else but at me. I cleared my throat and started again. I wanted a guy, I said, who I knew I wanted to fuck. I wanted to know that when I was sober. Then I wanted to fuck that same guy, but only when I was drunk. And I wanted no questions asked.

Chaz leaned back and smiled. He accepted the deal, he said. He would meet me at the Crow a few days later. Then he winked and I didn't hate the wink, seeing that it was only the last closing gesture to seal our joint prayer business deal. After I nodded in agreement there was an awkward little moment when he leaned in to kiss my cheek, but then drew back fast with a puzzled inward look, like he'd surprised himself by trying to slip a shoe on an amputated limb that had been gone for years. I offered him my hand instead and, following the natural order of the wink that had passed between us a few seconds ago, we shook on it.

A few nights later I walked into the Crow and Chaz caught my eye and tipped his head up once in my direction, just slightly.

So slightly that no one else could catch it. I was as comfortable as if I'd been vacuum-packed in plastic, knowing I wouldn't have to think about Chaz until roughly four hours later. Then it would be last call and I wouldn't be thinking at all. For now I was safe. I had the knowledge that after 2:00am there would be a waiting receptacle. Something I could dump everything into, everything that was me, and everything that had become too much me. A stuffed piñata would be waiting at the end of the night. I didn't need the candy. I just wanted to beat it until it cracked. Or until I did.

That was how Chaz and I started fucking regularly.

We always went to his place. Chaz's room contained nothing besides a huge bed and what looked like a thousand black socks. In sad little piles they dotted the perimeter of the bed, like autumn leaves slimed and black from rain. The socks were from his work uniform, the dressy black shirt and pants he wore as a waiter. I couldn't imagine him in regular day-to-day attire. I couldn't see him out in the real world, period. Chaz standing in line at the bank maniacally rocking back and forth on his heels? Chaz grocery shopping and bouncing those tiny pool table keys incessantly as he moved up and down the predictable aisles? When I saw all those black socks circling his gigantic empty bed—a shrine to Chaz the Waiter—life suddenly seemed hilarious.

I liked Chaz because he made Lo happy, for a while, and so in a way he brought me peace. Ground rules were laid out from the beginning. We didn't exchange phone numbers, agreeing only to rely on our frequent run-ins at the Crow to make contact with each other. It was a sex-only relationship, with neither party depending on it to blossom into something else. I thought it was perfect. Lo had reinforced my ideas about compartmentalization, sex in one box and everything else divided into others. But beyond the sex, there was a dynamic at work between Chaz and Lo that I couldn't comprehend.

According to Lo, it was impossible for one individual to love another without any ulterior motives. Lo's voice went high and shrill as she drilled this into me. Believing that one person could love another solely for themselves—for being only that he or that she, only what is, not what could be—well, that never happened. And believing any of those things—she paused for emphasis and looked straight at me—that was the height of stupidity.

This was the way of the world: When one person outlived his or her usefulness you moved on to another who served your needs better. Usefulness came down to what someone else could do for a person, how they contributed to either inner sensation or outer status—the only two ways to be diverted from the heady knowledge of onrushing death. I knew status was false as cheap plywood, but it appeared to divert most people. It never diverted me. I carried the knowledge of my own death like a lump behind my ear. Sensation was all I had left after Lo.

Looking back on my past, I remembered the people who had hit me, who had lied to me, who had never ever listened. Everything was clear now. I'd been doing it wrong the whole time. I'd acted like a little girl who expected a magical mother and father to swoop out of the sky and fix everything. My expectations were immature and unreasonable. Love was a matter of biology strung together with economics. Frogs spewing glistening strands of frail eggs and hard-eyed grayfaced people in bread lines. Lo's voice pierced me again. People could be friends, good friends even, but risking anything for anyone else was playing the fool. Dramatic as always, she finished with a flourish of her small white hand. This was the unspoken—the one and only—unchangeable rule of the world.

I fucked Chaz at least twice a week for the next six months.

Chapter 11

I had always been fascinated by Beautiful Women. Big tits, big hair, high heels—I wanted to know how it was done. My mother had gone through two different rounds with cancer, stretching from the time I was two years old, until she died when I was eleven. She lost all her hair, twice, had both breasts removed, and later had a total hysterectomy. I don't remember ever seeing her wear high heels. When she felt well enough to get around she could usually be found out in the sprawling vegetable garden she cultivated, in jeans and sneakers.

I knew my mother was a beautiful woman, even without the tits, hair, or high heels. She loved me totally, completely, and unconditionally. She always listened, even when she was exhausted from chemotherapy. She treated everyone with kindness, even when she was in pain. She never tried to hide the absence of her breasts, or her scars. She never wore a wig to hide her lost hair. She was just herself, all of the time, in whatever form that took at the moment.

After my mother's battle with breast cancer, my little brother was born and then diagnosed with leukemia at age four. He died right before his seventh birthday. A few months later my parents divorced, my dad quickly remarried, and then my mother soon after was given the news that she had ovarian cancer. She died three years after my brother.

I had always seen clearly what my mother was, the rarity and beauty of her soul. But I wasn't so sure my dad could see it. He worked so much when I was growing up that I hardly noticed when he moved out. I still saw him as much as I ever had after that, maybe more because the custody agreement said that I was to spend every Saturday with him. My father was a surgeon, and an extreme workaholic. Every time I was around him he seemed distracted and disconnected. He often mumbled to himself, focused intently on figuring out some surgical puzzle in his own head. He forgot things I told him one minute later and could barely remember the names of any of my friends. As a young child, I always had to remind him to hold my hand when we crossed the street. I knew if I didn't he would walk on without me and leave me stranded.

I was well aware that my father was some sort of genius, and so his brain didn't work like it did in other people. I could feel the laser-like concentration he directed inward, always inward, whenever I was around him. I also felt the raw agony of pain that enveloped him after my brother died. I saw how it made him run, from everything. He ran away from himself, even inside his own body. I saw and felt and knew these things without anyone telling me. I had always been able to do that.

But that doesn't mean that I ever had any clue what to do about it.

My dad had been having an affair with one of his nurses for eight years before my parents divorced. The divorce was final on a Monday in the spring of 1988 and the next day—Tuesday—he married the nurse. I met her a couple of months later.

My dad's new wife was very pretty. I could tell my dad thought she was a Beautiful Woman. But when I watched them together it didn't seem like they knew each other very well, even when they teased each other and tried to be funny. My dad still seemed to be his distracted self, and I saw my new stepmother subtly try to chase down his attention and grab it, just as I had been doing for years. Sometimes we would playfully argue over who got the olive in his martini, but I knew it wasn't just play underneath the surface. Anyone who was determined to fill a significant role in my dad's life quickly learned that the olive in his martini was one of the only things you could ever count on getting from him.

After the divorce my parents stayed friends. It was impossible for anyone not to stay friends with my mom. Even when she was angry with people, she still let them know they were loved. When my dad came over he walked out back with my mom to poke around in the garden or they sat on the porch and grilled steaks. After dinner they watched golf or part of a movie on TV or just talked with my grandma, who was always over at our house to help out. But my dad was still distracted, and he mostly talked about surgery and his patients, just like he always had. He still didn't seem to notice anything around him, like how my mom was heartbroken and dying. I wasn't even ten years old and I could see the heartbroken part.

After my mom died a couple of years later, my grandma moved into the farmhouse we lived in to take care of me. Then she died when I was 16 and I stayed there alone, until college. My dad stayed with my stepmother and had a new family. In all the years since, containing all those thousands of days, I had thought it out from every angle. But the more I thought, the more confusing everything seemed to be. Until Lo came along and made things simple. Easy to see. Why my dad had left us for my stepmother, who was a Beautiful Woman. Why he had continued to chase Beautiful Women after that. Why each new Beautiful Woman he found was never enough.

There was no explanation, Lo said. It was horrifyingly cold and simple. But—Lo interjected—at least it was only horrifying down to a certain point.

But I still had a lot of questions about Beautiful Women. What happened when the Universe took back its beauty, without mercy? What happened after the car accident, when the Beautiful Woman lost a leg? What happened after the house fire when the Beautiful Face transformed into a sheet of shiny pink scar tissue? What happened when cancer came and the Beautiful Woman had to choose between her Beautiful Breasts or her life? If being a Beautiful Woman was all someone had, where did that get anyone in the end?

I knew that I wasn't a Beautiful Woman. My face took on a sort of charming animation when I got excited, but any aspirations toward beauty ended there. Now though, when I went out to the bar, Lo dressed me as carefully as a doll. Some nights she chose black mesh and collars with dominatrix boots. Some nights it was pink satin and delicate curving heels. Whatever we wore, it was always accompanied by the black leather belted coat she had also picked for me that fell just past the miniskirts she so often preferred. Buried within so many costumes, I encountered all sorts of men who tried to solicit me. Guys offered to buy me drinks, paid me filthy and unbelievable compliments, and told me all about the make and model of their car and how much it was worth.

It seemed they, too, had bought into the illusion of the Beautiful Woman.

~

August of 2002 in Seattle was hotter than hell. I woke up one morning striped in sunlight covering me like a second blanket, pouring sweat. I cracked my eyes, blearily studying the motes of dust that lazily wheeled through the still air of the apartment like drunk and dirty gnats. Boredom came and settled on me like another layer of heat. I wanted—needed—something new. I dug the vinyl cat suit out of the back of my closet.

It was Saturday and so I knew Chaz wouldn't be around that night. He was with his girlfriend on the weekends and on a short leash. So once I got to the Crow that evening I grabbed a table with a good view of the windows to check out the prospects as they walked in. No one looked very promising. Boredom wound itself tighter around my brain, buzzing and whining. My armpits prickled with tension and plump beads of sweat broke out on my forehead. The insides of my thighs slicked against the vinyl, a reservoir slowly collected under each of my kneecaps. I needed a shot. I stood and began to move through the hot sluggish air, making my way to the bar.

While Kellen hunted around for a fresh cold bottle of gin I caught the eye of a guy down at the end. He wore a beige baseball cap and didn't appear to be any different than anyone else I'd seen all night, except that he was strikingly handsome. I seized on it, grabbed the thread and wrapped it around my palm, following it between waitresses with trays, through groups of loud frat boys, and under every regular's barstool. When I got to the end and saw the thread went into the guy through his navel, and attached to his guts by some invisible device, I decided to fuck him. The alternative was hell. If I was left with the boredom that had built up over the long slow hot day I might rip my eyes out.

I started my run on him.

My method with new guys was always the same. "Do you read?" I'd ask carefully and with chilly precision. If I still wasn't too drunk, on the better side of okay, I'd manage to edge my voice with an evenness that could easily be mistaken for neutrality. No matter what title the guy threw out, no matter what author he liked, I could get a conversation going. The guys who were really into books always gave me a name I was familiar with, an author I'd read. I'd pick detailed bits out of my memory and play it up. They were always impressed. This was the only bonding—the only sharing—I ever did with anyone else that was genuine. But it was always short-lived.

If the guy wasn't a huge reader but had experienced some pleasure at some time by picking up a popular novel at an airport kiosk, I could fake it. I worked at a bookstore and I knew every name there was to know in a drugstore paperback stand. I could spit John Grisham titles like a wood chipper cranked to full speed. Not one of those guys realized that I'd never actually read one sentence from their favorite popular author even though we were discussing his last ten books.

If the guy didn't read Lo took over the helm, and Lo was not interested in books.

The newest little animal, who told me his name was Jeff Tracey—Lo always demanded a full name from everyone, even if she thought it was a fake—was luckily into Tom Clancy. I chatted about submarines and spies for ten minutes and then ran back to Kellen to get more drinks. When I skipped off again I was intent on not losing any more time. I knew I might completely forget what Jeff Tracey's face looked like if I stayed on the other side of the bar for too long. Fortunately, he was standing in the same spot. I knew that spot way better than I recognized the memory of his face.

When the long arm of the clock headed toward last call we decided to get out of there. Jeff Tracey lived east of Seattle, across Lake Washington. We had to take the 520 bridge, and so we had to take my car, but first we had to find it. I thought I'd parked a few blocks down. But when we took a cab back to that spot, the car wasn't there. I ordered the cabbie to drive around and circle each block. During one of the circles I passed out. I woke up to Jeff Tracey pulling me roughly out of the cab and onto the sidewalk with a desperate unhappy look on his face. He looked like he might cry.

"I thought you said you knew where your car was!"

Two hectic patches of red flared perfectly on his sculpted cheekbones. I shook my head to clear it and got the spins. I sank down to the curb, holding my head in my hands.

"Will you shut the fuck up? Jesus. What the fuck. Where are we?" I said without looking up.

Jeff Tracey informed me that we were near Pike Place Market, that he hadn't had enough money to pay the cab driver, and that he wanted to go home now please. My mind was a blank. I was pretty sure at that point that my car had never existed, everything was surreal. Jeff Tracey was a complete non-person to me. Anyone could come along right at that moment and shoot him in the head, right in front of me, and I wouldn't care. The capacity to care had dumped out of me and into the street in one cold dead load. And then I heard a sniffle and Jeff Tracey's thin bleating voice intruded again and I began to pray that someone really would come along and shoot him. I wanted nothing more than to be alone.

Then I remembered I had a pint of tequila hidden underneath the driver's seat of my car. The thought of the taste of Cuervo hit me in the gut, electrifying every nerve. I suddenly knew where that bottle of tequila was. I was galvanized.

"C'mon!" I shouted. I dragged Jeff Tracey by one arm down the street, the black vinyl swishing viciously between my legs, a new fire in my eyes.

The car did exist after all. I slid into the driver's seat and groped underneath for the bottle. I took two long pulls, capped the bottle and slung it back under the seat, and then started the car. We were on our way.

I moved in and out of the blackout as I drove over the bridge, Lake Washington stretching off into an endless silver sheet of water and Eminem cranked full blast on the stereo. I hit the bottle of Cuervo and tossed it over to Jeff Tracey. The sips he took seemed to revive his spirits. But then a moment later I was safe away in a blackout and no sound, no light, nobody could touch me. And then it was back to the car again, back with Eminem as he sang to me what a bitch his mom had been to him. Jeff Tracey wasn't there anymore. I was alone behind the wheel, just me racing my car across the bridge, the moon on the water brighter and brighter...and then into the black again. When I came back this time Jeff Tracey was back too, fiddling with the radio and acting like he'd been there all along. I didn't mind his sly maneuverings. I was popping in and out of the party myself.

And we were still on the bridge. My entire life seemed to have been lived in that car, driving over that bridge. But I wasn't sure if that life was real, I only knew the level in the bottle of Cuervo was dropping along with the gas meter. When I used everything up I didn't know what would be left, or if we could even finish crossing this bridge. Aching now, I wished for a more continuous blackout and said a silent drunk's prayer to Jose Cuervo to get the job done. Then, as promised, I went back into the black.

When I came out of it we had finished crossing the bridge. In fact, it appeared we had arrived at Jeff Tracey's home and gotten to his bed. I was on my back and still in my vinyl top, nude from the waist down. It looked like Jeff Tracey was fucking me. He was naked, with sheets pooled around the lower half of him, but he wasn't on top of me. He was more set back, as if he'd been fucking me but then pulled out and rocked back on his haunches. He looked alarmed, his two handsomely arched dark eyebrows drawn together in consternation as a silent "o" puckered his mouth. It looked like he'd been watching me do something puzzling and awful. But I found no evidence as to what exactly Lo had just done to this poor man. No puke, no blood, nothing broken. I felt her surge up and buck and twist inside of me and then his face folded in like a closed door. When Lo hit me from behind everything went black again.

Then it was morning. I woke up alone and heard someone moving around downstairs. If I moved the pain would come and so I just lay there, rolling my eyeballs around the room in an attempt to gather more data. My gaze settled on a Polaroid picture by the bed. My brain started crankily chugging through the details of the night before. The guy in the picture was the guy whose bed I was in. His name was Jeff Tracey and he loved Tom Clancy. He thought *The Hunt for Red October* was the greatest book he'd ever read. The chick in the picture with him looked to be his mom. She was staring at me. I rolled over and groaned as the hangover comfortably settled its ass on my forehead. As if I'd flipped a switch, Jeff Tracey was immediately at the bedroom door.

"Hey!" he chirped. "Ready to go?"

His distaste for the slutty wino in his bed was obvious.

"Yeah..." I whispered. Talking hurt. "Can you give me a minute?"

"Sure thing!" he chirped again, and bounded off to what I could only imagine was a sunny game of badminton in the backyard, with people who had normal lives and clean hair, wanted to buy the newest trendy car on the market for the best price, and did not regularly puke on themselves during their morning shower.

I sat up, slowly. I gathered myself and pushed through the pain. I had to find my car. I kept this thought with me as I threw back the sheets.

I was covered in blood.

My crotch, my ass, the lower part of my back, the backs of my thighs, and the surrounding field of pristine, white, probably freshly-laundered-every-Wednesday-without-fail sheets, were covered in sticky dark red blood that smelled like a jar of pennies.

The bed was soaked. I saw some clots.

The possibilities raced through my mind. I'd gotten my

period, that much was obvious, but when exactly had it happened? I remembered the brief flash of having sex with Jeff Tracey the night before. I definitely remembered looking around for possible evidence of the latest horrific act perpetrated by Lo. There hadn't been any blood then.

As I thought about it more, and recalled the vaguely prissy and indignant air Jeff Tracey had about him, I realized it was highly unlikely that he would have known about my bloody gushing vagina and not said even one word. He had, in fact, just bounded into the room a mere two minutes ago freshly showered and with the perkiest of smiles. And while I knew he was understandably excited about the prospect of my swift departure, I also had a gut feeling if he knew what was in his bed, that same toothpaste ad grin would unhook itself off his face and slide away entirely.

There was only one possibility—he didn't know.

The instant I realized that he seriously, probably, almost-certainly didn't know, I shot up and out. I slipped my blood-covered, sweat-streaked ass into the vinyl while feeling around under the bed for my left shoe. The fluids on me, both new and old, helped me to slide into the pants even faster. I grabbed my jacket and found the keys to the car in the lining where I always hid them. Then I turned back to the bed.

It looked worse than it had when I was lying in it. Now I could see all of it, like an aerial view. The blood wasn't just in patches, it was in great mad splashes, like something had been killed there and had tried to get away the entire time it was being killed. It seemed to be soaked into the mattress beneath it. The clots looked like nightmare shellfish, beached and dying. I thought I saw little heartbeats in each one.

"Hello? You comin' down?"

It was Jeff Tracey. For what felt like the millionth time I begged the Universe to take him away. However, I was in his house and I knew my chances of never seeing him again could only increase once I got the fuck out of there. I took another brief look at the bed, cursed myself and Lo, and began to make it.

And I made that bed. I pulled the covers over the mess, straightened and tucked in the sheets and plumped all the pillows. It looked just fine and although I felt a twinge of guilt knowing that Jeff Tracey would go to bed that very night and find those eyeless bloody shellfish waiting for him, each with its little heart quite possibly still beating, I weighed the crushing majority of my feelings—as it seemed they had decided to sit on top of the hangover already sitting on top of my head—and found that truthfully, I just didn't care. I got the fuck out.

I didn't look at Jeff Tracey when I left, I didn't say a word. I walked quickly and surely to the car, parked out front. On autopilot, I started it and drove. Two miles later I remembered that I had no idea where I was or how to get back to Seattle. I stopped for directions and then hit the bridge going the other way, back to the apartment to tell Sadie and Bret all the horrible things I had done, yet again.

Chapter 12

By the fall of 2002 Lo was at full throttle, and when I was very drunk she could get ugly and violent. She switched rapidly back and forth between being out-of-the-blue mean and then full of pure charm. If the other people around us weren't just as drunk as I was, they usually noticed. They knew something was off with us, and that something was wrong with me.

But while I was busy trying to hide Lo from the world, she kept right on explaining the way it worked to me. Lo said any man could be drawn in by an unconscious physical characteristic of mine, something that corresponded to old memories or his half-forgotten dreams. Maybe I laughed like his first love, maybe I frowned like his barely remembered and long-dead aunt. Maybe my voice just sounded familiar. Whatever it was, said Lo, we pick the ones we want, in real life and outside of it.

Lo also said most guys picked their women like they chose an automobile: for type, potential pleasure, and the admiration of other men. But—I argued—some of the men I talked to had obviously already been broken by a woman. Lo drew her little mouth down in a furious bow. She then patiently explained that they only loved that past girl precisely because she had broken their heart. The pain that woman caused distinguished her from everyone else. Out of the grand swirling tapestry of phenomena in the Universe reflected and distorted through the filter of their mind, that old love girl from the past stood alone, a pure and shining beacon to help them find their way. But now they were stuck, Lo said. They were too stupid to think their way out of the fantasy they had created. The reality was that there were no beacons. According to Lo, you had to learn to live in the dark.

Letting Lo loose was always a dicey deal. Once she was out all bets were off. She pushed her way into my arms and legs after the first couple of shots. She sent electricity down my spine and through the roots of my hair after drinks three and four. From five and six on she kicked off her shoes and got settled. Paired with my fear of her—too delicious to be ignored—was the relief, always the relief. The crushing pain of the boulder on my brain lifted, if only for a matter of hours. And that was when Lo was in control again.

Sometimes I got 86'ed from a bar, like the night I got caught in the window. But I didn't seem to be in danger of losing any of my regular spots. Bret and Tom remarked how eerie my quick-change personalities could be when I was in a blackout, and my coworkers at the bookstore saw me come in hungover a lot of the time, but other than that life went on pretty much like normal. I let Lo out on the nights I drank and maintained my own self the rest of the time, when I had to move around in real life. I didn't realize yet that even when Lo was back in her cage, she wasn't sleeping.

That September Bret found her own place and Sadie and I fled to Queen Anne, a neighborhood on the edge of downtown Seattle, where I'd found an apartment with a view of Puget Sound, two bedrooms that didn't share a wall, and neighbors who were indifferent to the point of being comatose. It was perfect.

Now that I lived downtown again I ran a lot of mornings down near the water. I watched a few stringy old men take the jump into the Sound for an early morning swim, and then kept going down the pavement along the waterfront until I reached the end of Pioneer Square. Sometimes I ran five miles, sometimes ten. If I was too hungover, I didn't run at all. But no matter how much I drank, I averaged 25 miles a week, every week. Even if I had to stop to puke in the bushes, running was the only time I could think clearly about anything.

The bright mornings of that fall of 2002—Seattle in memory—are seen now from the sky. As if I'd been perched in a very tall tree and observed everything from that vantage point. There was a tall tree exactly like that right outside my new bedroom window in Queen Anne, like the tree I see things from in my memory. I could see the Sound from my bedroom window too, and out in the water the scaffolding that the cargo ships used when they came in to dock, its rusty skeleton standing darkly in relief, raising its arms to the sky.

But my memory of night in Seattle is maybe all dream, a dream of Lo, and a dream of wet gray coins of light, silver puddles in black alleyways. Water angels knifed by blades of orange light flickering through the darkness. Night in my poor dream of Seattle was tied to the street but had wings beating inside, and was always trying to fly, out and away, over the land...but the black water was everywhere. That's the last thing I remember.

~

As time went on the sex with Chaz got crazier. I did anything I wanted, and to him, I was only a mad slut from the bar, so he got to exercise complete freedom as well.

One of our games was rape. I'd put up a struggle and Chaz would pin me down, pretending to force me. If he hurt me a little bit into the bargain, so much the better for both of us. I was usually so drunk anyway that my vagina was actually numb, which no one else had ever seemed to understand before Chaz. Hard, fast, and violent penetration was the only thing I wanted— it was the only thing I could feel—and Chaz got that. He got me too. He understood I had absolutely zero interest in oral sex for the same reason. I couldn't feel anything. Two months into it we stopped going to his place and started going to mine. Sadie was a bad drunk like me and consequently, a relatively free thinker. I'd grown tired of the snotty glares of contempt from Chaz's uptight roommate, but even having a place to ourselves couldn't hide the fact that things had begun deteriorating. It seemed now that I was deteriorating too.

Every night I spent with Chaz spanned about four or five hours, and out of that time I only ever remembered maybe an hour or two. By the time October rolled around I was down to 45 minutes of memories, and even that was a compilation of random snippets of scenes. It was impossible to recall anything substantial that ever happened between us. I might remember handing a shot of tequila to Chaz. Or talking to a stranger and getting a jealous look from him. Sometimes it was the slam of his car door, with me waiting inside the car. For what? For who? Where were we? I never knew. And then it was Chaz in my bed and me on top and then him looking for a missing sock in the half gloom of the moonlit room.

And then always, it was morning again and I was sick. Real life resumed.

One night at the beginning of November I ran into him when I was dressed as the dominatrix again, wearing my vinyl cat suit, but this time Lo had paired it with a red wig. The Crow was almost empty and he was by himself, shooting a game of pool. After last call I was safely installed in the front seat of Chaz's small black truck, on the way to the apartment in Queen Anne.

When we got inside I barricaded us in the bathroom and tossed the wig on the floor. I turned on the bathtub faucet, full force and cold as it would go. I demanded Chaz strip and sat on the toilet lid as if it were an armchair, crossing my legs and talking to him while the tub filled up. I told him how I was in the middle of reading *Pnin* by Nabokov and there was no one I could talk to about it. There was no one who understood how much it was fucking with me. The way Nabokov dealt with memory felt... unsettling. It made me deeply uneasy in some way that I couldn't understand. I wanted to throw the book across the room, tear it in half, but I couldn't stop reading it either. Did he know what I meant? Did he understand at all? Finally, I looked at Chaz, really looked at him instead of looking right through him. He stared back at me blankly. Are you crazy? he asked slowly. I have no idea what you're talking about, he said.

I ordered him into the tub.

Chaz opened his mouth and then closed it again. He looked at the tub and then looked back at me. I hadn't gotten undressed. I watched him without pretense. This was his limit and I would push him past it. If he didn't believe in me, he would soon learn to believe in Lo.

And somehow, bizarrely, he did. He set his face slowly, carefully. And then he got in.

I'm not sure how much time passed. I went back to thinking about my problem with *Pnin* and was only finally aware of him again when he chattered at me through blue lips, asking if he could get out of the tub. I decided to let him out but told him he wasn't allowed to have a towel.

I marched him to my room and then I fucked him. And then the veil came down. But even so, some memories still got through. The next morning I remembered hauling off and socking him across the face as hard as I could, yelling at him that he was a bitch. But because I only felt the shadows of emotions through the veil and only my own—no one else's emotions like I got in sober life—all I could see in the memory was me drawing my arm back, drawing a line that was precise and measured. Then the pure force, a ribbon of silver energy unlooping in huge concentrated coils, shooting out of me and into whatever was beneath me, a slab of white foam, a wave of meat, a body that was Chaz.

Later, how much later I never knew, we lay in each other's arms like two lovers, except that he was the wrong lover. Or rather, I was calling him the wrong name. Barely conscious of it the first time, the second time the name floated on the air before it disappeared. I was only sure of its echo, of the place where it used to be. But the third time I said it the name came out dry, flat and sharp. It was a smack in the face, a fan snapped shut, cutting everything short. I heard the name clearly the third time, heard myself saying it—*Jared*—felt the ache throbbing through it like the hot fever of blood poisoning. A red sticky heat, the wailing buzz of anger—FLOOMP—exploded out of Chaz like a lick of fire, up and under the veil, and into my eyes. And then Chaz was gone. I didn't remember him leaving.

I also didn't give it much thought the next morning. Chaz had been angry with me before, livid in fact, and it never affected Lo's agenda one bit. But when I ran into him at the Crow a few days later he acted like he didn't know me. When I pressed him, it didn't work. When I changed tactics and got mad, he didn't care.

It was like I didn't exist. Like I had never existed.

I took a cab home, alone.

There is no worse feeling than to find out you're nothing but a loser while you're fucked up and alone in the back of a cab. The night and the city streamed past me in ribbons of orange through vacant streets that felt like they went on forever. I could feel death on me, eating away at me, and all this time it had been fucking me too, but so slowly I didn't know it, I hadn't even felt it. Death had apparently not gotten the memo about my numb vagina. I tried to talk to the cab driver but he wouldn't speak to me either, and I knew then that he felt it too, death there in the car with the both of us.

Even Lo had gone away and left me. Now, too, it seemed that maybe I'd been alone the whole time. And I couldn't argue with that, because it was precisely when Lo was strongest within me that it was like no one else could see her at all.

Chapter 13

When Bret and I discovered the Cellar we started going there more nights than we went to the Crow. It was a grimy biker bar in Pioneer Square and the sign out front boasted it was the oldest saloon in Seattle.

A bar snaked down the main room of the Cellar, and in the back, the place fanned out into a small stage and a dance floor littered with a few pitiful tables and chairs. The two windows in front were crammed full of junk. The glass in one was blacked out and the other held a mannequin, dressed in fishnets and a faded costume disintegrating from age. The mannequin leaned on a rickety silver tinsel tree propped up in the window that shed its dead glitter over the bar.

The Cellar had a particular smell, and since that time I've always thought of it as the smell of a real bar. It's the musk that hits you right in the face when you cross the threshold of any dark den. It's solid, meaty and warm, and smells like hot moist parts working and squirming against each other like a litter of animals, moving together in the fight to reach the teat. The Cellar smelled like a hole, but it was a refuge. I liked it because I could see it was comprised only of bare elements, life eating life inside of it.

Jerry was the first regular we met at the Cellar and he immediately latched onto me. A guy who looked kind of like a muskrat, I pegged him as a small-time crook even before I spoke to him. His head was round like a Muppet's and almost bald, with just a few scrubby patches of stubble still clinging on, crawling down his face and onto his neck. Like a concentration camp survivor his face seemed to be all skull. Starved by life and disappointed early on, now he cheated whoever he could out of habit. Just like how Lo and I collected people and stories, Jerry collected tricks.

Like me, he possessed what I thought of as an "unconventional morality," but with Jerry everyone knew it just by looking at him. After we became friends I visited him frequently at the bar next door, Harry's, where he worked as a cook. Harry's was a notoriously dangerous place, in small part because all the gangsta types showed up every night for the hip hop, and in large part because happy hour stretched from 2:00pm to 11:00pm during which whiskey drinks were only two bucks. I found that Jerry loved hip hop, and rap like I did too, and that he sometimes felt more at home in the black world than the white. But the Cellar, full of bikers and druggies and freaks, was Jerry's real home more than anyplace else, just like it was becoming mine and Bret's.

Cassady was buddies with Jerry too, but they had formed their relationship based around her coke habit. Jerry sold coke sometimes, but mostly just weed. The coke business was a good way to get laid though, and so he never entirely gave it up.

I knew by this time that Lo was a vampire. If we met a person of interest we had to have their story, even if she had to manipulate it out of them. If pushed, we flat out stole it. With men, it was always easy. My sex was the bait, and while they were busy trying to sleep with me Lo started drinking them up, word by word and drop by drop.

Some men gave something away by a certain look—an uncontrolled twitch, the flicker of a single frightened eyelash—and then

Lo preserved it with her photographic memory. She stored each one of these frozen images way back in the small of my brain, until she had an entire file cabinet all her own filled with unconscious moments from men. As they attempted to get my smile, my sex, whatever that something was that they wanted from me, they had no idea that I was taking it all from them. In fact, some of them I only slept with out of pity, a form of hidden payment for what Lo did to them, for the parts of their selves that she stole from them.

Lo took everything she could get. If she could have had the whole of their soul, leaving them nothing, she would have taken that too.

I never slept with Jerry but he was a person of interest nonetheless. I liked the sound of his voice and I liked that he had decided to take on the degenerate role. It was a tough one to play well but he was good at it. Sometimes I chased him off when I had my eye on someone, but Jerry was as resilient as a rubber ball. Nothing I did could ever injure him. Maybe that was why I liked him so much, because I knew that I was a huge phony and he seemed to be the real deal. Every expression on my face was a fake, my clothes nothing more than a stupid costume. My voice and my attitude and the attacks on any hapless individual that Lo used to entertain herself—it was all a sham. But Jerry knew without me telling him—knew without even knowing he knew it— that the pain I tried to cause him didn't mean anything at all.

All my life, people had told me I was weird. It usually happened right after I did something I thought was normal but everyone else thought was extremely bizarre. Jerry never called me weird. Sometimes when I was drunk I wanted to go to Rat Alley, and I took Jerry with me. Rat Alley was the go-between alley that served as a shortcut between the Cellar and the Crow. If you drove through it at night with your high beams on dozens of rats streamed from the flanks of the buildings. When I went there with Jerry I'd find a dead blown-open rat and pick at the guts with a stick. To me, the shiny pink, plastic-looking rat innards looked like shredded pieces of glistening pink balloon, flowering out of the cement. I had to know what that balloon flower made out of guts felt like. It meant something that when I poked around inside a rat, Jerry never called me weird.

Instead, Jerry looked at me with a knowing glint in his eye, as if to say: We are the same. The experience is everything, there is nothing else.

On some levels Jerry understood me better than anyone.

But then just as I was really getting to know Jerry, he slipped away. He was charged with statutory rape after he blacked out at a party and woke up in bed with his boss's 14-year-old daughter. When the case was wrapped up Jerry got 12 months jail time. Soon it was like he'd never existed. We never visited—not me, not Bret or Cass. We talked about Jerry a lot and said we wanted to go see him at the King County Jail, only a few blocks away from the Cellar. But visiting days were arranged alphabetically by prisoner's last name and we kept getting the days and Jerry's last name mixed up and we didn't even know which part of the jail Jerry was in. If there had been an open bar at the jail I'm sure we could've made time in our schedules, but jails do not have open bars and the people who work there are depressing. We gave up every time before we began and decided to just stay at the Cellar and get drunk instead.

Cassady met the new love of her life, V.C., through his wife, Shelley. They started dating and it was okay because Shelley and V.C. were swingers. V.C. stood for Vampire Cowboy, a name that I made up for him and then stuck. V.C. was over six feet tall and lean as a long dry bone. His face was warm and friendly, but with eyes set too wide apart and black like liquid pools of ink, he had a cool sinister air to him too. He was always entirely clad in leather. His body was an instrument of such long clean lines it seemed he could probably fold in on himself, like a tripod with large, dark, searching eyes.

Life for V.C. and Shelley was the same as it was for us, nothing but time, and simultaneously devoid of time. Seconds crawled by like a thousand insects scuttering over the clock face, leaving behind snail trails of destruction and waste. Shelley and V.C. spent their days and nights watching the clock—waiting for it to be over—just like the rest of us.

As swingers V.C. and Shelley got to have sex with other people and it was cool. Sometimes the other people became steady boyfriends or girlfriends, sometimes they didn't. What remained was the rock solid friendship between V.C. and Shelley. They had long ago dismissed the illusions they had for each other and instead, foisted these illusions onto other people. Passion for strangers grew, fired up and then died, as all things that burn too high finally do, but the friendship between Shelley and V.C. remained as blank as concrete, as impassive as a stone.

When I met V.C. he was sober. Cass told me that he'd checked into rehab the year before, but then escaped and fled to the mountains where he grew a gigantic beard and got well on his own. Shelley worked as a bartender at the Cellar, but V.C. was still completely dry.

Later, when V.C. was gone and Shelley too, I looked back and remembered V.C. sitting at the Cellar holding the same glass all night long. The club soda he held—a glass filled with clear fizzy and a bruised and tired lime—looked like a gin and tonic. I saw him at one of those little black tables on the sidewalk right outside the Cellar's front door. In memory he protectively encircles his watered-down mess with one hand and his two huge black eyes peer out of a face mostly covered by a big bushy beard, even though I never saw him with that beard in real life.

In my vision V.C. is the one silent spot in all the noise, the calm center in the screaming madness and anguished mayhem of the bar, the night, and the street. Surrounded on all sides, the quiet inside him brings him so much pain that he can hardly breathe. The club soda he clutches is a rope, a foothold, a tool to wrestle sanity for himself from the suffocation of the world. But he hates that drink. He hates it because it's nothing. It's worthless. Unable to change the world, it changes no flat and pointless interaction within it. It doesn't make colors brighter, stifle nausea, or get you through. It's just club soda, not magic. It even tastes like the void. In memory V.C. keeps his hand in that frozen half circle on the glass, and I see him wanting to cry.

After a few weeks Cass was officially V.C.'s new mistress, the steadiest girlfriend he had. They partied, socialized, and went around as a group all the time now with Shelley and her newest boyfriend, Gene, a big guy with full red lips and stretched earlobes and wandering hands. And so it was that Cass was formally introduced to the swinger scene in Seattle, and so it was that V.C.'s period of sobriety abruptly ended when things got more serious with Cass. He was drinking again inside of two months. At first it was a secret and only Cass knew, the club soda in his glass discreetly replaced with gin or vodka. And at first V.C. was only drinking again with Cass, but then she started waitressing at the Cellar and we met Dante, the coke dealer in residence, and then both Cass and V.C. had access any time they needed it. And so it was, the clock ticked on and a thousand more insects made their way by.

~

Dante controlled a good portion of the coke trade in Pioneer Square and in Queen Anne. He was an old school player type who was a supplier but also a dealer, meaning he got large quantities for other dealers in order to be a re-up man, but he also went out to the bars and the clubs and sold on his own.

Dante told us that once he became a dealer he had to pretty much give up the rest of his life. Most customers bought in small quantities, and they always wanted more when they had done it all. Cokeheads have no loyalty, he said. They won't wait. If the need comes they'll buy from anyone, so if you're in competition with another dealer, you just have to make sure you're the one who's there when they need it. A lot of the regulars at the Cellar were also cokeheads so staying at the Cellar until last call every night worked out pretty well for Dante. With his cocoa-brown skin, spotless white Nikes, and impeccably ironed clothes he stood out a bit, but everyone knew him and accepted him as part of the scene. What made him stand out even more was the fact that he was never drunk, never high, and always well spoken. The rest of us alternated between manic and screaming or passed out in the bathroom.

Tom had moved out of Jared's house months ago and into a sprawling, crumbling apartment complex on First Hill called the Montecarlo. Pockmarked with abandoned courtyards that none of the tenants ever visited, the Montecarlo was blanketed by an eerie, almost total silence during the daytime hours, and haunted by the wild howlings and desperate moanings of drunks and junkies at night. Dante also kept an apartment there. It was one of the many places that made up the complex web of secret bases he kept ready and waiting around the city, because Dante was prepared to go underground at any moment. It was also where he kept his pit bull as the dog only barked at night.

Some nights I stopped by to see Tom and we ran over to Dante's to help him package product before we all went out. With three of us the work went faster. We established a ritual with Dante weighing everything out and then Tom and I helping to divide each individual portion into tiny bags of $40, $60, or $80 value. Each bag was marked with a different color and I was responsible for bagging. That is, I opened every tiny little fucking bag that was needed. As time went on I developed the trick of placing an open bag on the tip of each finger while Dante weighed and divided. Then I could quickly hand off each bag, opening more and tenting them on my next five fingers while Tom carefully sealed the last round.

Since we had gotten to be such good friends with Dante it wasn't long before Cass and V.C. were doing more coke than drinking. Then Shelley took on another boyfriend, a young biker named Simon, and she started spending more time with him than anyone else. If possible, she was even more distant than before, indifferent to who V.C fucked or how many. A few weeks later V.C. did too much coke and had a seizure on Cassady's bathroom floor. Cass calmly folded his six-foot frame in half, picked him up and put him to bed. Then she called me. She couldn't call a doctor, with the amount of coke and other drugs in the apartment it wasn't a place for anyone from outside. V.C. eventually regained consciousness anyway. It seemed she could just as well have left him on the bathroom floor.

In line with Lo's obsessive need for life to be sliced up into separate compartments, I now separated everything I knew into different transparent cells. Like Dante's tiny little fucking bags of coke, these compartment cells were labeled in ascending order of value. Lo's voice was the constant running tape in my head that quoted the price of each cell to me. To shut the voice up I fell back on my old routine, losing myself through my five senses.

Chapter 14

One night Bret and I were at the Cellar when I ran into a tall, ruddy-faced rocker guy I recognized by sight but had never talked to before. He had long red wavy hair and looked kind of like a skinny Viking. He was also covered in tattoos. He told me he was in the process of having most of his skeleton outlined. He said his plan was that after he died he'd be skinned and then his skin would be hung somewhere, either in a museum or someone's home. His first name was a common one I couldn't remember, his last name I couldn't pronounce. I settled on calling him Blanzenewski, a name I could only recall because I was the one who made it up.

Blanzenewski pretended to work at the Cellar. With unflagging enthusiasm he helped out wherever needed. He gathered and cleaned ashtrays, picked up glasses, and ducked back into the kitchen to wash up a fresh batch of silverware when everything was out. I watched him show up behind the bar like a ghost runner, mixing up a swift rum and coke for an impatient customer, banging open the cash register as nonchalantly as any of the real bartenders did. No one ever told him to stop working. Probably because all of us were insane one way or another. It was my insanity to compulsively come to the Cellar to methodically take my poison. Apparently, it was Blanzenewski's insanity to compulsively clean up after me without pay.

That night he had whisked away an overfull ashtray a split second before I put my elbow down into it, and I started talking to him. Him being a flamboyant rocker guy, I didn't bother with my standard book line. I just asked him what he was doing. He said he was emptying the ashtray and then smiled at me with complete open-eyed innocence. Coldly, I smiled right back.

"Why?" I snapped, not caring if he decided to hate me. My tone passed unnoticed.

Blanzenewski bounded to my side, tail wagging.

"The Cellar's my place man! Are you kidding me? I love helping out!" He leaned in closer and started asking me questions. I loathed questions. I drew the topic away to his many tattoos, and in a space of seconds he was hiking up the back of his too-tight metal shirt and showing me the half-finished map of his vertebrae. When he turned back to face me, boredom hit me between the eyes. I needed something new—RIGHT NOW—or I was going to fall apart. I could already sense the paste that was holding together my papier-mâché, in-public personality growing sodden and weak, soaking through. With Blanzenewski caught in mid-sentence, I ran for it.

A few moments later I came back to myself. The boredom was gone, replaced now by a scattering of black raindrops and bracing wind, burning my eyes. I'd ended up in Rat Alley. I hadn't even noticed if I'd accidentally kicked any rats or how far they went if I did. But I didn't care. I was free again, busted out of the lights and expectations of others. Here. Alone. I kept running. Then I crashed.

Going down I knew I'd hit another person. I'd heard the audible and unmistakable pumpkin thump of my head against someone else's. I landed on my back and lay there for a few seconds with a sudden and unexpected appreciation for the full blackness above, flanked by the narrow brick buildings on either side. Then I remembered the rats. I flew up from the alley floor and patted the lining of my black leather coat. I had created secret pockets in the lining, and that's where I always hid my essentials whenever I was out with Lo. As I patted myself down, I also remembered the other person. I snapped my head up and peered around, skittering my eyes over the gloomy darklit alley.

He was half in the shadows, a tall guy slumped over. I could tell that whoever he was, he was extremely drunk. He listed sideways as he cradled one side of his head in his hands. But then through the grainy gray veil of light between us I recognized the pained and familiar grin fighting to surface on the guy's face. It was my friend Joey, one of the punk cooks with burning black eyes from the Crow. I helped him up and dusted him off. When he saw it was me, he gave me a hug. We decided to get martinis.

We backtracked up Rat Alley and then slid down to the Martini Bar, slung below street level and full of gigantic tanks of all sorts of tropical fish, aquariums straining out of the walls. We tucked into a dark booth in back and ordered two gin martinis with no vermouth and extra olives.

For the next hour we talked and drank. Joey turned out to be overwhelmingly interesting. My guard was down from the very beginning. First he told me stories about his dad, who was a bank robber, and then his sister, who was a heroin addict. Then he told me he was moving to New Orleans and asked me if I wanted to come. I knew that I couldn't. My time in Seattle wasn't up yet, and as fucked as I was in the head I knew—in that unnamable way I had of knowing things with dead-on certainty—that I wasn't yet supposed to go. I shook my head sadly, but I didn't try to explain it to Joey. He seemed cool, but I didn't know him well enough to start chattering about voices inside my head that spoke to me and told me what to do and how to live. I gulped more of my martini.

As the gin hit me I started to relax and feel normal again. The groove repositioned itself and a better song played through me. I thought about what it would be like to go to New Orleans with Joey. The idea of it seemed like a green plant in the middle of a dying and pissed-on city, full of dirt and cars and people, constantly moving, like ants. Or rats. The vision of New Orleans, the possibility of Joey, breathed fresh air and golden sunlight into parts of me I'd assumed were long dead.

Joey and I finished our martinis and I stood to go. The gin had flushed out and cleared my head and I suddenly remembered I'd left Bret at the Cellar. Now she was probably stuck with Blanzenewski. I'd run out into the night without a word to anyone.

Outside, Joey hugged me for a long time. Something inside constricted and lurched into my throat. It felt like indigestion. But with my face in Joey's chest and the smell of him all around me, I realized I couldn't stop thinking about New Orleans. That little green plant of an idea was rooting down into me like an obstinate pig, snorting and grunting relentlessly into my heart. I tore away before anything else could be discovered lurking around in there.

When I got back to the Cellar I found Bret in a circle of bikers, all of them talking, laughing, and smoking while Blanzenewski hovered at the edges of their circle, dipping in and out like an irrepressible moth, grabbing ashtrays and empty finger-printed glasses. It was almost last call. My accidental meeting with Joey had blown any chance I had of losing the rest of the night behind the veil. The insides of me started boiling over, everything kept shifting and I couldn't regain my balance. But then Lo stalked silently into view and tossed me a single angry glance. I wasn't going to New Orleans.

She squatted down and shouldered her gun, sighting Blanzenewski through the crosshairs, squinting dispassionately as she took aim.

Before I left the Cellar with Blanzenewski he dipped

behind the bar to grab a rucksack of alarming size, shouldered with an even more alarming familiarity. We loaded the enormous pack into the backseat of my car and made out in the front. As he felt me up I straddled him and touched his long red hair, tied back in a ponytail. I wanted to know what was in it. After a few soapy strokes I determined it had to be pomade. It was most definitely disgusting. My hand couldn't even make it from top to bottom, which ended somewhere around the middle of his back, without sticking on the layers of coarse wax. I was repulsed.

I was also sold. I told Blanzenewski I'd take him home and fuck him.

When we got to my place I pulled Blanzenewski back to my bedroom and latched the door. Since I never slept well when I was drinking I usually chugged two sleeping pills the moment I got home. The sleeping pills helped me to sleep without a panic attack hitting before dawn. This night was no exception, and I swallowed the capsules dry as I tugged at Blanzenewski's zipper.

When I checked his penis at work a few minutes later I noticed something sticking out of the side of it. I looked closer, it was a dick ring. I laid back and tried to feel something, but dick ring or not, the only thing I felt was the same vague-yet-pleasant piercing thrust I always detected during a fuck, like a dull blade right through the middle of me. This was the high bright point I sought from all sex activities with any man—the penetration and the pounding. Something inside of me was way too sharp, like rodent teeth that won't stop growing until they puncture the poor creature's lips and cripple him. Razor teeth that had to be worn away grew from inside of me too, shredding my body as they exploded into others standing nearby. The fuck was one of my ways to fix it.

After half an hour I felt the sleeping pills take hold. I got drowsy and heavy. I'd gotten my fuck for the night and now I was done. It was obvious though that Blanzenewski wasn't, and I knew it was a matter of minutes before I lost consciousness.

"Look, uh...You gonna be done soon?"

The red that colored his face from exertion deepened to the light plum of embarrassment.

"I'm sorry...I...it's the booze...I...just had a little too much...you know how that is..." He tried to joke with me. I remained unamused.

"Well, I'm going to sleep." I yanked his dick out of me and rolled over.

"I...I—" he stuttered, and I cocked my head back his way.

"I'm really sorry," he finally spluttered out. With the eye that wasn't already shut and sleeping I peered at his large and red, still hard, and looking-embarrassed-now-too, cock. I pitied it.

"Look..." I lethargically moved in his direction. "How about this—I'm gonna go to sleep and you can jack yourself off on me. If you aim right, maybe you'll hit a tit." I winked at him and turned away again, then thought better of it and turned back.

"Oh yeah...and clean me up afterwards or no rides home in the morning." I rolled back over. There were a few seconds of silence and then, slowly, I heard him begin. Satisfied, I smiled to myself and went to sleep.

And so even though Blanzenewski was apparently good-looking, and tall and muscular and a rocker and all that, after we slept together (and even after I found out he had a huge dick with a huge dick ring in it) I still found him to be nothing but repulsive. And while it was nothing he did, it was exactly everything that he was.

The morning after, when I dropped him off in Pioneer Square on my way to work, he turned back to me before slamming the car door.

"Thanks for not treating me like shit," he said quietly.

I wanted to get out of the car and push him down in the street and bloody his face with a rock, scrubbing his cheeks and lips with its jagged edges. Goddamn it, fight for yourself! I wanted to scream at him. Don't let someone like me treat you this way! And because he couldn't see it, couldn't see what I really was, couldn't see Lo behind me with her hand over my mouth, I wanted to kick him in the teeth. Because I had treated him like shit. I'd abused him horribly and he didn't see that either. Or worse, he chose not to.

Chapter 15

In April, I took Joey to my apartment for the first time. The bars had closed, the night was late, but we couldn't sleep. Joey stood in my living room window, his back to the black water of Puget Sound and the black sky. He smoked slowly, letting the cigarette hang between his fingers and then his lips. He curved in sadness, drooping even more than usual when he told me about the girl who left him, who was also the girl he thought he was in love with. I sat on the couch and methodically ripped can after can off the plastic rings as I worked my way through the six-pack we'd picked up on the way home.

Caught in memory, I look up at Joey and let him talk. The lamp in the window lights him from behind, but the light falls away, drizzling like quick-moving sand through the screens down and down, onto the street far below. Edged in gold and black night, Joey hangs between me and everything else, poised on the lip of something better than I am. Silver blood and love and hurt, a million tiny fish scales are in his eyes—the girl gutted him. And what comes out of him now...I find I want that too.

Joey slept on the couch that night. There was some sort of

glass wall between us that I didn't dare to break through. But I saw him more after that, or rather, I noticed him now every time I was down at the Crow.

He seemed to come out of nowhere. The entire place would be empty, with only me sitting by myself in the far dark corner of the bar huddled beyond the late-afternoon sunlight leaking in along the floor and the one TV set droning sports scores in the background, and then he was just suddenly there, slouched over the jukebox, picking over the selection for anything punk. Or I'd be at the Crow all night, trekking back and forth between the pool room and the bar countless times, pacing the floor the way a cow plods over the same little field, searching for any sign of new grass. I talked to everyone. I saw everyone. I moved through every clustered knot like a heat-seeking missile, and just when I knew there was nothing to be had, that was when Joey was suddenly there again, slouched near the kitchen with a half-chewed tortured cigarette hanging from his lips, that same constant wince of pain around the eyes. I never saw him walk through the front door.

And just as quick he could be gone again. Even if we were in the middle of taking shots, his shot was left on the bar in a pathetic widening pool of cold sweat. If we were in the middle of a conversation, my sentence was left hanging half finished, wiggling viciously out of the corner of my mouth. Nothing could make him stay.

I never knew where he went when he was gone. There was always the vague suggestion of more interesting people to meet— wild paint to splash on canvases and bursting wineskins to be drunk on grassy knolls. I never asked. In this new life with Lo I never asked anyone anything that I really wanted to know. My only recourse was to watch them, and wait.

But Joey was hard to watch. His habit of materializing in random places instead of walking through the front door was one thing, but the true roadblock was that he never really lived in one place. He was always staying with friends or living out of his car. Also, Joey was a punk. He mostly hung out with other punks, who didn't smile fondly on the Crow. Joey was cool with the Crow because he worked there and the booze was free, but his presence was never consistent.

The more I tried to watch Joey, the more I thought about going to New Orleans. The obsession of moving had descended upon me like a cloud of bloodthirsty gnats. I wanted to follow Joey. I wanted to walk behind him, just near enough to be protected by his magic. As with Jared, I wanted to be inside of him and knew that I couldn't. And so instead of trying to crawl down his throat and share his body, I settled for hoping to solder myself onto him like melted wire to take what he had that way.

I was in love again.

But Joey did not feel the same way.

He'd just been dumped by a mysterious punk girl who had a scene on Capitol Hill and who was, according to Joey, a goddess. Also, Joey wasn't interested in me. He didn't care about my cleavage, my corsets, or my acid-tipped tongue. My arguments didn't intrigue him. I only had two hooks that might get me in—Joey was an alcoholic too and he loved books. As I got serious about Joey I put away the tits and concentrated on my Dostoevsky.

Cocaine fever spiked higher every day that spring of 2003 in Seattle. Dante's business was so hot he could barely keep customers satisfied and I had to tell a few of my favorite bartenders more than once to wipe their noses as they poured my shots. Everyone was doing it. And Joey was no exception.

Every night it was the same thing. First it was a couple of people, then a clique, and finally a whole herd running off to the bathroom every ten minutes, just as I was feeling the first high light buzz from the whiskey. The coke interrupted our conversations, our cigarettes, even the waitress taking the order for my next drink. The bar wasn't the spot anymore, now it was the bathroom stall. But I still had no interest in coke. I had never done it and I didn't understand why anyone would. A person had to be insane to want to be any more alert in this world. Also, the relentless coke chatter I had to endure every night bored me to tears.

One night, after hanging out with Joey at the Crow until last call, we decided to swing by the Cellar to pick up Cass. But when she got in the car we discovered she hadn't been able to get anything from Dante. Business was so good he was selling out of everything he had well before 2:00am these days. With gritted teeth I settled in for the long hours stretching out in front of me. I knew we would have to hunt and wait, holding our breath and then hunting and waiting again, driving from apartment to house to club to apartment. I would be trapped in the car for all of those long hours on all the same dark, wet orange-shine city streets with the same furious thoughts circling maddeningly in my head.

Around 5:00am—three hours later and long enough for me to feel unacceptably sober—we finally found an eight ball.

Cass and Joey were positively jubilant. Cass chattered and giggled as she threw the car in reverse and squealed away, and Joey bounced on the backseat in an easy rhythm, his face intermittently pitching up into the reflection of the rearview mirror. His eyes met mine and splattered light and sparks at me. For once, he was genuinely smiling. My tongue felt like carpet and I wanted to throw up. I slid my head into my clammy hands and lay limply against the passenger-side door as I tried not to think anymore.

We ended up at Joey's current place, and it was crazier than even I had imagined it might be.

We got in through a small red door. Set low in the middle of a squat, nondescript gray building, the door seemed like it probably led to a warehouse that housed janitorial supplies. But it actually opened onto a bizarre underground bunker-type system of tunnels, like something out of a post-apocalyptic sci-fi novel. Somehow, it was located invisibly in the middle of Broadway on Capitol Hill, one of Seattle's busiest streets.

The tunnels belched us out into a cement-lined cavern that looked like a huge empty hall underneath a castle, or a strange underground garage meant for storing nuclear arms. A ladder propped against the far wall fed into an opening that appeared to have been chopped into the wall. The edges of the hole sprouted arcs of bent metal, crumbling wiring jutted out of the ragged sides. A soft rain of dust sifted down, flouring the ladder and floor below. Dim greenish light emanated from inside. I thought there was a good chance it probably headed to Seattle's sewer system. Two minutes later I found out it was Joey's room.

One by one we negotiated the ladder. We catapulted ourselves through the hole, into the greenish glowing darkness beyond, and then emerged into a small cement room, a box of space that had four cement walls, and a cement ceiling and floor. There weren't any windows. It seemed plausible that no air from outside had entered this space in decades, if ever. A pile of clothes was heaped along one wall and a collection of blankets along the other. It was all Joey had and looking around me, imagining sleeping and waking up in this room, where there was never a daytime or an evening, where there was no time at all, I suddenly lost my breath. I thought of my own crowded apartment. The stacks and stacks of books on every available surface, the old plastic alarm clock I'd carted around with me for the past seven years. I shuddered in revulsion at all the things I needed, all the stuff it took to keep me going. Joey only used two piles. I knew he could leave those pitiful piles that very second and never look back. Cornered by admiration, I was dizzy.

Cass took the score and cut out shares between her and Joey. I watched each of them take their hits and then pass the plate to the other. Soon they were talking and talking and I knew it might be a couple of hours before they stopped. I buried myself in one of the piles and slept fitfully, cement breathing through my pores. When Cass shook me awake she showed me the tiny blinking window on her cell phone. The sun was up outside, the party was over.

The next day, Joey left for New Orleans.

Chapter 16

By the beginning of that summer Tom was going to the Avatar a lot of nights without me. I found myself avoiding the place. The Russian Mafia had taken it over and big guys—monstrous guys who looked like they played rugby with semi trucks and snacked on rabid raccoons—had started popping up in uninhabited corners. These new guys wore sunglasses inside the club and you could tell they were always sober as a giant rock. The sunglasses didn't scare me, but the iron clad sobriety unnerved me to the bones. It meant they were watching and filing away what they saw. I didn't know who was poring over the files in the end, but I didn't want them holding mine. I stopped going altogether and Tom pulled farther away.

I also stopped going to the Montecarlo to see him. The place gave me the creeps. Every time I was there I heard whispers carrying on the night air like screams and saw evil white eyes glowing everywhere. Tom's new best friend, Flaco, had moved in with him and that added to my reasons for staying away. I knew Flaco already from the Avatar, where he was known as Little Flaco, and I didn't like him. Vietnamese, slender as a teenage girl, with a shock of fuzzy coal black hair,

Flaco was a meth dealer. He was also a coke dealer, an E dealer, a pot dealer—an everything man. He had the hooded eyes of a criminal paired with an open boyish face that made him look oddly vulnerable. Flaco was a lot like Tom and they needed each other, but I didn't see that. I only saw Tom using meth, and I saw Flaco supplying it to him for free in exchange for a place to stay.

I still ran into Tom here and there at the Cellar, before he took off for the night to the Avatar. Sometimes he was antsy and tweaky, and sometimes he was irritable and cranky. He had stopped sleeping and eating on a regular basis some time ago. As the spring turned into summer he lost weight and meth rash started cropping up on his face. Deeper, interior changes rooted and twined around his center, growing thicker and ropier as the weeks passed, cutting off his air by millimeters. I had a hard time realizing just how serious the situation had become as it was happening. It was like trying to measure the growth of a vine from second to second. I just couldn't see it.

Then Tom started laying down condescending judgments every time I saw him. He was dismissive of everything. And then he started lying, and Tom had never lied before. Telling me a dozen times he was clean, that he hadn't been out all night doing meth, when I'd already talked to people who said he had, who had seen him do it. When he met me at the Cellar nowadays I saw the red-eyed meth monster staring me down, letting me know it would have more of Tom, exactly as much as it wanted, until one day it had all of him. And letting me know too, that there was nothing I could do about it.

Because of the meth, Tom's concept of reality limped along like a tired old dog with three legs. He had stopped completing most sentences and jumped randomly from topic to topic. He was always paranoid. He repeated himself constantly. The scraps I was able to stitch together collided at crazy angles. I didn't know if most of the pieces were missing, or if Tom was just growing cancerous holes in his brain. I thought it was probably both.

One morning on my way home from the club just before dawn, rounding the curve toward my apartment in Queen Anne, a guy caught my eye on the side of the road. He flagged me down, two big arms slicing together in mad scissor strokes—a rescue signal. It was Tom.

I pulled over and Tom exploded into the car.

"Drive." he ordered.

He tapped five fingers on each leg in what I'd already come to loathe as his newest nervous twitch, while shooting quick little scared glances into the rear and side view mirrors and sharp looks behind us. Tom was always checking for a tail these days. I drove.

When we got to my place Tom sat on the edge of the couch, tapping all ten fingers as he explained that he'd been with Flaco, they'd been chased by the cops, and Flaco had run across four lanes of oncoming traffic in both directions and then jumped off the Ballard Bridge, abandoning Tom and two other guys in the car, leaving them to deal with the police and Flaco's disabled vehicle.

Tom was convinced the cops were after him, even though he had actually spoken to both officers at length and ended up forging an awkward but amiable camaraderie with them over his past service in the Marines. It didn't matter that they let him go, and it didn't matter that they went out of their way to call a tow truck for the vehicle Flaco had dumped on him. It most certainly didn't matter that Flaco cleanly got away with all the drugs on him. Tom was high and everyone was out for him.

I asked Tom point blank.

"When's he moving out?"

"Who—Flaco?" Startled, his hands were still for a moment.

"Yeah, Flaco." I countered, exasperated.

"Why? Why would I want Flaco to move out?" Tom's face

remained blank, but his hands stirred restlessly again on top of his thighs.

"Because Flaco sucks Tom. This bridge business is ridiculous. You could have been killed. He jumped out of a moving car, as he was driving it. And he left you there! What the hell? He sucks."

The tapping started full scale again. Tom's face twitched out of its stone casing for a moment.

"Awww, Flaco's all right. He means well. He really loves me you know? We're like brothers." Tom paused, his hands frozen in mid-air for half a second.

"I can't let him live on the street." he finished, and resumed tapping.

I let it go. And then with it, I felt myself begin to let Tom go too.

~

Across from the waterfront in downtown Seattle ran the Viaduct, an elevated freeway that twisted along the contours of the city and then emptied out onto I-5. At night, it resembled a huge mechanical snake that had come to life, roaring with the echo of a thousand cars speeding through its steel belly. At 3:00am I frequently parked underneath it and took dead-hour shots of tequila all by myself. A lot of bums and crackheads lived under the Viaduct and sometimes it got to be box city or even just blanket town, everyone lining up to get a space, because it was one of the only places in Seattle you could get out of the rain. The reverberation of semi trucks flying past above us sounded like a giant piece of shimmying sheet metal shaking in the sky. That noise—the promise of motion—was nothing but a phantom, trails left by the commitments of invisible others to the road.

Sometimes I stopped by the circle of homeless people who had one boom box shared all between them—old Sue and her gang

—behind Pike Place Market. Sometimes I shared a joint with a guy named Sam who lived in a box and always offered me a crack rock with the same deferential elegance a butler would use when offering someone a cup of Earl Grey tea. I knew a lot of people around the area of the Viaduct. But I could hardly remember any of them for very long. The blackouts had become an old friend now too, and I couldn't be sure of anything.

One night, leaving an after-hours party around 4:00am, I ran into a hunched woman with the face of a mole and round glasses that shone like two spinning coins. She grasped my arm and turned me around.

"Lo!" she exclaimed happily. "How are you my darling?" I'd never seen her before in my entire life—but it seemed she knew Lo.

"You must think I'm someone else. I'm—"

"Oh no!" she cut me off. "Not that again, Lo! I wouldn't forget you. You've been under the Viaduct too late too many times for me to do that. It's dangerous you know."

"Yeah..." I didn't know what else to say. I had no memory of this woman.

"Well," she finally sighed. "I guess I'll let you go."

She moved away, cantankerously and with a lot of grunting, the way homeless people do when they have too much to carry and no shopping cart. Like a big tired turtle with all of her stuff on her back. I touched her briefly on the arm and she turned.

"Wait—I mean—thank you. For looking out. Thanks."

"Goodbye Lo." She smiled at me serenely and was gone.

I knew she wasn't really talking to me.

Chapter 17

I woke up one Saturday morning in July already knowing I was late for work. I didn't need the clock. I could tell by the long sun shadows running across my bedroom ceiling that I had overslept.

No time for a shower, I slipped on a pair of shorts and the cleanest shirt I could find in the chaos of my bedroom floor. It was a massive t-shirt pitted with holes and emblazoned with the logo of a construction company. I couldn't remember where the shirt came from, but when I put it on it fell way past the shorts, reinforcing my belief that some guy had probably forgotten it in my room. I considered pants for a moment, but then ran a hand across the greasy beads of sweat already popping out on my forehead and decided against it. The bookstore didn't have air conditioning.

I never brushed my tangled mass of curls, even on a good day, and so I swept the hair off my face with my hands and tucked it behind my ears. It would have to do. Feeling the familiar burning in my gut I vomited once, quick and neat, before leaving the house. I scrambled out the door and ran downstairs.

When I got outside I was immediately dismayed. My car wasn't there. I froze, thinking it had been stolen, and then the night before came back to me. There had been no veil and no blackout. I'd just been extremely drunk. My brain had only been warming up for the past half hour, now it was up and running.

I'd lost my keys. I remembered realizing I lost them shortly before the bars closed and madly dashing between the Cellar and the Crow in a desperate hunt to find them. I remembered finally giving up and calling a cab to take me home. I remembered my car was still parked near Pioneer Square, underneath the Viaduct.

I ran back upstairs and found the spare key. Then I called a cab to take me downtown to my car as I shot one eye toward the clock. I was so late at this point it didn't matter anymore. I groaned and thought about how I wanted to transfer out of my life.

The cab came less than ten minutes later and I ran down the stairs again. All the running and the hangover oozing out of my skin had considerably dampened the oversized t-shirt I was wearing and it clung to me, sticking to my back and armpits while the rest of the material billowed out like a sail. Because I was sweating so much, I could smell everything I'd drunk the night before seeping out of me in steaming sour whiffs. I tasted leftover bile in my nose every time I breathed.

Impatient but already dreading the scene waiting for me at work, I threw myself into the cab and slid crazily to the other side when my sweaty thighs hit the cool vinyl. I crashed into the opposite door and one of my slip-on shoes flew off and out of the car. I boomeranged after it and then crashed back in. I slumped down into the seat in exhaustion, dropping my head back and closing my eyes.

"Hmm hmm."

Who said that? I opened my eyes. The cab driver's head was pivoted around toward me.

"Where are you going miss?" he politely asked. He was Middle Eastern, trim, 30ish, and well maintained. I was a piece of shit who couldn't even hold onto the fact that I was now in the cab that I'd called to my home and I needed to direct the driver to take me somewhere. I felt badly for cabbie, it was going to get worse.

"Well..." I wheedled. "First I need to go to the Viaduct." Cabbie remained silent and kept staring at me. He was obviously waiting for me to give him another, more specific, point of reference, as the Viaduct spanned almost the entire waterfront and contained no addresses, only cardboard boxes and tent city.

"That's the thing..."

And with that I launched into my story of the night before. How I'd gotten incredibly drunk, lost my keys, and now couldn't remember where I'd parked my car. As I was going through my explanations, a new and different and quite horrible complication struck me. My car alarm was on. It was always on because the car had been stolen twice before. I had the spare key with me now, but I didn't have the remote to deactivate the alarm. The only remote in existence was attached to the set of keys I'd lost the night before. The alarm was state of the art and went off if anyone so much as breathed on the car, but even if I could get inside the damn thing it wouldn't start because the alarm shut down the car's engine when it went off.

I was completely fucked.

By the time I'd finished my story and realized the true state of affairs, we were halfway to the Viaduct. I ordered cabbie to turn around. When we got back to the apartment I told him to wait for me, I'd be right back down. I ran upstairs again, producing a fresh coat of sweat that smelled faintly of old vomit. I knew I'd have to puke again soon. I said a silent prayer that it wouldn't have to happen on Cabbie's car floor and grabbed the phone.

After sitting on hold and being transferred through various departments of the car alarm company, I got the information I needed. I bolted back down the stairs and smashed into the back-seat of the cab again. I told Cabbie to head down to the Viaduct as originally ordered and on the way there I hooked him into my plan.

The car alarm company had told me there was a magic deactivation switch underneath the steering wheel of the car. When flipping this switch, while at the same time—the same exact quarter of a second—turning the key in the ignition, the alarm could be deactivated without using the remote. The car could be started without all hell breaking loose.

I didn't trust the car alarm company though. The guy on the phone sounded annoyed and like he was quite possibly making up the story about the magic switch and the attached promises that it really worked. I knew there was a good chance I'd still need to take the cab to work and so I needed Cabbie to wait for me. I also knew there was a good chance, if the magic switch story really was made up, that the car alarm would go hysterical and I'd have to cut the wires. I was too big of a fuck-up to just go cutting wires willy-nilly underneath the hood of the car, I'd need help.

So, I chatted with Cabbie the whole way to the Viaduct, making him like me and then pushing it one step further—making him want to invest in me. I didn't see how it could possibly work. I was still slightly drunk and I smelled awful. The shirt had dwarfed my shorts the moment I put it on and so he probably thought I was naked underneath. I reflected that he was probably impressed I'd even managed to put on shoes. My hair hung in dry crispy straw-like chunks around my bloated cheeks, and my tongue was white, so white that I knew he could see the pale fuzz on it when I talked. I reeked of tequila and vomit.

But I desperately needed his help. And so I smiled and laughed and asked him about his life, but I had to warn him I might puke out the window at any time. He didn't seem particularly affected.

We arrived at the Viaduct and drove through the parking lots underneath it until we spotted my car and Cabbie pulled over. I told him about the magic switch and the only requirement of perfectly aligning the flip of the switch with the turn of the ignition—at the exact same quarter of a second. To my delight, he put the cab in park and got out.

Following me, Cabbie moved toward the car just as slowly as I did. I'd experienced the alarm going off before and I knew what we were in for. I walked and crouched at the same time, the way I would approach an intoxicated sleeping gorilla.

The moment I lifted the door handle, the alarm sounded. Great high shrieks filled the air above us, widening and strengthening and rippling outward as they hit the Viaduct, and then falling in a shrill umbrella of sound, raining shards of pure noise all around us. Staccato beats followed, puncturing the air and stabbing us in the ears. The alarm dropped back, revved up, and rose again in a crescendo. And then the entire cacophony was repeated.

I was right. The guy at the car alarm company was a total liar and there was no magic switch. There wasn't even anything resembling a switch and now that I'd turned the key in the ignition the car's engine was shut down, everything except the alarm. I looked at Cabbie and pressed my lips together. It was go time.

"Get on that side! Lift the hood! I'll pop it!" I yelled over the alarm. He got into position and did as ordered. The hood was up. I ran to the other side of the car and stood across from him. I handed him a spring knife I'd retrieved from the backseat. I had a pair of kindergartener's scissors from the glove box.

"Look for the alarm! Cut the wires!" I screamed at him while making cutting motions across the air in front of my face. He nodded jerkily and started hunting with his eyes. I noticed a light sheen had appeared on his forehead. I wondered briefly if this was similar to detonating a bomb, and decided it probably was. The alarm had numbed my ears and now I saw more and more people, some of them tourists, pausing on the waterfront across the street, shielding their eyes and staring in bewilderment. A few pointed at us.

I looked back at Cabbie to see if he'd noticed. He was too excited to be distracted by the people across the street, now organizing themselves into suspicious little clumps. Cabbie's eyes were big and he was smiling broadly. He pointed to a small black box near the windshield on his side. The box was imprinted with tiny white letters that spelled out the name of the car alarm company. I nodded frantically and Cabbie snipped the red and green wires that fed into the thing.

The alarm blared on.

I shot another look across the street. A definite crowd had gathered.

"There's got to be another wire!" I screamed. "Check under the car!" I pointed downward desperately and then hurried over to his side and pushed his shoulders down and screamed into his ear.

"Down there! Get under! The other wire! THE OTHER WIRE!"

Cabbie shimmied under and the top half of his body disappeared. I waited a few seconds, watching the crowd across the street. It was getting bigger. I waited two seconds more and then kicked Cabbie's legs in a series of quick little jabs. He surfaced as I glanced across the street again. A couple of official-looking guys in uniforms were starting toward us. We had 45 seconds, maybe a minute if they got caught at the light, but only a minute at the very most.

"RIP IT OUT!" I screamed at Cabbie, pointing back at the black box under the hood. I ducked into the car to grab the few necessities I needed.

I slammed the driver's side door shut and checked on Cabbie. The light sheen on his forehead had turned into fat drops of sweat that slid desperately down into his eyebrows and streamed off the wings of his nose in a fine banner-like spray. He was breathing hard—I could see his nostrils flaring with the effort—and small veins stood out on his temples. The muscles in his arms bulged as he tried to hoist the thing out. He heaved and then mustered his strength again. The alarm was not only supernaturally powered, it was also apparently super-glued into the car.

I looked out at the street again. The light had changed and the two officials were halfway across. It was time to abort mission.

"LET'S GO!" I screamed and pointed at the two guys. I bobbed my head so frantically that I almost fell over.

Cabbie jerked his hands out from under the hood just as I slammed it down. His adrenaline pumping, he shot to the driver's seat of the cab in less than a second. I was right behind him. We took off as the two officials sped up to a trot and banged on my window. I laid my head back again and closed my eyes. The cab was just as cool and beautiful and peaceful as it had been when I'd first entered it only an hour ago. Without opening my eyes I instructed Cabbie where to go.

On the way there I almost did puke in the backseat. I burped and sat up abruptly as waves of nausea gripped me. I burped again and this time it was wet. Cabbie being of no use to me now, I let him know just how wet it had been. He seemed amused.

And now, I noticed something else. Cabbie kept darting quick glances at me in the rearview mirror and asking me questions. He seemed excited and happy, like we'd just bought our first home together—like the experience was risky and definitely heavy, but we'd come out of it okay and the risk was worth it. I reflected that the past hour was maybe the most exciting time he'd had in a while and I groaned to myself. The horrific fuck-ups of my fucked up life were always way more exciting to other people.

Cabbie kept at it with the questions. He wanted to know why I had gotten so drunk that I had lost my keys, why I had planned on driving home last night in that state anyway, and why I was so sick now. I patiently explained the whole story to him again, and that I was an alcoholic and that things like this happened to me all the time. I punctuated my point with another gurgle and burp. He told me he was of the Islamic faith and so he never drank. He'd never been drunk. He wanted to know what it was like.

"Well...it's like flying in a way. But only at first...and not for everyone. It's bad and it eats at you, but it sets you free too. It's really horrible."

Cabbie asked me if it was so horrible and made me so sick, why did I drink so much?

"Because I guess I love it more than anything."

This seemed to satisfy him and he fell to musing for a few minutes. I burped again through my fingers and smelled them. I seemed to be rotting on the inside. Cabbie took up the conversation again.

"Does it make you...ah...you know—loose with the men?"

"Nah," I waved my hand at him and burped again. "I'm a slut. That's my own prerogative. I do it on purpose. I do everything on purpose." I dropped my head into my hands to block my eyes from the streaming scenery outside the car window. I was very close to becoming violently ill, but I didn't mind Cabbie's questions. They were more interesting than anything else anyone had asked me in a while and a welcome distraction from the churning in my stomach.

Cabbie made a small "hmm" noise and refocused his eyes on the road. We rode the rest of the way in silence.

When we finally pulled up to the tiny corner of the strip mall that housed my bookstore I was almost three hours late. Any trace of drunk had worn off and I felt like I was going to die. An actual stench now emanated from me.

Cabbie leaned an arm across the divider.

"So uh, hey—you wanna go out with me sometime?"

I stared at him incredulously. Was he serious? Was he sick? I had to be the worst piece of shit he'd ever laid eyes on. I laughed harshly and it came out in short little ragged barks.

"I don't think that'd be such a good idea."

Cabbie shrugged his shoulders and said he'd knock $20 off my fare anyway. I had, after all, shown him a good time. He smiled good-naturedly and I smiled back at him. We were friends now.

I sighed and thanked him. I paid the discounted fare and threw in the extra $20 as a tip. I knew I'd get out of that cab and go into the bookstore and lose him even as I'd just discovered him.

And that's exactly what happened. Like all the others, I never saw him again.

Chapter 18

The original Falcon nightclub had closed in February of 2001 after Seattle's big earthquake crumbled one side of the building into a pile of dusty bricks. The owner, Arthur, had gone on hiatus until a new space could be secured. In the months leading up to summer of 2003 Arthur had stockpiled, trained, and built his forces into a silent towering pyramid of influence and power. Now, he officially began his new reign as the divine king of Pioneer Square.

Arthur's wife was Samantha, a darkly beautiful young witch with thick, waist-length black hair streaked with rainbow color. Arthur was nearing 50 but Samantha was around my age, maybe 24 or 25. Samantha didn't work at the Falcon, not really, but she was always there. She stayed mostly silent, sweeping her deep black eyes in never-ending circles around the room, slowly stroking the long black-red-blue-violet hair that lay on her neck like a pet boa constrictor. I had just finished reading Fitzgerald's *Tender is the Night* and I thought that Samantha, like Nicole Diver, "gave an impression of repose that was at once static and evocative." I wondered if I should plan to feel badly for Samantha, just as I had felt badly for Nicole at the end of the book. Things with Nicole, and her husband Dick, had not been what they seemed.

Arthur owned a black and looming turreted castle a little ways outside of town and when he married Samantha, she'd moved into it. The castle boasted a fully-equipped dungeon, a snake room, and rubber sheets on all the beds. Arthur and Samantha headed the great unofficial council of swingers in the Square.

The Falcon was also a castle of sorts. With three levels and five full bars, after it opened there was nowhere better to go to drink and dance. Live music played on the main floor and upstairs, while electronic beats spun downstairs on the basement level for more intense dancing. Everything was wrought iron, every floor connected by a spiral staircase. With his long black hair, deep-set black eyes and handsome wizard's face, Arthur stalked through the crowds of frat boys and their dates come to slum. He parted the seas between the industry people who came to see the staff and the regular drunks bumming around, looking for a change from the Cellar. He passed through them like smoke, floating like clouds over the sea.

Everyone at the Falcon had a schtick. There was the girl in a pink wig who only wore corsets, the pissy goth guy with slick black hair and wire-rimmed glasses, the loud-mouthed spiky-haired bitch in the basement. You didn't just wear a costume to the Falcon—you were the costume. At least until further notice from Arthur, leave yourself at the door please and thank you. There was the promise of sex. There was coke, sometimes, and whiskey. There was always dancing. There was nothing else, except the mask assigned to you and the finely graded adjustments you made to it every night.

Often I stood on the third-floor balcony and watched Arthur on the floor below, standing unnoticed in a forgotten corner, arms crossed. Watching. His small grandfatherly spectacles acted like curtains. Falling over his hawk-eyed intelligence, they glinted back two blind discs of light at anyone who looked too closely. I knew he was aware I was watching him, just as he watched the masks swirling and biting at each other through the fog machines that turned the air a smoky blue. On those nights, when I went downstairs to dance afterwards, I could still sense Arthur standing on the floor above me. I could still feel him watching everyone within his realm.

~

After the Falcon opened V.C. got Cass a job bartending there and now they didn't need to depend on Dante for regular coke. It was everywhere. With every day that passed their relationship became bound by a thousand more threads of cocaine, as if they were being cocooned together, against their will. By midsummer the web had coalesced into an indestructible net, cradling both of them and swinging back and forth every night from the midnight disco high to the 4:00am dark gutter fights.

V.C. had a friend named Nikki who he delivered coke to on the regular. Apparently they went way back and V.C. felt like he owed her. Cass agreed to help him out and met with Nikki whenever V.C. couldn't. Nikki lived in a townhouse that was paid for by a shadowy and mostly nonexistent husband who lived full time in New York. Nikki was around 30, but she didn't work. It seemed that, for the most part, she curled into herself in the dark townhouse day after day and shot up massive amounts of cocaine.

To me Nikki looked like a porcelain doll. Her skin was pale and translucent and she had red hair the color of beaten copper without any of the attendant freckles most redheads have. Her face was almost obscene in its perfection. Her body was like a mannequin's. Nikki was hard, hard all over. Her arms were round and white, and the glint in her eyes said she was made of stone under the shimmer of that blinding snow-white skin. Her gaze was flat and sharp, like a jagged piece of slate. Every time we met with her I felt she was turning more completely into a human-size piece of rock.

Cass and I met Nikki on small deserted streets that wormed out from Pike Place Market or down windy alleyways close to Puget Sound. Nikki was always eager, too eager—and grabby. She was done with conversation and finished with being polite. Nikki wanted her stuff and she wanted it now, two minutes ago, yesterday. In the darkness of Cassady's car I saw her face change from week to week. She had the by-now-easy-to-recognize paper skin I'd seen stretched across dozens of sick skulls at the Avatar. Her porcelain head looked like it was on the verge of cracking. Her white round arms became gray sticks. Her hair had lost all its illusions of sun and glory and dragons, now it looked just like the dead thing it was.

Cass started to feel weird meeting with Nikki, but she didn't dare refuse. Nikki and V.C. were good friends and he watched the lavish townhouse whenever she spent weekends in New York. Plus, Cassady hated offending people or hurting their feelings in any way. Even though I personally thought Nikki reminded me of one of those lizard creatures from that old sci-fi TV show "V," Cassady saw every lost soul as a puppy waiting to be rescued. She knew that for some people, addiction was all they had left.

One night toward the end of summer, when V.C was housesitting for Nikki, he announced to me and Cass that we needed a night out—a good night out, a normal night. No fighting, no screaming, no crazy. He told us that we were going to be pretend to be different people. Cass and I looked at each other, excited and starting to smile. This sounded like fun. We would sit and sip our drinks contentedly, V.C. went on, not reach for things we couldn't have or grasp at those around us. We weren't going to flail around in our own heads this night, or circle each other like vultures, cawing our ugly songs as we dug into fresh dead meat. This night would be different. But the deal was—and here I was the one who spoke up—they had to stay away from the coke.

So we went out to a new bar that night, and an hour into the plan Cass and V.C. disappeared from the table. V.C. had brought along a buddy for me, a blond guy with large vacant eyes named Zip. I sat with him and kept both eyes on the bathroom door. I could already hear the flap of vulture wings, the hollow thump-thump of them landing all around me.

As I monitored the door, Zip droned a steady whisper into my ear. I picked up "wounded," "bomb," and "bloody explosions." Not sure if he was talking about a war or something, I smiled politely and nodded like the plan had been all along. He increased the whispering and the air blown in my ear went from warm to damp and hot. I swatted at the whispers halfheartedly, already giving up hope they would change direction.

Finally V.C. and Cass showed up again. Apparently they had been outside, knowing I would pick the bathrooms as my first choice for surveillance. They moved from the front door to the table like a reel of sped-up film. Both of them looked like they had slammed facedown into a dinner plate of coke and then rolled around in it like a cat in dirt. So much for normal. Half an hour later the fights began.

By last call I was sure Zip believed himself to be a Vietnam War veteran. He hadn't specifically said the words, "I'm a Vietnam vet," but his oblique references to "before," "back there," and "when I was—you know," pointed me toward a limp and humid scene in the Asian jungle where Zip crouched behind a giant fern with a submachine gun and a blown-off leg, half mad and waiting for the unseen enemy. I peeked under the table for the telltale prosthetic but decided not to question him and went with it. So what if he was only 23 years old and thought he'd been in Vietnam somewhere around 1972? I had two different beings fighting it out inside of me, and I still wasn't sure that Lo wasn't going to win and banish me into oblivion. For Christ's sake, I just wanted to fuck the guy. The shrapnel tearing through his head was none of my business.

We got to Nikki's townhouse around 3:ooam. As usual, the thick velvet drapes were fastened securely over every window and I felt like a lap dog dwarfed by the matching overstuffed velvet furniture that sprouted everywhere, the ottomans like bloated and fashionable toadstools underfoot and tassels hanging from every available surface. V.C. and Cass, now totally lost in their coke frenzy, cut up what they had left and argued briskly and neatly between them about who got more. Zip stared into space like a zombie. I thought he was probably reliving a particularly bad run-in with the Vietcong. I went to the kitchen to root around in Nikki's fridge and came up with a half bottle of old white wine. I sucked at the end of the bottle and surveyed the scene in the living room. Everything was going nowhere.

I gulped the last of Nikki's dead wine and tugged on Zip's clammy dead hand. I pulled him toward the bedroom, the one room of the townhouse I'd never been in.

We made it there in the dark and I started to fumble around with Zip's belt and top button. He'd withdrawn almost totally into the rice fields, but I knew most penises lived and worked independently of the person they were attached to. However, it didn't change the fact that Zip was shaping up to be one of the most difficult fucks I'd ever pursued. He wasn't helping with his clothes at all and his total silence was spooky. The half bottle of wine had fuzzed over my high clean tequila drunk and I felt myself getting sloppy. I just couldn't locate the top button of Zip's pants and Mr. POW was congealing ever faster into an extremely frustrating slab of weird jellied meat. I could feel the penis, it was there, but I couldn't get to it. In a final snap of irritation, I reached for the silhouette of the lamp by the bedside and switched on the light.

Instantly, I went blind.

Apparently, Nikki never settled into bed with plans for a cozy evening reading a good long book by the warm glow of her bedside lamp. In fact, it seemed the lamp was only there to blast away vampires and blind anyone else who wasn't lucky enough to have cataracts. The bulb had to be 3000 watts, no less.

After the dots swimming in front of my eyes faded, I was able to make out the room and its contents. Zip and I were enfolded in a huge canopied four-poster bed. The posts were solid mahogany and looked like they were carved by pioneers, maybe Nikki's Puritan ancestors. The canopy was white eyelet lace, the bedspread was white eyelet lace, the pillows even had shams and they were white eyelet lace too. The entire contraption dripped and oozed and sparkled with white eyelet lace. I felt like the one red farmhouse buried in fields of virgin white snow, the mahogany posts trapping us in a frozen frame.

Under the searchlight I finally figured out the snaps and buttons on Zip's jeans. His eyes had definitely lost what little focus they'd displayed earlier, but I figured it was because he was staring directly into the beacon Nikki called a bedside lamp. A tiny slivering string of drool hung from the corner of his mouth, but once I pushed my mouth up to his he halfway started to kiss me.

I tried for ten minutes and then I had to stop. Zip was an unresponsive robot with post traumatic stress disorder and I was trying to fuck him on a bed that looked like Pennsylvania in winter. Even with my eyes closed I could see Nikki in this room. I could feel her cold breath all around me. There were two scenes going on here. The first was the one with me and Zip—which was sick and sad in itself—but we were only faintly overlaid on the scene below. The one on the bottom was Nikki, alone night after night. A small capsule of pain, curled in on herself and drowning in the middle of that bed. I knew—I saw in that other scene beneath us—that she kept the light so bright because she was afraid of vampires, she was afraid of whatever thing was eating her soul. And like everyone else who has lived with fear and taken it compulsorily under their skin, she knew the end for her would come at night. The end, the death fear, it always comes at night.

Zip and I balanced ourselves on Nikki in that bed. We rocked back and forth on top of her rocking herself back and forth beneath us. Everything was white—I saw it now through her—as far as her eye could see, as far as space could go, there was nothing but this horrible blankness, this eternal field of white where no other thing lived, and where she slowly burned. I knew then that she would burn herself down, in all that white, until she died. I'd had enough.

I ran screaming. My cries broke Zip's stupor and sent him stumbling out of the room not far behind me. V.C. and Cass barreled down the hall—two wild and angry chimpanzees with fangs bared. I tried to explain, but no one understood. Zip regained his precarious normalcy, ordinary life infusing his cheeks with a slight pink glow and all traces of dead zombie-eye and spooky slivers of drool gone. Even V.C. and Cass, once they settled down from the shock of my screams, crossed their arms and appeared uncharacteristically reasonable in the face of my broken bizarre story. The wine blunted my words and now the entire incident was surreal. Everyone was A-OK, totally all right, and I was the freak again. Helplessly I repeated, "Pennsylvania in winter...the bed...you have to see the bed to know..." When they started exchanging looks with each other over my head I knew it was over.

I found a warm well-lit corner in the living room, far away from the bedroom and where I could keep an eye on everyone, and then I passed out.

Chapter 19

As the summer of 2003 wound down the fights between V.C. and Cass got longer and uglier. They grew a skin of thick, brown, scabrous boils. But even through the nastiness that had taken hold between them I still saw that V.C. was one of the most thoughtful people I'd ever met. By thoughtful, I mean he actually thought for himself. Cass could see it too. He never hid anything from her. But, just like us, he couldn't prevent the pain that came to everyone around him from what he was doing. His need was too great; the pure immediacy of demand it planted in him too beautiful to pass up. No one would ever be allowed to come between him and his addiction. And Cass and I understood that too.

The aftermath that unerringly followed the smoke and slaughter of the fights was a hangover no drink could cure. The day after a really bad fight, Cass always felt like shit and wanted to kill herself. Without any particular reason, I frequently felt the same way. So on these days we went to 6 Points, and the best time to go to 6 Points was in the morning. That's when you could really get a fix.

The windows of 6 Points were covered with neon signs,

blocked by the huge jukebox, or just plain blacked out. The booths were big and roomy, once securely settled in you were sure to stay unseen. That was exactly why we went to 6 Points in the morning, because it was a place to go to hide. We needed a hole to crawl into that summer. Strapped into one of those booths, we were officially missing persons.

Walking into 6 Points was good. First came a loosening in the torso, a relief we hadn't even been fully conscious of pursuing. The promise of a stiff and spicy double Bloody Mary lifted the heavy shadow that settled right over our eyebrows during a hangover. The dimness of 6 Points masked Cass's blotchy cried-out skin and the smeary streaks of mascara that ringed her eyes. On our way from the front door to a booth I noticed that the other people in 6 Points never looked up for long. It seemed they only looked up at all because the message hadn't yet gotten from their brains to their muscles that they actually didn't care anymore. Those people didn't count as other people anyway. I'd be them in a couple of hours, looking up even though I didn't want to at the newest waste walking through the door. You just never met anyone good at 6 Points. That was the whole point.

Some mornings morphed into long hours filled with nightmare cartoon tunnels materializing out of a sinister green fog, both of us being chased and caught and killed, and then resurrected all over again. Hostile grinning faces with sharp teeth and huge eyes floated out of the void and then dissolved into invisible poisonous snakes, only entering our bodies at very certain points, like under the fingernails, where it really fucking hurt. We saw witches with long knives and children who wanted to eat us. All of it eventually lost under the veil.

After bad binges like these I woke up in the middle of the night, not sure what time it was, not sure what night it was, with no idea how long I'd been out, how many days had passed, how I got home, or if Cass was still alive. After I regained consciousness those precious few moments of confusion were almost immediately crushed to a fine toxic powder by the strong black cramps squeezing my gut. Then the retching came. My body screamed for water and whimpered for food, but as I leaned into the toilet and held on through the shakes my mind only raced faster and faster. What time is it...how many days...? Where could she be...? I got home, but when and how? Where's Cass? Why'd I do this again, HOW could I do it again? HOW long was I out? HOW LONG was I out this time? HOW LONG was I GONE???!!!

After the first major bout of retching I had exhausted the last of my meager resources. My body was spent and sore and my ribcage now contained a set of shiny new department store knives that twisted and sliced at me with every shallow breath. Sleep was an impossibility. But although my body was apparently dying, the motor of my brain only whirred around faster. And because I had abused us so badly this time, it could only move in circles, like a senile man with a lame leg.

I wanted to die.

Coming off a bad binge feels a bit like dying I suppose. There's the pain, but most of that is bearable. The physical pain isn't so different from a normal hangover. But when you're in the really bad shit the pain comes with something else: a revulsion that cuts into the soul like acid slime. The feeling of me, moving around in my dying body, the shadow of the carcass to come, was abominable. It felt like I'd found some dead rotting girl by the side of the road, decomposing and stinking and pussing and steaming and just FESTERING, and like I'd taken out my trusty pocketknife and sliced her open from throat to crotch and crawled right in and slid around, settling into the slippery reeking mess like it was home.

This partying-inside-a-corpse feeling wasn't the limit either. It was disgusting to continue living inside my poisoned body, but the loathing I felt for myself was almost unspeakable. It was a total contempt that went way beyond hatred. I didn't want to punish myself—I wanted someone or something to blot me out, every single atom and without a twinge of hesitation. And then I wanted the tiny mark from the blotting out of my existence to be erased entirely too—leaving nothing but a wide empty expanse—as if I'd never been there at all.

I sat and rocked back and forth in my dark apartment, and paced and retched and massaged the corners of my eyes where my tear ducts ached so terribly but seemed to be completely empty anyway and I watched the moon shine on the water of Puget Sound and wished that my life had never been at all, and most of all, if it had to have been, that I wasn't here to see it now.

It wasn't all bad at the end of that summer. Some nights were good nights without us even trying. The mornings after those good nights we all woke up in Cass's apartment, the screen door half open and flies buzzing lazily through the heavy heated air.

It was a good morning. It would be a good day. We were going to the beach.

After flying down I-5 and swerving over the West Seattle Bridge, V.C. floated us down like a silent cloud to the boardwalk. He always found the perfect parking spot, right in front of our favorite boardwalk bar.

V.C. ordered his first drink as we were shown to the table. During the approximately three minutes it took the waiter to get the drink he reclined back, his long snaky body one lean line of black, drumming his fingers wildly on the tabletop, and then shot straight up, an electrified rod, thrumming and humming now, zeroing in on any server who chanced to walk within ten feet of him.

"Vodka cran? Vodka cran?" he asked helplessly. Eyes blank,

fingers still but ready to drum madly again as soon as he was denied, V.C. held his head high, waiting for the one and only thing he wanted, waiting to recline again—to breathe—and breathless, he waited.

Finally it came. While Cass and I ordered our drinks and took menus from the waiter, V.C. downed that first vodka cran and ordered another, slipping it quietly but urgently into Cass's order and then looking away, like the stage manager caught on set replacing the fake apple in the plastic fruit bowl when the lights go up. We avoided each other's eyes, looking everywhere else, suddenly interested in reading the cheap tin signs around the room and looking over the menu one more time, but mostly checking how the bartender was coming with those drinks. Time had slowed down again.

Lunch lasted at least two hours. Over the span of those two hours V.C. took down around seven vodka crans. If it was a good day and we were at the beach, I could limit myself to three or four drinks. I could stay away from the shots and Cass could too. After we paid the bill we ambled across the street and down to the beach. V.C. shed his leather pants and the three of us laid out for the rest of the afternoon. Cass and I passed a joint back and forth and V.C. jumped up every 30 minutes to flee the baking sun-spilled sand for the ice-wash waters of Puget Sound. Bounding back a few minutes later, he resumed his calm flat immobility on the two sides of the towel stretched between me and Cass. None of us said much. We weren't exactly happy or even okay, but on those days, at the beach, we weren't in pain at the moment either.

That was enough to just not talk about it.

Other mornings Cass and I got drunk by ourselves and stumbled downtown to the Déjà Vu strip club. We sat around on back countertops with the employees inside, telling them we wanted to be jizz moppers when we grew up and dangling our feet like two lost third-graders, milking them for stories. Then we journeyed on to Taboo Porn on the edge of Pioneer Square. All of the customers at Taboo looked like child molesters. They hunched into themselves and had squinty eyes. Their skin was thick and reptilian. We were sure that some of them had tails.

Cass and I got to know the dude who worked at Taboo during the day. He wore wire-framed glasses and had a neat blond ponytail. He had stories about jizz mopping and he was interesting. He and the girls at the Vu had such great stories I sought them out especially, just to hear what they had to say. Not just about jizz mopping, but about everything. They'd seen so much that I hadn't. They hoed huge loamy fields filled with mushy green plants no one had ever seen before. I was sick of my backyard garden with its assembly-line tomatoes that I could buy in any grocery store.

After we went back to my apartment and passed out Cass and I usually woke up a few hours later in a giant pile of shiny new porn. Video and DVD cases were opened and scattered around us like a poltergeist had hit the room. Monstrous neon-green and purple dildos, quivering jelly thimbles and cock rings and butt plugs fanned out from us like shipwrecked debris on a beach, all of it non-refundable.

But it still wasn't as bad as the nights I woke up alone.

Cass and V.C. broke up at the end of that summer. One hot August morning after a four-day coke-and-booze binge they had their last fight. Sitting in V.C.'s long black car, they watched the sun climb higher, drenching them from above and frying them like ants, and screamed at each other until they were hoarse. Cass slammed out of the car finally, wounds streaming, circling the oven of the parking lot. There was nowhere to go. She sat down behind the long black hearse and V.C. drove off and out of her life, the last of him floating away like the exhaust fumes that hit her in the face. Later, when she told me what happened she got caught on that part of the story, like a machine caught on something and about to burn its motor out. "I've been exhausted," she repeated to me, over and over. "I've been exhausted."

I knew she was talking about the fumes, about sitting on the scorching pavement behind that long black car and watching V.C. leave forever, but I knew what else she meant too. He'd taken everything.

Part Two

September 2003 to August 2004

The idea of pure independence has become an insanity with him: the thought of dependence in any form is a torment...And Ahab has his reward. He gets not independence but isolation.

—On Captain Ahab, from "Herman Melville" by Newton Arvin

The Edge...there is no honest way to explain it because the only people who really know where it is are the people who have gone over.

—Hunter S. Thompson

Chapter 1

A round the bars of the Square in Seattle in the autumn of 2003 a strange looking girl began to be noticeable to the characters that frequented the dark pockets of the street and the sad saloon where Kurt Cobain made the first in a long line of supplications to a world waiting for death to come to him and translate his words into something everyone could understand. Visionary eccentrics of past generations had scarred the walls long before she got there...where she came from nobody knew, nobody cared.

In September of 2003 Lo and I were at the Cellar at least four nights a week, and I was reading Kerouac's *Visions of Cody* for the third time. The stabilizing power of liquor seemed to balance out the manic high I experienced after reading each section, and the mental toll the book was taking on me overall. After getting off my shift at the bookstore, I got to the Cellar early in the evening and sucked on a beer to pass the time. I watched the door and cracked jokes with the bouncers, welcoming the bikers as they flocked in—

their leathery wings flump-flumping as they landed around me, beards wagging up and down as they picked and squawked at each other.

There was always a band coming through and I watched them too, as I got steadily drunker and waited for Lo to fully occupy my body again. As the opening band started packing up the stage, I kept my eye on the drummer, the bass player, and the guitarist. They filed by with speakers on one or both shoulders, miles of cord wrapped around half a body, and instruments that knocked and clanged against everything on the way out.

If the band had never played at the Cellar before they didn't know the rules. Rule number one was that if you wanted to park your car—or a huge band van—you had to park in back or on the side street, never in front. Because around 8:00pm or so, the bikers started showing up and they always parked in front. If the guys in the first band that played that night didn't know the rules, they more than likely emerged out onto the street with all of their gear, ready to load and get out, only to find their van surrounded by almost 20 motorcycles. No one was going anywhere until last call.

But because I was almost professionally in the business of scoring before 2:00am, I definitely didn't have the luxury of staying in one place until then.

Restlessly walking the streets one Saturday night, just to get out of the Cellar for at least a couple of hours, a line from a song I'd been listening to lately ran through my head. It had caught on the groove in my brain that always picked up snatches of rhythm and odd bits of phrases. The line wasn't going to let me rest until the groove was worn down smooth.

I ran the lines through my head again now. The singer complained that love kept trying to find him, but he wouldn't have it, he didn't want it. Instead, he invited someone to get in his car and go home with him, challenging that they were the same as he, out prowling the streets for sex and kicks.

I could relate.

I stopped by McLear's, a pub just a couple of blocks away, and ran into Don, a bartender from the Cellar, on his break and sucking down Mind Erasers. Don was an older guy, but not really old. He had gray hair and a gray mustache, and his face was lined, but he still seemed young. I hardly ever saw Don when he wasn't smiling or laughing or cracking a weird funny joke. His poofy hair refused to be cajoled into lying down flat and even when he was being serious you could see the corners of his mouth twitching. Don looked like he could have been a friendly carpenter hammering out toys for the neighborhood children, but somewhere along the line he'd chosen to do large amounts of coke instead.

Don's favorite funny story was from years ago when he'd been working at a bar up north in Washington where the men's bathroom was covered in pictures of naked women. Huge glossy tits and pink glistening vaginas decorated every wall, with a few shaved buttholes thrown in for the connoisseur. But in the midst of all this a smaller picture was pinned up, of about 30 women on motorcycles, all topless. Each woman and her bike were no more than a centimeter high. The set of tits on each chick measured at only a millimeter, maybe. 60 tiny boobs.

One night Don walked into the bathroom and caught a guy jacking off. He thought the guy was getting off on the centerfolds strung around everywhere, but when he approached him he noticed the guy's nose was almost touching the wall. He was staring intently at the 60 tiny boobs and going to town on himself. Don told me that the guy made him laugh so hard he left him alone and let him finish his business.

After a few more of Don's stories, I left him sitting at McLear's and told him I'd see him later, at the Cellar. Then I made my way back into the night.

Five hours later, just past last call, I was planted in front of the

Cellar on the sidewalk with the bums. They had closed and locked the doors maybe five minutes before I got there. I watched red-faced frat guys and their shrieking stumbling girlfriends surge outside from the meat market bar next door, and then turned to watch the gangsta guys mean mug and shit talk each other over on the sidewalk in front of Harry's on the other side.

I stood up and looked around. Last call and I had nowhere else to go. I started pounding on the Cellar's door and Cass saw me and let me in. Inside, the place was a circus. The staff had partied hard during their shift and various comrades had stayed after to continue the party. The water was on full blast in both sinks in the kitchen and the trapdoor to the manager's office in the loft hung open above. People clambered up and down like wasted monkeys as they went upstairs to do lines. The bathroom door to the women's restroom stood open and a pool of bright pink vomit rippled on the floor. The one buzzing fluorescent light that still worked in there flickered green on the puddle, turning the pink into shades of unnerving orange.

In the middle of all this, with eyes glazed yet oddly focused on the pool of stagnant vomit, stood Don. Like a tall swaying tower, he loomed over the insane metropolis below. One hand was thrust deep into his pocket and he held his other hand over his heart. He wasn't talking to anyone. I thought he looked a little dead. I pushed through the madness and pulled on his sleeve, staring up at him until he came back to himself. Suddenly, he jerked forward.

"Oh...hey! Hey Lo!" His face lit up like a tree on fire and then extinguished just as fast, like a cold bucket of water had hit him.

"Why—Cap fired me." he said.

Don was beyond drunk. He was in that special state of homicidal madness brought on by long term resentment and hours of Mind Erasers. No employee ever got upset when Cap, the owner of the Cellar, fired them. He fired people all the time. The

Cellar only employed cokeheads and drunks, and they were always drinking up all the booze, leaving coke trails on Cap's desk in the office upstairs, and forgetting to lock the place at the end of the night. But just because Cap fired someone, it didn't mean his career at the Cellar was over. Cap was a drunk and a cokehead too, and so he also always drank up all the booze, left coke trails on his desk upstairs, and forgot to lock the place at the end of the night. He just got cranky sometimes when other people did it. Don would have his job back tomorrow when Cap sobered up.

But the Don I knew was gone. No jokes in his eyes and no belly laughs. The corners of his mouth fell into still sharp lines that cut coldly into his skin. Like all of us, Don had a red-eyed reeking beast inside him and on this particular night, he happened to have fed it too much liquor.

"The worst thing is," Don continued lifelessly, "is that Cap hasn't paid me. He owes me."

I wasn't fooled by Don's surface complacency. The beast was stamping the ground and ready to charge. I wasn't surprised when Don's usually cheerful voice fell into an almost guttural snarl.

"But I got him. Ohhhh I got the bastard. Yes indeedy. Gonna be FUCKED tomorrow. Yes indeedy, oh boy." With that, Don pulled out the hand thrust deep in his pocket. It held a thick wad of cash. I whistled low.

"Don...is that the money from the till?" I raised an eyebrow at him.

"You BETCHA. Ohhhh boy. Oh yeah. Gonna be FUCKED tomorrow." Don stuffed the wad back in his pocket and commenced rubbing his hands together gleefully. They made a dry rasping sound that scraped over my ears even through the chaos of noise in the background. I slowly backed away and waited for Don's eyes to lose their focus again and go back to swimming at a point just above my head. I'd seen the beast before, in fact, I already had my own to deal with. I didn't want any part of it. I slunk my way to the front door and then slipped outside.

It was now after 3:00am. I glanced around at the shapes moving in the shadows and clutched my coat tighter and crossed the street. It was time to see what else I could find.

Chapter 2

Since the meth took over, something behind Tom's eyes had closed up. A sly giggling demon was using his body now, and speaking with his mouth. Every time I saw him he was high.

One night at the Cellar we had it out. Bret and I had just arrived and started the first round of shots when he showed up. First he ordered a beer, and then some water. Then he ordered a soda. When he got those drinks he ordered another beer, and so on. After 15 minutes Tom had ten drinks, all untouched. The liquid in each glass trembled delicately as he tapped-tapped-tapped his fingers on the bar. He looked behind him, nervous. I wanted to let go a wild scream and then slice the scream into razor thin strips and use them as a cat o' nine tails to beat him until the thing inside him, the thing behind his eyes, was black and bloody.

I hated the new Tom.

"Tom—" I eyed the cluster of glasses in front of him. "What the fuck? What are you doing?"

I could feel a lump in my chest, something that threatened to come out in one hot sad gush. Suddenly I felt very close to crying.

"Huh!" he started. "What? Oh, ah—yeah—what?" The thing

161

swimming in his eyes tried to focus on me. It couldn't and swam away again.

"You're fucked up Tom. Right now. You know it." I clenched my fists. "Flaco's got to go."

The thing in his eyes circled and darted back. It was going to fight me.

"Listen, Flaco's cool. That's it. It's done! Flaco's cool. He stays." He gave a small cracked laugh at the end of his speech. I heard each sentence like it was the final chop of a knife, every word a tiny slaughter.

I blew up.

"And what about Jared? Jared was real cool too, huh? That motherfucker never cared about any of us, not even you. He was always out for himself and no one else. And what about Sid? He broke Cassady's fucking nose! He was super cool too, right? Tom, you have got to see these people for what they are..." But I couldn't say the last part—I couldn't say what they really were—because all of us had been barnacles on Tom's great honest whale-wide world-weary hide. All of us had used him. Maybe none of us had meant to, but we did it all the same. The thing behind his eyes shrunk back and Tom was there, in his own eyes again, for a moment.

"Maybe I'm so lonely anymore I don't care."

Fat tears welled at the corners of his eyes and fell in slow motion. My heart broke within me. This innocent man who was destined for despair, this awkward hero whose actions up until now had been so gentle, so brave and kind, how was it right that he was so lonely? He was only alone because he refused to use someone for his own end. So, there it was. Everything Lo had ever taught me was true. Even inside the purest love, someone was always the user and someone else was always getting used.

Dizzying waves of hatred rose up and packed themselves into the air between us. I wanted to jump into Tom's eyes and kill the thing coiled there, its tail lazily swishing and taunting me, waving like an alien flag planted on the moon.

I turned and walked out, because I already knew. That thing wasn't going to let Tom go.

As the weather got colder and rainier Tom got worse. A lot worse.

He lost more weight. His cheeks just about fell in. Whenever his face was at rest the skin flapped like dirty yellow sheets. He got pale, so pale that his teeth started to look yellow too. And now, even when he was under the dim bar lights, you could see the meth rash cropping up high on both cheekbones. It was impossible to keep Tom focused on any one thing nowadays, conducting a conversation to its end wasn't even an option anymore.

The worst was when I saw him get lost in his own thoughts, when he didn't know he was being observed. Standing on the edge of our close bubbling knot at the Cellar, Tom looked like he was beyond despair. Like he'd seen enough of the world and he didn't understand why it hadn't mercifully crushed him to dust yet. He looked how I thought someone probably looked right before they shot themselves in the head.

Then Tom got evicted. He lied at first and told me his lease was up and he needed to find another place to stay. I found out later what really happened from Cassady. Even the totally indifferent landlady at the Montecarlo ended up telling him the drug traffic in and out of his apartment was just too much. I was shocked the Montecarlo actually had a landlady.

By October Tom was homeless. He never said the word and none of us used it around him, but it was a fact. He was now one of the many who lived in the Pioneer Square clubs at night and couch surfed by day. But even though Tom's life was falling apart, he still wasn't technically poverty-stricken. He had access to mass amounts of meth through Flaco, and in the Square that was better than hard currency. So, he kept bringing more customers to Flaco, who kept compensating him with more meth.

Now all Tom did was go on and on. That was all he desired, to go on and on and on and on until he died. His eyes were limited to two shades—blank and sneaky. Robotically, he marched into the clubs, brutally murdered his time, chopped it into tiny pieces and fed it to the vicious slavering wolves of his addiction, night after night.

Some nights Tom called me every few hours, and every time he left a message that seemed to indicate he was totally unaware he had already left me half a dozen others. He called at 12:00am, 4:00am, 7:00am, and 10:00am, each time from the club. Every message sounded casual yet forced, as if it were 10:00pm on a Saturday night and he had promised friends I was going to show up, instead of it being 7:00am on a Wednesday morning and him high out of his mind on meth and lost under the strobe lights, miraculously still going in some dark Seattle basement.

The only time Tom laughed now was when he was high. He laughed like maybe he'd seen someone laugh on TV a decade ago and memorized the sound. Like an alien would laugh trying to ape a human being. And when Tom was sober now, he never ever smiled.

I thought a lot about other people. People who weren't drunks or addicts or criminals. People on the outside. I assumed most of these other people thought that screwing all sorts of different surfaces one encountered in the world was wrong. I didn't think it was or wasn't, but I also didn't think any higher power had any place to tell me anything before I decided for myself. And so I wondered about these other people and what they thought about their higher power.

I guessed that the people I saw represented by smiling faces in TV ads were probably burning and bleeding inside too. They probably didn't know what was going on either. Maybe they couldn't trust themselves, just like I couldn't. But I also wondered if they believed the Universe had a set of instructions hidden somewhere, and if you did things a certain way—bought the right car, went to the right school, picked the right mate—then the instructions led to Nirvana, just like another set of instructions could produce a clean and sanded-tight birdhouse with each bird hole the exact same size.

I knew that a lot of the instructions posted were worthless. At least the instructions most other people seemed to see, the ones about the right car and right school and all that. They didn't lead to a happy life or a perfectly built birdhouse. All there was at the end was an assembly line of cheap square boxes, all the same. What kind of bird wanted that shoddy fake piece of crap for a home, with only one hole that was going to close up like a sick swollen eye once the bird was trapped inside? No, those instructions weren't for me. They just didn't apply. I was a bad drunk, and getting worse every day, but I wasn't living in a fucking box and trying to convince everyone else it was Nirvana.

Chapter 3

That autumn—despite my daydreams of Joey blowing back into town on the rainy wind in Seattle that smelled like night and water and the Sound—I really wasn't sure Joey was ever coming back. He'd already been gone for over four months. As to his current whereabouts, I had no choice but to operate on the scant information gleaned from the kitchen punks at the Crow. Some of them said he was still in New Orleans, and some of them said nothing. Realistically, I knew Joey could be anywhere.

I was going crazy inside my own head, obsessing over instructions that worked and instructions that didn't and finding nothing I could use in my current state of life. If Joey never came back then help wasn't coming from that quarter either. Perhaps, I reasoned, if I got to know someone normal, someone on the outside of life in the Square, I could find the clues that I needed. So I set about locking down on a normal guy. Someone around my age, who wasn't a drunk and wasn't an addict. Someone who lived in one concrete location and lived there legally. Someone who— for whatever bizarre reason—could come to develop an interest in me. It seemed impossible from the start.

That's how I ended up loitering at the Cellar one slow Monday night, strictly monitoring my alcohol intake. I stood in the rear, in the shadows, and examined each choice as it passed by. I was just starting to think about scrapping my plan and ordering a shot, when I spotted my ticket.

Two guys strolled in and went directly to the bar. Both of them had short hair, no visible tattoos. They looked to be in their late 20s, and even better, I could tell one of them was wasted by the way he kept keeling over to one side. Already seeing the hook gliding into that one, I licked my lips and decided to throw my line.

I walked over casually, making sure not to saunter, and stood at the elbow of the more sober one until he noticed me. I was careful not to demand my presence, not to demand anything.

I smiled generically and said hi. The sober one told me he was Allen and his friend's name was Antonio. Antonio leaned toward me lopsidedly and clumsily shook my hand.

Close to an hour later we were buddies. Allen whispered to me that Antonio didn't normally drink this much and I inwardly checked off another point on the list and congratulated myself. We talked about good beer and movies as I bit back comments about my drinking habits, avoided eye contact with the regulars who passed behind us, and steered clear of any discussion of books. But one thing still puzzled me. With Allen everything went as expected. He gave me a once over when he thought I wasn't looking and then his eyes got brighter each time he looked back into my face. But that wasn't the case with Antonio. He was just as friendly, but he wasn't giving me any looks. I was spinning around, announcing myself as prey—but while Allen had predictably noticed and then just as predictably started circling me—Antonio stared off into the distance, his wings folded behind him like a statue.

When I talked to Allen I could feel the bright warm streams

of his self coming at me. They curled around my head and shoulders, and playfully poked into my mouth and up into my nostrils. When guys were interested they all acted the same way. Their eyes changed. They looked hungry, like Allen did now. But Antonio looked like he was getting three square meals a day and then some.

My curiosity was piqued. I dashed off my number on a napkin and handed it to Antonio. On the periphery I saw Allen's face fall, just a fraction.

When Antonio called a few days later I suggested we meet at the Cellar again, like it was no big deal. But what I was really doing was going to meet an almost total stranger at a prearranged time and place to do what everyone else did—get to know each other. Technically, it could be called a date. I'd never done anything like that before.

That evening I chose an appropriate costume, a long demure black skirt and a halter top. I passed over the collars and the mesh and the dominatrix boots. Instead, I settled on sensible black pumps. I studied myself carefully in the mirror and decided my disguise fit. I looked pretty normal.

I got to the Cellar early. I showed up everywhere early. It was essential to scope everything out before things started happening. I sat at a table in front, staying away from the bar, and slowly sipped a beer. I watched the door and trembled. My hands shook and when I raised the bottle to my mouth the glass chattered violently against my teeth. I planted the bottle firmly back on the table and forcibly splayed my hands flat, ordering them not to shake. They stayed still, but the vibration traveled up my arms and into my chest until I felt my shoulders start to tear and come loose. I needed a shot, badly.

I gave in and went up to the bar to order a martini. Beefeater, up with an olive, very cold. While I was waiting for my drink someone tapped me on the shoulder. I spun around. It was Antonio. His eyes shone full of joy. Real joy—I could feel it coming at me.

In a flash, I went into nothing. I felt myself going there, felt the movement there, like you do in your stomach when an elevator changes floors. That feeling of nothing—of being inside nothing— it happened all the time now. I pasted on my game show hostess smile.

"Hiiii...Antonio...Wow, you're here! How—uh—wonderful!"

I bit the inside of my cheek and waited for him to finish his predictable response. I found a point slightly above his eyes, toward the middle of his forehead, and concentrated on it while I listened for the sound of his voice to cut off. Then I realized I wasn't acting very normal. What I was trying to do was muck around in Antonio's private inside parts and comb through what I found. Once I caught myself, I drew back sharply. I started over.

"So, uh..." I paused awkwardly and tried to remember a question normal people always asked me. "Uh...what do you...do for a living?"

"Oh...I'm, uh...I'm a stockbroker." He cut his eyes to the side and cleared his throat. He looked uncomfortable.

"Really." I said. I didn't know what to do with that. I didn't know anything about stockbrokers. It hit me now, in fact, that I'd never given a single thought in my entire life as to how a person conceivably entered into that position. I hunted around for the next right thing to say. I didn't know what the next right thing to say would be.

I excused myself and said I had to use the restroom. I kept my smile stiff and stretched wide as I turned, shouldering my way through the thickening crowd, but then I dropped it and began chewing the insides of my cheeks as I forced my way through to the bathroom.

Once inside I ran my hands under the cold water and then brushed them through my hair. I breathed deeply and let the burn of the hastily-downed martini seep into my stomach. I looked at myself in the mirror and was perfectly still. The muffled crashing and pounding of the band outside the bathroom door faded into silence. The answer was clear. I ran a quick hand over my face and closed my own eyes like I was a corpse and needed the help, just this one final time. When I opened them again I carefully set my face in the mirror. I turned to walk back to my evening with Antonio.

I started in full force on the martinis. After four more, it was time to proceed.

We left the Cellar and Antonio told me we were only a few blocks away from his building. I chatted with him about light ordinary things and made exclamations forgotten as soon as they came out of my mouth. Although I didn't listen at all to the words he said, I picked up on the rhythm of his speech and smiled and laughed at all the appropriate moments. I waited for Lo to completely absorb the gin and gather the power she needed to come out of hiding. It wouldn't be long now. I could already feel her stretching her long limbs and cracking her knuckles.

Antonio lived on one of the top floors of a very tall building. There was a doorman to greet and there was an elevator to take. There was a long hall to trek down and then there was a lock and deadbolt and another lock to get through. By the time we got inside I was safely seated in the back of my mind, knees drawn up to my chest, arms comfortably around my knees. I was able to see everything, but powerless to act. The martinis had done their work.

Slowly turning my head around to Antonio, I barked the first command. We would see how he took to it.

"Where are your condoms? Get them out!"

He fanned his hands out in front of me, palms up.

"I don't have any." He sounded apologetic.

I laughed harshly. It scraped the back of my throat as it came out.

"What? Why? What's wrong with you?"

Antonio opened his mouth to speak but I started in on him again before he could.

"Wait—ah, ah. Don't tell me. I don't want to know."

I considered for a moment and then decided.

"Go get some. You have 10 minutes."

He looked at me.

"GO." I ordered.

He went.

The door snicked shut behind him. I waited 30 seconds. I ran to the door on stockinged toes and opened it onto the hall. I peered down the corridor in both directions. The hall was empty. I closed the door again and threw one of the locks.

Now we had a bit of time and Lo knew it. She decided she wanted to take things slow, even though I pleaded with her. I warned her Antonio was coming back. I looked down at the street far below and showed her all the nearby convenience stores. He would be back soon.

Lo wasn't interested. She wanted to take her time. If I didn't give her all of my faculties for the search ahead she would force me.

She started with the kitchen.

Lo opened every drawer, every cabinet, and every cupboard. She opened the fridge and sniffed each little jar, every piece of forgotten Tupperware. She lifted the burners out of the stove and poked around underneath. She read every scrap of paper pinned to the fridge and examined all the photos too. She scrutinized the contents of every hidden space.

Then she searched the bathroom, the bedroom, and finally the hall closet. She lazily fingered each item, smelling or tasting it if she could. She handled each tiny thing cursorily, but deliberately.

Without haste, but with complete dismissal for the object the instant she ceased to touch it. The only things that noticeably delayed her attention were the pictures. She went through photograph after photograph, some off the fridge and some found in a kitchen drawer. Antonio with what looked like his friends, Antonio with an old girlfriend, Antonio with nieces and nephews, Antonio with someone who could only be his mother. At this last one Lo twitched and then was dangerously still. Feeling something coming, seeing the shadow of it like a black storm on the horizon, I held my breath.

Then she shoved me.

Hit hard from behind, a long blast of cold air tore past me on its way to the front of my mind. I reeled and hit a far wall, and then stumbled and fell. I was bleeding.

I wiped warm blood out of my eyes and looked up. Lo stood at the helm. The cold air had settled over her like a fog, turning her as white and perfectly clean as snow. Only her eyes moved. They skittered crazily back and forth and then rolled back into her head. I bent into the huddle of my knees and cried softly. When I looked up again Lo swung herself over me as if she were on suspension strings, hideously and with slow precise grandeur, a huge arachnid made out of ivory. As a spider, her taut abdomen was shining and bloated, her two arms divided into four and another four legs appeared to form a cluster of eight crooked limbs. She crouched above me, waiting for me to give her blood.

But then everything was back to normal. Lo was the same as she had always been, a warm and flesh-colored, beautifully cruel woman. I wondered at myself and why I'd been so distraught, why I had thought something was so wrong. Everything was fine, Lo was here. The veil would come soon.

During Lo's excursion through Antonio's kitchen she'd found a bottle of Maker's Mark in the cupboard above the fridge. I took a pull off the bottle and licked the edge, sweet like the top of a soda can. Then I went to the door and unlocked it. I sat on the edge of Antonio's couch and waited for him to come back.

When he walked in two minutes later I was fully composed. I kept the whisky bottle with me, not caring if he realized we'd been through his stuff. I expected him to be wary, but his eyes were still open and clear. He was ready to forgive anything it seemed. He clutched a slippery crackling plastic bag. I saw the clean shine of the brightly-colored Trojan box and snatched the package from him.

"Where in hell is all your porn?" I growled at him. "I've looked damn near everywhere."

Antonio grinned at me and fanned his hands out again. He shrugged his shoulders good-humoredly.

"I don't have any porn."

I spun toward him, incredulous.

"What the hell is WRONG with you?" I demanded. Antonio remained silent but continued grinning.

He stood with his hands open in front of me and seemed totally unafraid. I wondered if he'd ever had to shove his hands, curled into tight ashamed little balls, deep in his pockets so no one else could see they were shaking. I wondered if he'd ever been in a situation where someone else was studying his hands for just that slight shake to them, that small but firm telltale sign of weakness. I wondered if he'd ever gripped his hands into such fists of rage that he'd cut himself without knowing it, only noticing later the thin delicate lines of red flowing from the tiny raw crescents in his palms. It sure didn't seem like it, not now.

But that wasn't true. Lo lies—she always has, and always will. I have to back up now to tell you what really happened.

Antonio stood in front of me, yes, that part is true enough. His hands were out, in front of him and between us. But they didn't stay open, not like before when each palm blankly presented itself to me with unflappable steadiness. Now, as he stuttered and tripped over his words, navigating clumsily around my demands, his hands clenched and unclenched. His eyes smiled, his face was open and easy, but I knew he couldn't stop his hands. I was suddenly sure he had shook and stuffed and bled from those hands just as I had. I saw it all at once and the fight went out of me. Lo began a high-pitched keening shriek deep inside, and I lurched as I felt the kickback of the last of her strength.

"Well then STRIP." I ordered.

Antonio dropped his hands and obeyed.

He kicked off his shoes while unbuttoning his shirt. He half folded the shirt and laid it carelessly but neatly across the arm of the sofa. Hesitating, he looked at me. I stared back and then bared my teeth, just slightly. He gave a small shrug and unbuttoned his pants and shook them off. Almost as an afterthought, he removed his socks. I noted that he paired them carefully and laid them out just as neatly as the shirt. He stood looking at me in his shorts and bravely managed a smile. I could see the edges of the corners of his mouth twitching. Instead of triumphant, I only felt tired.

"Leah…" he started. He smiled again and then faltered.

"I don't feel right about this—you're really drunk. I just don't —it's not—"

He groped for words.

"It's just not right is all."

I shoved my hands into my coat pockets and as I did, my fingers brushed cold rounded metal. On one of my visits with Cassady to the porn store during a daytime drunk, I had bought what I thought at the time was a mini-vibrator made for a woman, but when I got it home and out of the package I saw that it was actually designed for a man. It was a vibrating bullet. Small and silver and streamlined, it came with a cock-and-balls, jelly-like ring that looped the whole thing together and deposited the bullet right underneath the shaft of the penis but above the ball sack, where it was supposed to remain, according to the instructions in tiny script on the back of the package, "during intercourse."

Not having any immediate use for the device, I had pocketed the bullet in case it might come in handy later. And now, it was later.

I pushed Antonio into the bedroom and down on the bed with one hand and yanked my skirt up with the other. The streetlamps outside drove sharp knives of light in through the windows and my shadow fell across him as I pulled his shorts down and mounted him. I moved through stripes of black room and white light as I rode him for a minute. Then I paused and just sat there. I held the bullet in the cradle of my hand, using it as a net to test the weight of what was about to happen.

I rose up and arched my back, holding the bullet behind me as I planted my other hand by Antonio's side for leverage. I could see his face washed in stark relief from those white bars of light still pushing their way into the room through the blinds. I could tell he didn't notice I was hiding anything. I kept the hand behind me, and then, just as he shifted his position, I struck.

Holding onto the end of the bullet, I pushed it effortlessly between his ass cheeks and into the anus. As it penetrated him, I saw Antonio's eyes widen and flutter and fix on me. His mouth remained open and slack. He seemed okay and didn't try to throw me off of him. He was still moving, and so I forged on.

I started by pushing the bullet gently in and out. Antonio kept his fixed stare on me and gave no other facial response. I began to wiggle the thing from side to side. As I wiggled, it suddenly occurred to me that it was supposed to vibrate. I found the miniature switch on the side with one fingernail. I flicked the tiny lever and to my extreme delight, the bullet immediately hummed to life. I gave up wiggling and pushed it in again.

And then it was simply—gone.

I felt it go cleanly, half sucked into Antonio by his pink

rubbery anus and half propelled a good way into the lower part of his intestine by my violent probes. It really didn't matter how it happened. It was gone.

I glanced down into Antonio's face again. Now there was fear. His mouth still hung open, but it wasn't loose anymore. Now it trembled in a rigid little "o" shape. His eyes widened and then narrowed, back and forth, almost imperceptibly with our movement. I held him with an iron steady gaze and made sure he kept his eyes on mine.

I plunged two fingers in and groped with the nails. Nothing but hot slimy skin that wanted to close over the fingers and take them off. I adjusted my position and shoved in the ring finger. I pushed farther and then farther still. I pinned Antonio to me with my eyes and ignored the naked terror ready to explode out of his face. If I wavered now, if I thought for one fraction of a second that the thing might not be found, then I knew I would lose it forever. I had to keep him with me.

"Careful...careful..." I murmured to him as we rocked back and forth and I dug deeper. Careful of what I didn't know, but at a time like this I didn't expect him to ask me. I had fully four fingers up his ass now and I could feel my nails scraping and shredding flesh that felt as easily scratched and damaged as wet clay. Somewhere under me Antonio groaned.

I went for it.

We rocked back one last time and then forward and I thrust with the momentum, catching the bullet, still vibrating, by the tiny lever that told it to vibrate and caused all the trouble in the first place. I hooked it down and pinched it between two of my fingers, methodically pulling and twisting until I'd worked it all the way out. It dropped tiredly from Antonio's anus and sat gleaming on the bed in a warm little lump. It jittered and shook as I sat on top of him, until I realized the thing was still on. I reached out and flicked the switch and the bullet finally died. I kicked it away and heard the distant thud as it landed across the room, burying itself into the carpet.

I looked back down at Antonio and sighed. He wasn't moving, and he still looked a little scared. I hoisted myself off of him and went to wash my hands. When I came back I sank down on the edge of the bed and hung my head, too tired to hold it up anymore. I laid back and pulled my coat to me. Drawing it protectively over my head, I breathed deep. It smelled like the Cellar and that was good. The bed was soft, and inside my coat it was dark and safe. I was in a small sealed-off pod. Cheerfully, I came to the conclusion that nothing outside my coat was real anyway.

When I woke up I was still in the dark. I was, in fact, still under the black leather of my coat. But small bright white shafts of light razored in through the chinks in the worn out garment and hit me in the eyes. I heard whistling and butter frying in a pan. I smelled meat cooking and it smelled good. I poked my head over the rim to inspect the situation.

It was morning. Inwardly, I wished I could live somewhere where it was always night and there were no people, like maybe above the Arctic Circle.

Antonio was in his shorts, but he was freshly showered and alternately whistling and humming happily as he flipped eggs with expert ease on the stove. He felt my stare and turned to greet me.

"Well, good morning sweetheart. I hope you like elk. I'm cooking some steaks up right now."

He turned back around and whistled and flipped something else. For maybe the first time ever when waking up at a strange guy's place, I was curious. A clear insistent pulse beat right behind my eyes. I had to know—what kind of a person cooked elk steaks for breakfast?

So, against my better judgment, I asked.

For the next hour, as we munched on elk and eggs and as I

surreptitiously scoured the apartment for any sign of Lo's wild search through his things the night before, Antonio told me all about his weekends.

During the week, Antonio worked downtown in Seattle as a stockbroker. He lived in the high-rise building we were sitting in now. He wore a suit and tie every day and he forgot about what he wanted. Instead, he concentrated on what he was supposed to be doing, on what he was supposed to have. But on weekends he was free. Every Friday afternoon he jumped on his motorcycle and took off for the mountains. He made camp wherever he found a spot that called to him and he set about being alone. He hunted deer, birds, and elk. When he'd killed enough to eat and enough to put away he skinned and cleaned the animal and took the meat back to the city with him. He separated the body in the forest and packed each tidily wrapped square back into his freezer in the city. When he needed the magic, when he was hungry for sustenance, he ate part of what he'd killed.

We finished our steaks and I let my eyes stop roving around the room. I looked at Antonio without fear. Now I understood why he wasn't focused on me. That was the barrier I'd run up against in his mind before, that was why Lo couldn't touch him. It was why I didn't get anything from him that first night and why I couldn't, no matter what I did it seemed, wrench the smile off his face—because Antonio wasn't really there. He wasn't present for any of it.

He lived far away, in the mountains.

Chapter 4

Winter in Seattle threads itself through falling dusk in the late afternoon, pink and gold and gray. Empty clouds leave lonely tracks all over the sky before they're ripped to death by the wind and leave reflections twisted and torn on the surface of the water. Time is suspended and then frozen. The buildings downtown tower over the city, over the people, half frozen themselves by the steely drops of rain just beginning to fall and blot out the dusk. Sun and shadow wash over the cold streets, waves of pale light and black space, and the city turns and sees its own face for a moment. Caught in a scream, eyes wide and terrified. Then the clouds settle and the city settles too, huge wings folded over it, the feathers pink and gold and gray.

I wandered through Seattle that winter in search of people. This person, that person, every person was the next person who might be *the* person. I couldn't stop myself from catching people and then letting them go again. I had to catch them to be able to really look at them. And sometimes when I trapped a quick lively bit of color, a wingtip caught out of the corner of my eye, I didn't expect it to be much more than a wood moth. But when I opened my hands—surprise—I encountered a real butterfly.

Dylan was one of these.

I'd known Dylan for almost a year before we started sleeping together. He was an on-and-off bartender at the Cellar and good friends with Cassady. Dylan was an abnormality at the Cellar because he was a hippie. He had a curly brown mop of hair that looped in ringlets around his ears and warm brown eyes that were wide and clear. He always wore some sort of hemp jewelry, a necklace or a bracelet, something that flagged him as a hippie to all the rockers and bikers and punks surrounding us at the bar. He was from Montana, short and solidly built, a sturdy playful little boy who had been magically zapped to full grown man. But the best part about Dylan was his voice. Deliberate and nasal, that voice was easy to believe. When he told you all about your hopes and dreams he made it sound like it had all already happened. I knew that if any of us got out of that place it would be Dylan. Because he still had faith that something good could happen.

One night I told him I wanted to hang out with him after last call. His eyes lit up as he took my hand. He looked like he thought we were going to have a slumber party. After the bar closed, I waited upstairs with the last of that night's coke swirling in wisps of windswept patterns on Cap's desk, looking like a desert storm seen from space. Dylan popped up an hour later and still had that oh-boy-we're-going-to-build-a-tree-fort look in his eye. All of a sudden I realized he was a friend. I took his hand and we climbed down.

But the next morning I was sober again. My warm friendly feelings had vaporized. In the bright autumn sunlight I didn't like Dylan anymore. I eyed the window. I pictured myself kicking it out and jumping to the pavement below. But Dylan didn't seem to care that I'd suddenly turned into an absolute bitch in the light of day. In fact, he was giving me the same look I often gave crazy people, like they were a fabulous exotic egg I wanted to turn around and around in front of me, an object of great interest. I realized that, maybe for the first time, I was the object and not the other way around. The thought that Dylan might be like me—not knowing how to treat people like people instead of eggs—wrapped around my heart and lungs and squeezed hard.

I calmed down. Nicely, I asked Dylan for a ride back to my car.

I saw him around after that. We started sleeping together almost twice a week and when Dylan's face turned over into a sunbeam I found myself smiling along with him. Before I knew it, it felt like we really were having slumber parties together. Somehow, we were becoming good friends.

Like me, Dylan was an addict. Also like me, he was a slut. So we had a lot in common.

Some nights Dylan called me late and came over to smoke pot and make late-night snacks. We talked and had sex and then passed out together. Some nights we went out to different bars around Seattle, both of us fighting the despairing pull the Cellar had on us. On those nights we got drunk at those different bars and talked, and then went to his place for sex. Those were the good nights, the nights when neither one of us got too drunk, when neither of us went into a blackout, and when we joined forces in fighting off the chill black water lapping around our ankles.

But some nights were bad. Some nights I got too drunk. Held hostage behind the veil, I said horribly cruel things I didn't mean or I got so violent it was all Dylan could do to get me out of the bar. Some nights Dylan called me late but when he showed up there were no snacks and no talks, there was no sex. There was just Dylan after hours and hours of coke. His dick limp and him ashamed, hands folded protectively in his lap over the zipper, hunched in on himself. His whole body was curled by shame, like a piece of burnt paper, his eyes empty. When I looked at him it was as if he were looking back at me from the end of a long tunnel, his eyes wet and pleading, the rest of him already having given up.

When he showed up at my place on Halloween night he looked totally shitty. His eyes were vacant and he agreed with everything I said without really hearing me. I could feel pieces of him breaking off in chunks, as if something as gentle and massive as a glacier was perhaps demolishing his soul. I sat down across from him and took his hands. His pupils looked like they were actually vibrating. When I looked down I realized I was holding two giant, fluorescent-green, plastic monster hands. It was still Halloween and I was still in my wig. Both of us wore disguises for the world to see, but we were still the same old fuck-ups underneath it all. And really, we had been in disguise from the first moment we met: Dylan as the happy hippie and me as whatever Lo chose for the night, be it dominatrix, vixen, or whatever else camouflaged crazy—real crazy—well enough. But right now we were just exactly what we were and what we couldn't get away from. Scared and lost, beyond lonely, we were tortured souls dragging our unwilling bodies into death with us.

I dropped Dylan's hands.

A couple weeks later, just before his 29th birthday, Dylan borrowed his sister's car and then totaled it. He hit another car, but no one was hurt. It was one of those accidents where no one is injured, no one comes away with even so much as a scratch, but it's obvious everyone could have been killed. It's the moment every serious drunk has when we see the twisted smoking hulk of close death. The moment when we're faced with the blackened wreck as it moves by on the tow truck, breaking off the other decimated vehicle with a sickening crunch, and the whole time it winks steadily at us—flash, twinkle-twinkle, flash—you did this you did this—you you you.

The next day, when he got out of jail, Dylan called me first.

I didn't know what to say. I heard something that scared me in his voice now. How things had changed, and how things were probably going to change even more. Dylan wanted to get better. He was beginning to care about how far he took things. But my part in this was simple and unalterable. In Lo's world there was only one thing—one line, one thought, one way.

We did not care. Not about anything—especially not about how far things went.

That was the whole point.

Dylan got assigned to court-ordered AA. But all drunks know AA won't stick if you don't want it to. And like I said, Dylan was only beginning to care. Like Lo, the Pioneer Square scene was merciless when it came to crushing out dangerous sparks of light or hope. Dylan was still on the coke, he didn't stand a chance. I wasn't worried about losing him—losing people was what it was all about. There was no way around losing somebody. Fortunately through Lo I'd found a way to hasten it, a way to kill that sick surprise. Dylan and I were in too deep, too far out in that black water, to slow the show down now.

But Dylan seemed serious. He went to an AA meeting every day, even though he still showed up at the bar afterward. He talked more and more about turning his life around, making a total change, becoming a new person. All the sunbeams were gone from Dylan's face now. He wasn't the happy hippie anymore, he was just disheveled.

We still had good nights and bad nights. The good nights I played along with him, I pretended at normal and Dylan told himself it was real. But nothing was normal. The bad nights still reared up like monsters in the distance, black dragons bellowing against the horizon. And every next morning we forgave each other everything again because we both knew how it was.

Suicide is never easy on other people.

∼

After the accident Dylan's younger sister—whose car he had crashed—told him he was a drunk and a cokehead and she hated him for coming so close to wrecking both their lives for what seemed to her like no good reason. She was partly right. There are no good reasons when you're an addict, but there are definitely reasons. Each and every reason wants you dead, until you figure out that's really the only reason. Sometimes destiny wants you to be pulverized.

So, when Dylan's birthday rolled around, I wasn't surprised when he told me he was going to spend it not drinking. But then a couple of days later he told me he was having his birthday celebration at the Falcon, on the night of the Genitorturers show. That was when I knew everything was back to normal.

The Genitorturers were a gothy industrial band that did weird shit like perform blowjobs and have orgies onstage during their shows. Needless to say, they were enormously popular with our crowd. Their cool beyond cool couldn't be denied. So cool I had to stand in line for a fucking hour, I muttered to myself, waiting outside the Falcon that night. When I finally got in I could barely move the club was so packed with people. For every nipple that winked by there was a chain attached to it, and every other person was on a leash. I felt like a square in my old standby vinyl cat suit.

I made my way through the sea of people, breasts, and tongues to the stage, where two members of the band were fucking to the music. I watched them hypnotically for a moment, feeling the crowd around me move and work with them. It was like we were one giant black pulsing organism writhing all together. It creeped me out.

I broke away. I had to look for Dylan.

I found him lolling on a couch in the rear of the club, his whole body limp and his head thrown back. A couple of chicks sat on the arms of the couch and a guy I didn't know was beside him. The girls were laughing and teasing each other and the guy looked bored. Dylan was smiling, but his eyes were closed. I sat down next to him, pulling his head forward to shake his curly mop. He laughed when he saw me and I knew he was drunk. I was glad.

We sat on the couch together and got more drinks and soon I was drunk too. We talked a little but mostly watched the crowd. It was a Cellar-type circus. We tried to guess who people were from the flashes of exposed crotch or tit we got. The tits were the easiest to identify—even if we thought we'd never checked out the rack of a mutual acquaintance, it turned out our unconscious mind had been scoping it out the whole time—we were dead on about almost every pair. The crotches were harder because they mostly all looked the same.

As the clock crawled toward midnight we stood up for the first time and all the drinks hit us at once. We realized how hot it was and how bad it smelled. Rivers of sweat crashed in a waterfall from the small of my back into the crack of my ass, and down the backs of my thighs. Dylan staggered and stumbled as he grasped at the arm of the couch to hold steady. I grabbed his sleeve and led him through the same squirming slippery crowd I'd gone through to get to him. We got to the door and grabbed onto a swirling streaming banner of cold air whipping inside from the street. Magnetized, it pulled us out of the club and landed us back in the night again. I grabbed a cab and steered Dylan into it.

The veil came gently this time, falling in soft folds around me, enveloping me in warmth. The smell of a litter of animals emanated from the veil, just as it had from the walls of the Falcon. I lifted it up and peeked out from under it, catching little glimpses of life. The next morning I filtered through the glimpses and real-ized the veil had given me something like 30-second movies to replay as memories.

The first happened in the cab. Dylan leaned, his head thrown back, with the same drunk goofy smile. His shirt was open and tufts of hair stuck out haphazardly. He told the cab driver where to go and the driver turned his head and laughed at something funny, something Dylan had said.

The next took place in a grocery store. I had no idea how much time had passed. We stood in the produce section and searched for the perfect something. Dylan's shirt was still open, but now he looked like a corpse underneath the all-night fluorescent lights. His mouth was pursed into a grim line, his eyes concentrated and feverish. He looked up at me, once, quickly, and looked down again.

"Help me. Please."

I knew what he was saying, we had to find it. The perfect something. I started hunting through tomatoes and then moved on to the lemons. Dylan tackled the grapefruits. The situation felt hopeless, but I knew I had to keep up my half of the task. If we didn't help each other everything would fall apart.

And then another cab. This time I was the one who was ordering the cab driver where to go, up the hill and then down again. Dylan's shirt was buttoned up now and he had his jacket on. He sat hunched over but kept his head up, his eyes focused on the road. He had the perfect something in his pocket. We'd found it, now he had to guard it.

The last took place in yet another cab and my god I was so tired. My eyes itched and my skin had grown a fine layer of bumps. Dylan looked like a zombie, but he was still conscious. His skin stretched across his face, shiny in spots, pale and gray in others. He had wide black circles under both eyes. He still hunched into a half moon shape, cradling the perfect something, guarding it from the world. We both knew if the secret got out that he had it, the world would come to eat it.

Then I woke up. It was over and it was morning. I was in my bed and I smelled someone familiar beside me. It was Dylan, last night's booze seeping out of him. I shook him awake to see if he could fill in what the veil had blanked out.

But Dylan didn't know very much either. He'd been in and out of a blackout too. He recalled a lot of cabs, and he seemed to remember that we'd driven all over the city the whole night long. He didn't remember searching for the perfect something, or guarding it against the world. He didn't remember the produce section. He didn't remember being a zombie.

I found Dylan's coat and rooted around in the left pocket, where I'd seen him hide the perfect something in the movie from the night before. My hand mushed into a juicy, pulpy mess. I snapped it back like I'd been bitten. Then I turned Dylan's coat pocket inside out and shook whatever was in it out on the floor. We both stared at it with disgust, and then with disbelief.

It was a pear. Or rather, it had been a pear at one time. Now, it was a battered mangled mess of murdered fruit. We looked at it, bleeding juice all over the floor, and then looked at each other. I knew we were thinking the same thing. Obviously, the pear was the perfect something we thought we'd found the night before. The question we silently asked each other now was if the pear really had been perfect when we found it and then we pulverized it, or if the pear had started out as that hideous monster, had maybe even been trampled on the black night sidewalk outside all those fluorescent lights, and because it was so awful, because there was no hope for it—because it was already pulverized from the very beginning—we'd recognized it at once. We'd recognized it for the perfect thing it was.

Either way, it was bad.

We never talked about it again.

Soon after that Dylan was rescued, from his life and mine. He called me one freezing starry night a week later and hurriedly asked me to meet him at the bar right down the street. He was out of breath and said he had something important to tell me.

Five minutes later I was installed in the first booth by the door. I craned my neck, watching out the window up the sidewalk for Dylan, and then I saw him. His cheeks were red and his hands were shoved inside his parka. His breath came out in quick little puffs and he was smiling to himself.

When he sat down he squeezed my warm hand in his cold one but didn't say anything, he just motioned the waitress over. After ordering a drink he looked at me for a long moment and then expelled his happy news onto the damp polished table in front of us.

"I got a job," he said.

I raised my eyebrows and waited.

"In Montana."

I let out the breath I'd been holding and grinned. I was ecstatic. But if I showed it everything would come off wrong. I held the corners of my mouth in so that I didn't smile too wide and asked him the details.

He'd gotten a job, a real job, he said—not in a bar—and he'd be based out of Missoula. He was going to be working for the public school system, sort of, but mainly he was going to sell software. He'd live in Missoula, but he'd be driving all over the country. He was moving out of Seattle in three weeks.

It couldn't have been more perfect. Now, without the threat of Dylan trying to repair his world in front of me, without the promise of his suffering, I was free. I was free to be friends with Dylan, free to fuck him, even free to love him if I wanted.

Then his phone rang.

He picked it up and I knew immediately that it was Cassady. His face shifted almost imperceptibly into tired expectation in the few seconds he spoke to her. Cass and Dylan had done a lot of coke together. But then he brightened when he realized it wasn't him she wanted and handed the phone to me.

"It's Cass. She wants to talk to you." I took the phone.

"Lo, get ready. Are you sitting down?"

Of course I was sitting down, I told her. I was at the bar.

"Joey's back. He called me last night."

Adrenaline instantly dumped into my system. Dylan caught my eye and gave me a questioning look. I pushed my mouth into a smile and fought for the straw as the waitress set another drink down in front of me.

Joey said he'd be back in town for a few days, Cassady said. He was planning on leaving for somewhere else soon, but he didn't know how soon, she explained. He wanted to see her to score, but he also wanted to hang out. He didn't leave a number or an address and she was sure he wasn't staying anywhere permanent. Same old Joey, she finished breathlessly.

I kept my mouth on the straw and sucked slowly, marking the delivery of information. I hung up the phone gently when she was done and handed the phone back to Dylan.

Lo rustled and stirred in the nest she had built, where she hid for most of the time when I was at least halfway sober. One leg thrust out obscenely as she dragged her new, huge spider-like girth forward and chomped on the bones of some forgotten man scattered around her den. I finished my drink and ordered another. All of a sudden I was thirsty.

Chapter 5

The section of Highway 99 that flows through metro Seattle and the northern suburbs is called Aurora. Winking with neon and snaking from Everett up north to Tukwila down south, it looks like everything else in America—every strip mall, every fast food joint, and every sprawling auto parts store—all crammed together. It is a straight shot. Everyone takes it sometime, because they want to avoid the hassle of traffic and the challenge of taking a more complicated route. The straight shot seems easy. But after being on Aurora for a while you start to feel weird. You start to feel tired. What begins as just a slight ache in the muscles soon drops into full-blown mental fatigue.

Driving north up Aurora from downtown Seattle, we pass Green Lake first—populated mostly with joggers and yuppies, and moms with strollers. Green Lake is a quick fix of filtered air, a blast of oxygen and relief coming through the car vents before it flits past the window and melts into the ghost of Aurora behind us. As we continue north the curves come, and on one of those curves we find Cheryl's Café.

Cheryl's is a shack of a diner planted on the edge of the road.

Inside, every free space on the walls is covered with artwork. Drawings, paintings, poems, conversations, fragments, all recorded on placemats and hung up wherever space could be found at the time it was created. The cooks and the waitresses, as well as most of the customers, are punks. No one wears hairnets, no one wears uniforms. Everyone has piercings, a score or more. The safety pin through the eyebrow is cool, the dirty Converse sneakers with no socks. The old yellowed undershirt on the hot young chick taking your order, that's cool too. Everything in Cheryl's depends on cool, and the middle of the night is the coolest time to be there. Cheryl's is a meeting place for everyone to be cool together, because when you're cool on your own, it doesn't really matter.

Let's get back in the car and keep on driving. Farther north on Aurora we'll see motel row. Places that mostly rent rooms by the hour or by the month. All of them have a small red sign that reads: Cable TV. All of them are close to the road. And all of them seem to house at least one person you know in Seattle, or one person that somebody else knows. None of them are a place you'd ever want to live in.

Then the casinos start dotting both sides of the street and that's when we know we're out of Seattle proper. The casinos are open 24 hours and, sitting on what might be the most depressing street in the Pacific Northwest, all of them look like carnivals inside. That's to make you forget. If we come in off the street— even at 3:00am—we can leave Aurora behind and come into the warmth of the lights and the bells and the feeling that we might just win something. Every casino has a menu that includes everything, to cut down on the risk of customers leaving for lack of choices. Because on Aurora, all of life is reduced to choices. This casino or that one. Lowe's or Home Depot. McDonald's or Jack-In-The-Box. A thousand different car dealerships, a million little holes. If you find one item on the menu that actually fulfills you—

even for two seconds—then you're lucky. Fulfillment is hard to come by on Aurora.

Outside, cars zoom past and rows of gray buildings face them hideously, the windows looking like the flat and scarred eyes of blind old men. The only human emotion found in this wasteland comes from the sky, who leaks slow gray tears, the drizzling ever-present rain of the Seattle winter. Driving up and down Aurora can make you want to open a vein. Walking up and down Aurora, friendless and without a drink in the middle of the night, can make you straight up want to put a gun to your head.

Aurora runs you down while you're running down it. You might not end up renting a room by the hour, but we all, sooner or later, end up on Aurora. We all sit at Cheryl's Café some nights, with someone we don't like, someone we don't really trust, drawing pictures on our placemats and inching them onto the wall space, covering up someone else. We all, sooner or later, duck into the casino because of the bright lights and because there are people there. We all scan the giant menu over and over again. Seeing nothing that we want, but trying to talk ourselves into it anyway. We all hate Aurora, but we take it day after day, because it's a straight shot. Because it obviously has everything we'll ever need. Whatever we wanted before we jumped on Aurora we will forget. It doesn't seem that important anymore.

We all, sooner or later, every one of us, walk down Aurora wishing for the gun in the middle of the night.

~

Late one rainy night I gave Tom a ride down Aurora. Cold drops of rain beat against the windows as I turned the defroster on and off and rolled the windows up and down to get rid of the fog on the windshield. I told Tom I was worried about him and flicked on the heat again, cracking the window another inch. For once, he wasn't high.

He said he knew it was bad. He'd gone out the weekend before and someone had spiked his drink with acid. He'd ended up trapped with the gangstas at Harry's—and then later the ecstasy kids when Harry's nine-hour happy hour had finally come to an end and after-hours started—until the sun was high in the sky and the acid had worn off.

When he stumbled out onto the sidewalk in the middle of the day he ran into Dante, who loaded him into a car and took him to one of his secret bases. He let him stay there until he was well enough to leave.

The unplanned acid trip was a revelation for Tom. He said he had to quit the meth. I let out the breath I'd been holding for over a year, it was finally over.

A few days later Tom moved in with Harrison. Harrison was a guy none of us knew who lived north of Seattle. His place was far away from Pioneer Square and Tom didn't have a car. Harrison seemed like he might be a good influence. At least, he didn't have obvious meth rash crawling up both cheeks and so Bret and I figured he was okay.

Bret and I visited Tom on his birthday about a week later and he looked worse than rock-bottom horrible. He'd been asleep for days and only roused himself to answer the door after we banged on all the windows of the house he shared with Harrison. But the sleeping was a good sign. He needed to catch up after going for over a year being awake for days on end. He was still skinny though, and obviously he felt like shit. His mouth looked as if it had hardened permanently into a brittle bone shell of a frown. Slight wrinkles had turned into deep lines painted on his face. His eyes were flat and almost colorless. All around him, emanating from within him, was the death smell like a wish blown out.

But Tom said he was clean, and I knew he was telling the

truth, just like the old Tom would. Bret and I lit all 33 candles on his cake, the plastic cover of the cake box sounding BARRRONG when we lifted it out of the way, thin drops of rain sliding off it fast, forming a small messy puddle on the linoleum. My hand trembled as I touched the precarious flame to each cheap little pink candle, the first ones already melting into the frosting by the time I reached the last row. Bret and I sang happy birthday to him in the empty kitchen, keeping our eyes fixed on the dark rainy night through the window above the sink. Tom blew out the candles and then said he had to go back to bed. We placed the plastic Safeway cover over the cake again without removing any of the candles and stuck the whole thing in the fridge. None of us felt like having a piece. Tom saw us to the front door and we left him standing alone in that bright square of light, with that same terrible look on his face.

When Tom called a couple of weeks later I answered. I'd promised him that if he needed support I'd be there.

"Heeeyyy Lo!" He said it like he hadn't expected me to be home. But before I could say anything, he barreled on.

"What are you doing tonight?"

I told him I was going to bed. I had to work in the morning. I asked him if he needed anything—where was he by the way?

"Well, I'm out—in the Square! But, uh..." He paused and breathed hard into the phone.

"Where Tom? Where in the Square?"

He was at Flaco's new hangout.

"I know, I know, I know—I know! But listen—listen Lo," he spluttered and started trying to explain. I didn't say anything. I let him stammer through his explanations and excuses.

"Tom?" I asked quietly. "What are you doing?"

A couple of seconds passed and he was quiet. More seconds scraped by and then when he did start talking again it was more calmly than he had during the entire monologue spilled out just a minute before.

"I can do it Lo. I can stay clean. I can."

But I heard the death wish, the silky smooth grain of it edge past his voice. Just like before, it wanted me to see it. It wanted me to know it was going to win.

"Fine, Tom. I'll call you tomorrow."

I gently released the phone back into its cradle and then stood gripping it. Finally, I came back to myself—away from whatever pulsing strobe lights Tom stood under now. I went to bed.

The phone rang two hours later, at midnight. Then it rang every hour after that, in punctual shrieking jabs at 2:00, 3:00, and 4:00am. Then there was a break, but it started again, ringing at 7:00, 7:30, 8:00 and then 9:00am. Fed up, I finally got out of bed to check the messages.

They were all from Tom. Hour after hour he'd left the same message. But instead of getting pissed that I wasn't answering, or depressed because I was out of reach, it seemed like he'd left each message on a different day, during a different week even. Every one was bright and happy. I heard people talking and club music in the background. In every message Tom said the same thing. He was with Flaco and it was a good time. He had some people coming down and he hoped to see me make it out. He gave the same hopeful goodbye at every ending, a shimmering whisper in his voice the only indication that each message was actually one of a series—somehow tied together by the thread of one long ghost trail.

The person leaving each message was a different Tom every time—he just sounded exactly the same. The Tom I knew—the Tom I thought of as the real Tom—was blind and exhausted from another night on meth. But the other Toms bustled around a dirty table covered with an oilcloth down in the basement of his soul. All of them hunched and grimy, with long bony fingers that clacked together feverishly as they rubbed their hands together under one naked light bulb with a single gray string swinging from it. Like insane Russian radicals out of Dostoevsky's *Demons* they plotted the impossible and absurd. They were conspiring to kill Tom. Each one planned on taking his body for their own, unbeknownst to the others.

Each one of these skeleton men had left me a message during that long night. And since Tom had never been there, not after that first real fix, he had no idea what any of them had said.

Then Tom disappeared again.

When he called me a month later it was early on a Sunday morning. Wide awake and hungover as usual, I answered immediately when I saw his number.

"Tom—where are you?" Panicked already, I cut straight to the point. Was he safe?

"Yeah, yeah...Lo...I'm fine." But he didn't sound fine. He sounded out of it. Like someone had come up behind him and whacked him a really good one with a crowbar. Like he had a concussion but didn't know it yet. Tom started to say something else, but then was interrupted by another voice in the background. It was a man's voice, muffled and indistinct, but I could tell he was mad. I heard Tom shout and then plastic clacking in my ear as he dropped his phone, breaking glass and then nothing. The line was dead.

I hung up the phone and let out a shaky breath. Had Tom and I really come to Seattle just to die? Any love we had started out with had fled long ago. It seemed there were things here that wanted to eat us. And now, they were intent on licking the last bits of burnt flesh from Tom's bones.

Chapter 6

I t was Christmas time again in the city. Two years ago I'd sat with Kellen at the Crow under safe twinkling lights, a strange warmth spreading through my torso, a small place of secure distraction in the middle of me.

Now Christmas was at the Cellar. The disintegrating silver tree in the boarded-up front window had a new set of lights thrown over it and someone had hung garland behind the bar, but that's where any similarity to the Crow and that happy bubble of time there ended. Most of the people at the Cellar didn't have families, or at least I assumed they didn't have families. I counted myself among them. I had a couple of real friends so I was lucky. But as the 25th drew near I mentally threw my lot in with everyone else, specifically to watch the decline.

I spent a lot of time with Lana that December. A bartender in her early 30s, she looked older but not really in a bad way. She was a Bette Davis type who had been beaten up, a dashing playboy sexpot robbed of everything. Lana had huge breasts, high and perfect, and a thin frame that fell into skinniness easily, and every couple of weeks or so. Her eyes were huge too, and beautiful, like the eyes of a great horse or deer coming upon its death all of a sudden, and all of a sudden understanding. That ephemeral death awareness filled Lana's eyes always, like tears ready to fall, balanced precariously on the bottom edge of her eyelids. The rest of her face was almost lost behind those eyes.

The death trip disappeared whenever Lana spoke. It moved lithely out of her eyes, and the movement transformed her into just another person again. Another bartender, another regular at the Cellar, another one of us. Lana's voice was smoke and splintered glass. The timbre told how she'd been used, the flat sharp edges told how she'd be used again. Lana had been ass-raped by life like the rest of us. However, unlike the rest of us I knew she'd never hesitate to bite off the feces-splattered cock that had raped her, if only just to spit it back at the world.

Lana was a harpy.

She hated life even more in December. She said the holidays reminded her of her family and her family hated her, so she hated the holidays. She balanced all the hate with coke and expensive tequila, and that was how I ended up keeping her company during her frequent breaks in the bathroom.

Sitting on the lid of the toilet with my legs crossed, my coat wrapped around me, looking up at her, I crossed my arms over my heart too. I had to protect myself from the pain coming out of her, it was bright green and radioactive.

When Lana was cutting up coke her eyes went dead. The large limpid pools of hazel dried up into hard cracked slits that held and measured each line, pinned it to where it couldn't get away, and then took their mark. The harpy in Lana's face came out then, unfettered by her sad animal eyes. During those moments her nose seemed even thinner and more hooked, her mouth solidified into pincers, a beak that was sharp as a knife as she spit every black word. I knew I couldn't help her. I couldn't tell her that all the people she thought hated her really didn't, she just hated herself. Her sad horse eyes and that hate were the only things she believed she really had. I understood. The only real things I had were Lo's experiences with strangers. Lana and I had a lot in common.

So, the end of that December I spent my time watching Lana cut up coke and listening to her talk about her family, her old loves and her hatred of the holidays, and then, when she was ready, I went back to the bar with her to help her finish off the tequila.

During the winter Cass and I stayed low key at 6 Points. We even stayed mostly within our own booth. People came to us now. Like large and impressive reptiles, we lay in one spot and slowly blinked our eyes as people stopped at the table to stroke our cool scaly skin. We watched the sun set in the middle of the afternoon and drank more every time we sensed any sort of feeling coming back. That year the end of December really felt like the end of everything. The dried-up, chewed-over stub that even the dogs won't eat. The end lived somewhere between our skin and the beginning of ourselves, it didn't look like anything but us.

Home in a cab on those nights that were really happening in the middle of the afternoon, I winced while humming along to Christmas carols on the radio. I thought about what the end of the world would be like, if maybe everything would just go very quiet and very dark all at once. I thought about how all endings—the end of this year, the end of the world I'd just dreamt up, all the endings given to me by other people, and all the endings I'd stolen —were all the same. Every ending was the only one there could be —my own.

In that cab, murmuring the words to "Jingle Bells" under my breath and against my will, I realized I expected less from everyone now. It seemed that I'd already met them somewhere, all of them, before.

Chapter 7

After the holidays Joey came back from New Orleans and I saw him only once, for no more than a few minutes, at the Crow one night. The place had been a madhouse, and as usual, he'd slipped away unnoticed after I'd spotted him. Of course, not one of the 30 or 40 people I questioned afterward had any idea where he had gone.

Cassady was right. Same old Joey, and I had no clue where to find him. The most definite place I'd ever known him to live was the mysterious underground bunker with the red door. A few people I'd talked to knew he wasn't living there anymore, but no one seemed to know where he was living, or if he was staying with anyone since he got back into town. My only recourse was to frequent the Crow just as much as I ever had in hopes of him showing up there again, like a mosquito drawn to the swamp. But I'd never had much patience for standing water.

One Saturday night at the Crow I leaned against a wall in the pool room and surveyed the scene through half-lidded eyes. Not much was going on this evening and I was already bored. Ratt Stilskin suddenly appeared at my side. I wasn't startled. Ratt Stilskin was always showing up at someone's side out of nowhere. Like

Joey, his preferred method of appearance was via magic material-ization, but unlike Joey, Ratt Stilskin was the opposite of lazy wandering smoke that gradually thickened into human form. Instead, Ratt appeared all at once, with a bright cartoon *POP*, smiling and winking and sizing you up all at once.

I continued leaning and yawned loudly. Ratt Stilskin was a friend, and it was always good to see him, but he wasn't Joey. He held no threat to me, and so he held very little interest as well.

"Hi Ratt," I managed through my yawn.

"Hello Leah. Bed this early?" His eyes twinkled. "I thought you had a fire in your belly. And now look at you, a prom date with the dress but no man. Sad." He grinned mischievously and the gap where he was missing an eyetooth flashed darkly at me.

"Guess so," I answered indifferently. My eyes continued moving sluggishly around the room.

"If you perchance discover some leftover energy within your shriveled self, you might rouse yourself adequately to come to brunch with me tomorrow."

I was only half listening, but Ratt Stilskin's pause at the end of this last sentence pricked me before I knew it. I drew in closer and really looked at him. There was something there...but then it glided away, fish-tailing its long black shadow behind it, and was gone.

"Yeah, maybe. Where?"

He gave a small satisfied chuckle. Rubbing his hands together, he continued grinning at me.

"The Chimera. 10:00am. You know the place, I assume."

I nodded and went back to scanning the room.

"Well my sweet, then I will see you tomorrow. Don't be late. And oh—yes—oh yes—Joey is meeting me there as well. Ta ta!"

I turned violently but he was gone. I looked in all directions. Vanished.

The next morning I woke up still drunk. I sprang awake

already manic and stood naked in front of the mirror while I tried my hair piled up on top of my head and then down. I looked out of my bedroom window onto the iron gray surface of the Sound. The wind-tossed water merged with the murky sky. Wet black tree branches, shining with rainwater, slapped against my window. I thought of Joey standing at the edge of the bar, his head bent, too drunk to hold it up, but even so ordering his usual, a Maker's Manhattan. That had been my grandfather's drink of choice too. I let go of my hair and it spilled down my back in thick knotted curls. I bared my teeth at my reflection and then shoved the mirror aside.

I was at the Chimera at 9:30am. I chose a dark booth to the side where I could watch the door without being seen. I ordered coffee just to order something and then poured packet after packet of sweetener into it to see if it would turn into one solid grainy lump of caramel-colored candy. I never drank coffee and didn't care if it turned inedible. My hands needed the activity. They trembled and spilled white sparkling crystals across the scarred black Formica.

10:00am and no Joey. No Ratt Stilskin either and nothing interesting had happened to the coffee. It had just turned thick and cold. Bored with it, I thrust it away and it sloshed over onto the table in front of me. I waited.

10:10, 10:15, 10:25. The minutes sat still with me and seemed to be waiting too. I was the only one in the place and the wait-staff kept glancing over at me and my disastrous coffee. I'd have to order something else soon or leave.

10:45. No one.

I waved over one of the waiters, a guy who was just a few years younger than me. His hair was cut at sharp angles and dyed a bright shiny black. I imagined ripping the ring out of his chic little tender nose. I ordered a Bloody Mary and made it a double.

By 11:15 I was on my second double and my state of affairs

didn't seem quite so wretched. I reflected that I could stop by 6 Points on my way home and make it a day. Ratt Stilskin and the aborted brunch didn't matter anymore, not even the rain, driving down now in sleek silver lines, mattered anymore. I was warm inside. Burning, in fact. Ah, but Joey. I stared down into the remnants of my second drink and watched the tomato and ice bleed together. Joey mattered.

But then, before I could think about ordering a third, something bumped my elbow on the outside of the booth. I snapped my head up, just fast enough to glimpse a tall black shadow floating toward the back. I recognized that shadow.

It was Joey.

The vodka working its courage in me, I flew after him and peered around the corner into the next room. Joey took a seat by himself at the window. He looked out into the wet gray street and bit his lower lip. I started to skid around the corner, but then stopped so suddenly that I almost crashed into the waitress station. I couldn't *run* to the table, I'd look like an idiot. He didn't know that I had known he was going to be here. He'd shown up with the expectation of meeting Ratt Stilskin for brunch.

I had to play the cards Ratt had laid out for me.

I ducked back into the other room and grabbed my coat out of the booth. I looked over the mess on the table and winced. Then I made my way back around the corner, and as casually as I could, strolled over to Joey.

Because he was still staring out the window, I got to the table before he saw me coming. My eyes lit up when I saw that he saw me. I feigned startled pleasure.

"Oh! Joey! Hi! Are you by any chance—?"

I swiveled my head around and pretended to look for Ratt Stilskin.

"—with Ratt?"

"No, but I'm supposed to meet him here for brunch."

He looked at someone over my shoulder and my heart sank as I pictured Ratt Stilskin's merry little face jogging toward us. I spun around.

It was the waiter. He'd poked his head in to see if we wanted anything. Joey ordered a screwdriver, a double. I sank down across from him and ordered another Bloody Mary, double. I clasped my hands in front of me and began the tedious process of beginning with Joey at the beginning, not wanting him to know I was crazy and usually began at the end first. I started by asking him how he'd been.

We spent the next two hours at the Chimera. Joey waited for Ratt Stilskin to show up and I pretended to do the same thing. He stayed strong on the screwdrivers and I finally switched over, sick of the thick taste of tomato juice coating the back of my throat. Outside, the rain never stopped. Inside, the first fluttering birds of panic hatched open in my head and began weakly pushing themselves into the core of my brain, leaving a shimmering snail trail of slime behind them.

Outlined in the white-gray, rain-skied window, Joey was more than perfect. He actually made sense. He was the same shiftless wanderer I'd fallen in love with last spring, but more worn and lonelier than ever before. I asked him how it had gone in New Orleans.

He leaned back and fingered his glass. One side of his mouth crept up in a slow smile, but his dark eyes stayed empty. He told me it had been good, he had been drunk all the time. He drank whiskey sitting on the shores of the Mississippi River. But there was no work and he finally ran out of places to stay. He planned on leaving Seattle again soon.

I brushed his last words away before they could even gain a foothold in my ears. Joey always said he was leaving soon. He was always in town "only for a few days" but sometimes he stayed for months before he found the next right place to go.

Time was running over itself again, like it did whenever I started to get really drunk, but I was still okay enough to see it was almost 1:00pm. Joey suggested we go to a punk bar down the street with pinball and hot dogs and heavy cold steins filled to overflowing with cheap beer. I agreed and we walked through the rain together, heads down, hands shoved in our pockets.

We sat in that bar for the rest of the afternoon and drank. Joey teased that I was going to blackout like I always did and forget everything we talked about, but I promised I wouldn't and stuck to the beer. Scrawny, pale and miserable, Joey sat across from me, smiling and wincing all at once. He was a Raskolnikov who laughed with magic dark mirth, a Rasputin who had joined the hippies and found the acid better than the murderous intrigues of the Czar. A die-hard punk who loved everybody, even the squares.

I asked him everything. Everything about the physical mundane details of his daily life. Everything about the grandiose monstrosity of his past and his nightmares. Everything about who he loved, what he loved, and why. Absolutely everything.

But Joey didn't seem to know how to answer me. At times he seemed not to understand the questions themselves, no matter how I rephrased them. It wasn't that he was dodging. I knew he was trying to be forthright, I could see it on his face. It was something else...a misalignment, a puzzle piece acting as a spurious fit that warped the whole picture. With growing horror I saw how much Joey looked like Jared when he tried to answer me, using half-formed shrugs and the same indifferent twist to the side of his mouth. Rasputin was gone and Joey was only a man again. Worse, I was only me. I ordered a shot of whiskey and downed it bitterly.

Uneasy now, I studied him. Joey's eyes moved restlessly around the room. He looked like he wanted to get away from me. I abandoned my line of questioning and dropped all matters of the soul. Maybe he just didn't want to discuss it, or maybe not with me. I shifted back to talking about people we knew in common and the hauntingly familiar Jared-like twist to the side of his mouth disappeared. His answers stopped skittering off to the side and became more concrete.

Then the subject of Cassady came up. It was almost 4:00pm and I knew she would be just waking up from the night before. She always had pot and both of us could use a break from the drinking. Realizing that a visit to Cass introduced a concrete objective that also served as a real excuse to spend more time together, I brightened immediately and suggested it to Joey. He agreed to go with me.

When we left the bar it was dark. We walked to Cassady's apartment in considerably better spirits than we'd been in earlier. The rain had stopped and now we were drunk as loons. Cassady poked her head out of the window when we whistled up for her, brushing her hands through her frowsy black curls as she yawned and smiled down at us. We clumped up the stairs and she let us in. She pulled out her bong and we took long slow hits, passing it around as Joey sat on the floor, his arms wrapped around his knees, catching up on all the latest news with Cass.

Before long, we realized it was almost happy hour. Joey and I looked at the wet black sky outside—it had started raining again—and then glanced at each other. Time to go back to the bar. We invited Cassady along.

Half an hour later the three of us were firmly planted at the Challenger, a hip modern bar on Capitol Hill. Outlined in thin tubes of neon light that bounced off the silver décor, the bar looked like the inside of a spaceship. Like somewhere Captain Kirk would go to get fucked up and lose himself.

I was really drunk now and glad Cassady had come along. She seemed to have such an easier time making conversation with Joey than I did. She never made him uncomfortable. But they also had a lot more in common, like coke. And that was the main conversation at our table. Who had it all the time, who had it only sometimes, and most importantly, who had it that we could get to right now. Cassady was out and Dante was unavailable, lying low at one of his secret bases.

We left the Challenger an hour later with drizzles of cold rain falling slantwise on our poor tired heads. We drove for the next couple hours, cruising through rain tinted a bright orange from the street lamps above. I sat in the backseat and watched Joey and Cassady talk. Whenever one of them got pricked by the idea of another possible source, their heads snapped back and forth in sharp discussion. Then the name was rejected for whatever reason and they nodded slowly again, talking of lesser things. As I listened to them plot our next destination I rested my eyes on the blurbs of neon that came shining out of the rain, and then were swallowed by the darkness behind us. It was early, but I'd been drunk for quite some time. The whole world seemed deserted.

After a while they came to the unavoidable conclusion: no one had anything. Cassady was ready to press on but Joey conceded defeat and told her to forget it. We made our last stop at the Falcon so Cassady could collect her tips and Joey and I elected to stay in the car, having been thoroughly beaten by the rain.

Because I experienced such strong emotions around Joey, my inner antenna was totally fucked in his presence. I could *see* into most people, even if it was only a glimpse. Sometimes I could sift through them and pick out the larger parts that had broken off inside, pulling those pieces out into the light for deeper inspection. But love for Joey scrambled my signal—just like it had with Jared—and I couldn't get anything. Both of them had that same terrible power over me. It was like being held in someone's fist and squeezed only at the times when you weren't expecting it. My antenna wouldn't work when I couldn't even get my breath. And without my antenna I felt like I was blind.

Sitting in the small black shell of Cassady's car, listening to the rain tap into the metal roof, and inside, feeling very small and cold myself, I still couldn't get anything from Joey. He sat in front of me, staring out the windshield as I nervously made conversation. I scanned the running wet shadows of the Falcon across the street, waiting for Cassady to reemerge, and desperately twisted my fingers together like cold dead rope.

But then Joey turned and leaned around the front seat. He craned toward me until he was two inches from my face. I froze like a panicked chipmunk. I flushed, my skin prickling, and dived into the next round of nervous chatter.

"So what—"

Joey crushed his lips against mine.

I gave myself a mental pinch. It was real. It was happening—or it seemed like it was really happening. Joey was kissing me. On the mouth. Voluntarily.

Then it was over and Joey faced forward again, as if he'd never moved at all. The car door flew open and a wet, cold black wind lifted my hair and a random scattering of cigarette papers on the backseat. Cassady was ready to head home. She started the car. Where did we want her to take us?

I opened my mouth even though I was reasonably sure nothing would come out. Then I heard Joey say, casual and like nothing had happened:

"Just drop us off at my place."

All the drunk went out of me. I'd been scared sober. Lo had fled to her own weird underground bunker and although I'd never wanted Joey to meet her, I already missed her. I was terrified on my own. I didn't know how to act and I didn't know what to do.

Joey directed Cassady up to Capitol Hill to a small apartment building, explaining that he was staying there with a friend. She dropped us off out front and Joey led me around to the back, the only place where the key he'd been loaned fit. Once inside, we made our way to an apartment that was almost totally empty but spacious and clean. It was enormously inviting after walking and driving through the rain all day. The kitchen and living room were bright and cheerful, but no one seemed to be home. He didn't show me any bedrooms.

When it came to Joey's friend, I didn't care who she was. Of course, I knew it was a she. I could tell by the way he said the word "friend." But friend, girlfriend, wife, a big man dressed in drag—whoever she was and whatever she was to Joey, I didn't care. I didn't want Joey as my own boyfriend. I was just in love with him.

The sex started slowly. I'd been drinking all day and I was absolutely filthy. I hadn't even showered that morning. Showers tended to bring out the hangover. If I was careful not to smear last night's mascara and started drinking early enough in the day, I came out looking much better. But that was my face, not my crotch. If I was going to fuck Joey, I needed to shower.

Joey led me to the bathroom and started the water. Then he undressed us both and showed me the way in. My mind snapped on and off—winking on with little lights of joy and then suddenly winking out again in black terror. My heart raced and my hands shook. I wanted whiskey but all I had was Joey, and why was it like this? I had the thing I wanted, the thing I'd suffered for and desired so much, and now here it was, naked and shivering and vulnerable in front of me, mine for the taking. And all I could think about was a shot of Jameson.

But other people did this all the time, I thought. And I could too. I'd do what I thought other people did. I'd lose myself—all my neurotic worries and the ever-present booze hunger—in the mind-blowing sex to come. But first, I had to figure out a way to make the sex happen.

The shower was so small that lying down was impossible, and once inside I realized Joey was even taller than I'd thought. He was at least 6'3" and I was only 5'3" on a good day. I stood on the very tips of my toes and flexed my feet with superhuman ballet dancer strength, but I still couldn't fit Joey's dick inside of me. Not even anywhere near where it was supposed to go. My toes cramped and I fell back, flat-footed and defeated.

Then Joey tried to pick me up, but that didn't work either. Both of us were still drunk and the shower floor was slippery. Either Joey's friend didn't have sex in the shower much or she was so agile she didn't have the need for the added traction of a shower mat for sexual escapades such as this. After the third try, when one of Joey's feet skidded out from under him and he dropped me on my tailbone and then slammed his head into the wall behind him, we gave up. We got out of the shower and turned to the living room couch.

The couch was old and had a comforting rough brown cross-hatch design that reminded me of outdoor carpet. Some of the stuffing was coming out of the cushions and there were good-sized gaps between them. We sank into it with relief and tried again. Lying down worked much better and it seemed like most of my awkward feelings were finally gone. Sex itself was comfortable for me, there were no secrets in it.

When we finished I sat up and immediately reverted back to watching him. I didn't know how he'd feel about what we'd just done. I suspected that, like most people, he'd now feel differently toward me in some way, either good or bad. Whatever he felt, I'd meet it with absolute wariness.

I pulled my shirt over my head and tossed his hoodie to him. Joey draped the fabric over his shoulders and fiddled with something small in his hands. I stood to go.

"Here." he said, and suddenly his hand was in mine, folding it over and pressing it gently. He was giving me something. A piece of paper, probably the number for a cab. I shoved it into my pocket. I'd already decided to walk. I felt more sober than drunk now and gave him a small wave before backing out the door.

Once outside I walked down the block fast without looking

back. I ducked around a corner and walked another two blocks and then took another corner. When I was safely on my way down the hill with the freeway in front of me, tiny toy cars zooming past in the rain, I checked behind me to make sure I was totally out of sight. Then I pulled out the crumpled bit of paper from my pocket and opened it.

Under the scrawl of Joey's name, there was a number. He wanted me to call him.

I bit my lip and tasted blood. I stopped on the overpass and stared north and then leaned my elbows on the railing. I looked down at the cars below and then all around at the sky.

Maybe I was happy. I really didn't know. I sort of felt like throwing up. Beyond that, I had the feeling of tying up loose strings for good, of finishing something and putting it behind me, of wide, white nothingness coming to settle over me again like a blanket of new snow. Maybe that was happiness.

Because of the rain, there hadn't been any twilight. Razor lines of water still fell, but the moon shone through, lighting up the layers of fleecy gray torn clouds, broken open and blown hugely this way and that, fast moving glaciers in the night sky. The lights from downtown sparkled one by one, twinkles of orange in the massy black and gray. I started walking again.

It felt exactly right to be alone in all that black and gray with the rain and the wind. Thinking of Joey, and the day behind us, a pulsing warm glow spread all through me. I realized I never wanted to see him again. I already knew how it would go. The Joey in my mind, the dark and pale Rasputin with full sweet lips like raspberries and the infallible great strong heart of a warrior stallion—that Joey would be reduced to just another guy over time, just another person. Someone who couldn't think of anything good to do on empty afternoons, someone who fought and cried and begged over his own little problems in his own little head, someone who couldn't think of one good thing in the world to want, not one single thing, and so ended up trying for the worst there was. He would be someone exactly like me.

The Joey in my mind would be murdered, probably shot on a wall right in front of me, and then afterward Lo would make me clean up the mess and burn the body.

I tasted ashes in my mouth and shuddered, sweating through the cold rain. Maybe I did want to see him again.

Chapter 8

I saw Joey one week later.

He was leaving Seattle again soon, this time taking off for New York. I had decided to come clean with him before he went. I had to tell him how I felt and deal with the consequences, even if he decided to hate me. We made a plan to meet that Sunday night. Joey said he'd bring his friend Xavier, who was a painter, and the three of us could all get drunk together.

We decided to go to the Challenger again and so I showed up early, like I did for everything. I sat at the bar and fingered the studded collar I wore and drank gin martinis. An hour after I'd been waiting, and only a half hour late, Joey materialized by my side, his friend Xavier standing shyly behind him, a tall skinny blond guy with colorless eyes who looked like a Polish refugee, someone whose real name was Stasiu Zyskowski, and who was living underground with an assumed identity.

I ordered another round of martinis, vodka for Xavier, and we started drinking. Then we ran into two other friends of Joey's, a surly punk named Billy with a dreadlock mohawk and his girl-friend, Magenta, who had bright red hair and seemed the happiest of the bunch. I didn't know if it was part of being punk-cool to have a constipated look on your face all the time, but I found it annoying. I felt like shit inside too, but it wasn't anyone else's business. I'd noticed the same thing with some of Sadie's punk friends. They wanted to let everyone else know how angry they were, how wrongly they had been treated. I already knew no one cared. I could kill myself and be found in a pool of slippery bright blood on the bathroom floor, shreds of flesh hanging from my wrists like birthday streamers, and the only person to get the point would be me. Everyone else had their own problems.

But I was with Joey, and him being a punk, and in cool with the punks, was his deal and not mine. The rest of his life had nothing to do with me.

After the bar we went to Xavier's apartment. He didn't have any furniture besides a mattress and a refrigerator, but the whole place was packed with his oil paintings. Drunk, I wandered in a surreal used car lot of canvases, one stacked on top of the other as far as the eye could see. Xavier painted like a virile ferret, even the walls were splattered. The rainbows everywhere reflected back to me in his clear colorless eyes. Silent all evening, he sat and watched us, gripping his short glass of vodka.

Waiting. All of it was just waiting. Waiting for the party to end, for Joey to get tired, for us to be alone. Waiting for a cab, waiting out the ride not talking much, waiting to get inside with normal fumblings at the door, with necessary small murmurs moving back to my room, waiting on the edge of the bed while he walked back across the darkened apartment to the bathroom. Waiting. And while waiting to get through it, missing that it was all of life. Still unknowing of it then, at that time the waiting was all there ever was for me.

In dark rippling pockets of deep blue night, I sat on my knees on the floor near Joey. He sat on the mattress, leaning against the wall, as if he were an old invalid receiving a springtime visit from an innocent young girl. I couldn't bring myself to touch him. Not until he told me that he actually hated me. That I'd never been interesting to him at all.

"Joey..." I started, already half biting back the hot gush of words.

"I...I have...feelings...uh, for...um, for you. I—I—it's been uh—well, probably since...last April? A long time anyway...I just—well, I—I didn't know how to tell you. How to say it, and I—that's it. I—well, see I..."

My mind's tongue formed the word's soft shaping—*love*—in front of me. The word floated up and glowed and then faded and was gone again. My real tongue locked and I knew—even if Joey didn't hate me, even if he said it first and it were all true—I'd never say it. It was poison.

Joey leaned forward, gently pulling me toward him. He held my hands and bobbed his head a couple of times. He was so drunk. He stroked my hair with one hand and leaned my head forward until it was touching his. Then, slurring, he said:

"I'dor ooh."

I craned my head closer.

"What?"

He made a slurping sound, clearing his mouth, and then repeated it.

"I—adore—you." He collapsed back, his hands dropped limply to his sides, drained from the effort to enunciate each word.

The craving—the outright BURNING—for a shot of whiskey hit me so hard I almost doubled over. I heard a light buzzing somewhere outside of myself. It was like being alone in the woods, struck dumb by unspoiled sacred tree and earth and peace and then hearing a chainsaw far off, an insect that is really a man. A comforting sound that was coming for me one day too, only with cold death and no comfort at all. A faraway person, someone I didn't know and never would, taking their part of the forest.

The rest of our exchange was hazy, the sex afterward even

hazier. My feeling of being alone and free came back the second he walked out the door. But before he did, Joey had asked me to come with him to New York. I'd said no. We were always so drunk...I thought there was a good chance he wouldn't remember what he asked.

He left for New York a week later.

Chapter 9

At the beginning of that February of 2004 I tried to cut out my morning drinking bouts at 6 Points, but then I just ended up somewhere else, at some other bar. I tried to stop drinking tequila because it made me too dangerous, but then I just ended up drinking gin. I tried to stop mixing liquor and beer, but then I mixed liquor and wine. I never tried to stop drinking.

Every morning of that bleak February I woke up watching the Seattle rain dribble itself down my bedroom window. If I had to kill someone to do it, I was getting out of Seattle in 2004. If I stayed in the Square for another year I knew I would die there. I had to get out.

I settled on the idea of San Diego. I had dreams of renting a little house, not far from the beach. I could drink things like margaritas and tall cool gin and tonics while I barbecued shrimp every night and studied the stars. In this new life I was at peace... there was no Square, there was no sad Seattle rain dripping down my window every morning. In this new life in San Diego, it was sunny all the time and I wore flip flops. I drank steadily, but I looked like the people in Corona ads on TV. There were no black-outs, there was no veil.

When a girl I knew from the Crow mentioned that she knew a guy who was from San Diego and planned to move back there in the fall, a guy who seemed nice enough, I said I was interested. When she said the guy was looking for a roommate I said I'd meet with him that very weekend.

And so the Saturday night right before Mardi Gras—when I should have showed up early and sober down at the Cellar to get an idea of the lay of the land, when I should have kept closer tabs on the drinking and held myself together—I was busy at a hipster bowling alley up on Capitol Hill meeting Ray, the guy from San Diego who was unexpectedly nice and who had, also unexpect-edly, immediately agreed to let me move in with him to the house I hoped wasn't far from the beach. I checked with Ray and found that he did, in fact, own a grill. I smiled and thought about barbe-cued shrimp every night for dinner. San Diego was just what I needed.

Bolstered by Ray's goodwill I let down my guard and started in on the mixed drinks. An hour and a half later I wasn't drunk—not by a long shot, not yet—but the sugary soda mixed with rum had muddled the high clean euphoria I usually got from straight whiskey or gin. It didn't matter though, everything was cool. Uncharacteristically, I'd left my car at home and decided to take cabs all night. It was the Saturday before Mardi Gras. I knew the cops would be out.

I ordered a cab to the Crow and stopped inside briefly, but when I saw how packed it was at the bar I wrangled my way through the crowd and made it back outside again. I cut through Rat Alley and came out on the other side by the Cellar, pausing to look around.

The sidewalks overflowed with people, spilling them into the streets. The line out of the Martini Bar was so thick I couldn't even see inside. Cars blocked the main avenue, and people crawled over and clambered out of them while horns honked frantically everywhere. It was only the beginning and it was already chaos.

Breaking into a run, I reached the Cellar a few seconds later. Possum, the door guy, waved me inside. I pushed through the swarm of churning, glistening limbs. I camped beside a barstool until the guy sitting there got up to use the bathroom and then slithered onto it and gripped it with all the speed and agility of a drunk just getting warmed up and cut off by circumstance. I hadn't had anything to drink in almost an hour.

But I was still blocked. Lana and Don were working, but the bar was so busy I could plainly see they weren't going to make it to my end for at least another 15 minutes. I blew sweaty wisps of hair off my forehead and growled low under my breath. A second later someone pulled on my shoulder. It was Bret.

After putting her in charge of guarding my coat and the hard-won barstool, I headed off to the bathroom to make use of the time I'd spend waiting for a shot. As I twisted my way through the crowd a face leered out at me and then lunged in my direction. I backed up quick and the guy with the face crashed into the girl in front of me. She yelled and pushed at him, but he kept staring at me over her shoulder. His leer stayed right where it was, the face rippling in front of me like a mask as I pushed past him.

Waiting in line for a stall, I thought about how painfully sober I was. I could hear clearly that the band was terrible, the lead singer was tone deaf, and the girl in front of me was talking about her burning yeast infection. The bathroom itself was filthy, graffiti scrawled over the mirror and walls, and some sort of sandy grime on the floor scraped under my heels. It was always like this at the Cellar, I just rarely noticed anymore. I missed the cotton batting a few shots of whiskey provided between me and the world.

On my way back to the bar the three bikers in front of me

suddenly halted and turned around, yelling to their friend by the stage. I waited and tapped my foot, trying to catch Bret's eye at our barstool, when something crawled up beside me.

It was the same guy, with the same goofy leer perched on his face. He leaned in and peered at me like an oily insinuating parrot. I was starting to get angry. It wasn't that he was threatening. With rare exception, men were never a threat. The only thing that really scared me was the supernatural. And it wasn't that he was sleazy. *I* was sleazy. Sleaziness was a non-issue. It was that I was angry anyway. I was always just a few steps away from blinding rage. For someone to make such aggressive unbroken eye contact was like tempting a wild dog.

Bret caught my eye and pointed to the fresh shots Lana had laid out on the bar in front of her. I forgot all about the loony guy and his leer. I pushed more forcefully at the crowd ahead of me and dropped under an arm when someone lifted a beer out of my way. In a moment I was back on the barstool next to Bret. I descended upon the three golden wells of Cuervo sitting on the bar. I took the first down as I listened to Bret. She yelled that she'd tried to find me at the Crow, but gave up and came to the Cellar. I took the second one and leaned forward to hear her better. She yelled that it had gotten even crazier outside and the streets were packed. I saw something move out of the corner of my eye and angled my head slightly, neatly finishing my third shot.

It was the same fucking guy. Somehow, he'd worked himself into a spot almost directly behind me. I felt the crowd surge and the weight of a hundred people pressed at my back like a huge steaming tidal wave. Crushed between the stool and the bar, I suddenly felt something crawling on me.

A hand attached to an arm—with ugly curly black hairs wriggling all over it—had snaked over and now lay like a dead thing between my breast and my shoulder. The weight of it pulled me from behind and dragged me backward. I already knew—it was that guy.

"Hey buddy. FUCK OFF."

I snapped one arm out and flipped up my middle finger, in case he hadn't heard, but the guy was gone. And now something clamped itself on my right wrist like the cold little teeth of a robotic animal. Then it bit my left wrist too, jacking both arms behind me. I was jerked roughly to the side as strange hands yanked me off the barstool.

It was the cops.

Still sober for the most part, I knew I needed to capitalize on my clear head. I had to find out what was going on before the tequila hit me. I'd skipped dinner and it was going to happen fast. But I was already being hauled out the door. Frantically, Bret ran after us as I shouted toward her.

"Call Cass! She'll have bail!" I knew Arthur would be at the Falcon tonight and he would loan it to her out of the till. I said a silent thank you to the god of drunks who had provided me with at least one benevolent wizard in my life.

The cop who had my hands pushed me harder from behind.

"If you persist in helping her to resist arrest, we'll arrest you too!"

She barked the order at Bret, who now stood rooted to a spot in the middle of the Cellar, my coat trailing from one hand.

"What am I being arrested for?" I asked. I tried turning my head but the cop wrenched me around like a doll being punished, a doll that was going to have her head twisted off in a minute.

"You're arrested for obstruction of justice!"

Apparently, she only barked at people.

"But..." I decided to ask my question slowly this time. "What does that mean?"

"It means you're going to jail!"

Then we were outside. The cops had the vans out tonight and

it seemed I was going to be loaded into the back of one, a small windowless vehicle that could have been a bread truck, or animal control. As she pushed me in, I finally got to see her face. She was pissed at the world all right, but there was something else there too. Something I knew was absolutely true in those last sober moments, because she tried to hide it from me. That woman hated me. And then she slammed the doors and everything went black.

$\sim$

Jail is the worst. It's not as bad if you go in wasted, but it's still pretty wretched.

The cops drove me around in the van for an indefinite period of time. There were benches on both sides but nothing to secure me to the bench, so with my hands behind my back and in complete darkness I rolled and smashed into the walls whenever the driver braked suddenly or took a hard turn.

After what seemed like hours we arrived at the jail. Enough time had passed so that I was definitely drunk, not starting to be or just getting there, but solidly wasted. With a start, I realized the jail was only a couple of blocks away from the Square—why had it taken us so many hours to get there? No one else had ever joined me in the back of the van. We hadn't stopped anywhere. For a moment the world slipped into a shimmering curtain of water and I thought of how easily a person could disappear.

As I waited to be booked, the cops sat me down on a bench inside the station. I slumped against the wall and hung my head, trying to gauge how many hours were left until morning and how long I had left in the cuffs. They fucking hurt, and moving around didn't help any. I could overhear the cops having a conversation behind me and then began actively listening in when I heard them snickering.

"That's how they are...every...single...year." One of them

stated flatly, as if explaining to someone that rain was wet because it was made out of water.

"What did she expect? That's what happens," said another in a told-you-so voice.

"Yup. That's what the little slut gets for exposing herself!" I snapped my head up in time to see a balding cop with a gelatinous gut pointing a fat sausage finger at me. With a twinge of annoyance, I wished him dead. He had no idea what kind of slut I was, and beyond that, I still had no idea why I'd even been arrested in the first place. Maybe I was guilty of a lewd gesture, but I hadn't flashed anyone and I hadn't planned to. Maybe that fat bald cop didn't know me but I hated him for labeling me in front of his cop friends. He was just another fake, his true self buried somewhere inside him by his own hands.

In fact, the only person who was nice to me at the jail was the lady who booked me. She smiled and said I had the smallest hands she'd ever seen when she took my fingerprints. I smiled back even though I was still in a blood rage. It meant something that she was kind to me. Things had changed rapidly in an hour. Now I was trapped in a place where there were two groups of people—the righteous and the free and the degenerate and captive. She didn't have to be nice. She was, after all, free. But she did it anyway and it meant something.

The rest were assholes.

But I'd always hated cops. Yeah, of course I'd met a few good ones over the years, but most of them were grown-up high school bullies looking for an outlet. Looking for a gun. Hardly any of them could think for themselves.

I was even more pissed that the whole thing was funny. It was actually laughable. I was a blackout drunk who regularly assisted in the packaging and distribution of cocaine to the low-life clusters of sick protoplasm that inhabited the Square. Plus, I stole all the books I could from the bookstore where I worked, whole boxes of them sometimes. Yes, I was a degenerate. But I wasn't sitting here in jail for any of that. I was stuck for I didn't know what reason and no one would tell me anything. On top of that it was the first Mardi Gras that I'd actually kept my clothes on, in years past I'd come home almost choked by the sheer weight of cheap plastic beads settling down onto my collarbones, like a giant iron ring around my throat. But tonight, I hadn't flashed anyone.

Time passed. They locked me into a room with a window in the door and no furniture, not even benches. My hands had been cuffed behind me for what seemed like hours. Even through the tequila I felt the sharp ache in my wrists. Finally, another cop came in and un-cuffed my hands. He gave me a jail-issue shirt and then left me alone to change into it. Then he led me to a cell, which was almost exactly like the room I'd just been in, but this one had benches and a bright crackling TV hanging from chains in one corner. He didn't say anything to me even when I tried talking to him, the only indication he existed was the slight ghostly pressure he applied to my arm to guide me through the door.

I scanned the room. It was filled with girls. Instantly I saw groups were divided between white and black and brown. Outside—among the righteous and free—I was a staunch liberal, even radical in my solidarity with all minorities. My attitude was always Fuck Whitey. But this was jail and I was captive now. Sensibilities didn't only demand a desperate re-adjustment— things had rapidly devolved over the last few hours to a state of slash and burn. My love for the minorities had to be swallowed and fast, otherwise I had the distinct feeling that I might lose some teeth. Like a whipped dog I slunk my way over to the white-girl corner and sat on the edge of one of the benches, trying to take up the least amount of space possible. The chick next to me had the most non-threatening face in the room. She looked kind of preppy and had a mohawk.

Time passed and I had no idea what time it was. Girls were

taken out of the room, more girls were brought in. I chatted with the girl with the mohawk who told me she was there for writing bad checks. I was grateful for her conversation, but I could also tell I was kind of freaking her out. I was still pretty pissed off. I proposed that we come back and bomb the place after we got out and elaborated my theories to her on exactly what type of person turned out to be a cop. She ran thin white fingers over the top of her mohawk and shushed me while casting anxious looks at the small window near the top of the door, like it was a portal, or an eye. When she started nervously tapping her feet and scootching by slow millimeters away from me I finally shut up just so she wouldn't leave.

I knew it was still the middle of the night. Outside anyway— back in the free world. But here and now, nothing spoke of time. There was no clock ticking away the minutes, only the constant buzz of the fluorescent lights overhead to mark the seconds in my brain. Hulky and huge, the TV threw itself forward against the taut chains that snared it to the wall and gruesomely stared at the entire room, as if it had been beaten into a comatose state and chained up to die in front of us. Static blasted across the screen every few seconds, interrupting the Matlock episode that seemed to play over and over with no end in sight. Because the TV hung so far above our heads, it was impossible to turn it off or change the channel.

The blasts of static and the buzz of the lights beat on me until something softened inside, like I'd gone through a meat tenderizer. It had to be a form of torture. Meant to appear as if it were there for entertainment—meant to seem as if it could kill time—that TV was the exact opposite. It *was* comatose and waiting to die. Time was killing it, and sooner or later Time would come after all of us. Whoever had chained the TV to that corner, whoever chose the Matlock episode that played over and over with the short bursts of static, like quick little screams in the middle of the night, wanted to remind us that, yes, of course time was passing. But it might as well have ground to a complete halt. We weren't going anywhere. Time would come to collect.

And so time passed. But it didn't, not really.

At one point one of the brown girls approached me and asked me to French braid her hair. I didn't know how to French braid but the girl was a lot bigger than me. I sat her down in front of me and started braiding. Her hair was greasy and full of tiny white moist grains, like a party of lice had thrown an orgy on her scalp and generated the white frothy stuff as a by-product of too much fucking. The white shit made her greasy hair slippery. Determined, I combed through the mess with my hands and fashioned it into something that at least resembled a braid. When she moved off I moved back into my corner, tucking myself behind the girl with the mohawk.

I sat and watched the room. I was just waiting things out now. I still had no idea what time it was, but I had sobered up significantly. It was a solid indicator that at least three hours had passed. I really hadn't done anything they could charge me with and they couldn't keep me forever. I knew I was in something like a drunk tank, and although I'd never been in one before it was like I was born with the knowledge of how they operated. Before getting there, I'd already known what they were like.

Finally another cop came and got me out of the cell and led me to a desk with windows behind it—another portal, this one to the outside. And then they told me I could go.

After I came out of the little room where I had changed back into my free-world clothes I appraised the situation. I was wearing the black satin evening pants, delicate heels, and lace top in which I'd started out the evening. My keys and my coat, and any money or credit cards left inside it, had been abandoned at the Cellar with Bret when I was torn off the barstool. It was February in Seattle and probably raining. I saw through the windows that it was still dark outside. Politely, I asked the man behind the desk what I should do. He looked up at me and smiled.

"Why don't you go back where you came from?" He stared at me coldly for a few moments more and continued smiling. Then he went back to filling out the paperwork in front of him. I was dismissed.

I wandered out of the double doors and into the dark streets, orienting myself by the Sound. I sniffed the air and found west, tying my soul back to the sea-silver cord of the water. I wrapped my arms tightly around myself as my skin prickled up into goose-bumps. It *was* raining, and it was cold. The King County Jail was only a few blocks away from the Square. I thought for a moment and decided that last cop had been right—the only place I could go was back to where I came from. I began trudging down the hill to the Cellar.

On the way I passed a clock on a building and noted it was a little past six in the morning. The Cellar would be closed, but Harry's next door would be open for after-after hours. I hated the ecstasy kids but I had no other choice. I had to find someone I knew.

As I turned the corner onto First Avenue I glanced across the street at the Cellar. It stood empty and locked up, rain beating mercilessly down on the skeleton chairs and tables shackled to the building. Only hours before drunks—just like me—had sat there, taking shots and yelling to the crowds passing by on the sidewalk. None of them with a thought of the half dead, strung-up TV hanging under cruel buzzing lights, or the people locked up, just a few blocks away. I hugged my wet cold arms to myself and thought about the lowness of my life. I was turning to Harry's—a meth den and gangsta lair at night, and a dance paradise for anyone still rolling on E in the early morning—because there was nowhere else for me to go.

The guy at the door knew me from around and cocked an

amused eyebrow at my drenched hair and clothes. I slipped past him with my head down. I pushed my way through the strobe lights and the skinny raver kids flipping around with glow sticks, concentrating on the solid square of unbroken yellow light toward the back, where the bathrooms were. There were two parties going on at Harry's, even at this hour, just like there were always two parties going on at the Cellar. The second party was for the cokeheads in the bathroom. If Cass, or anyone I knew from the Cellar, were here, that was where I would find them.

The minute I walked in I saw Cass, and then Lana too. Suddenly I was crying all over the place and I couldn't stop. I choked out the whole story to Cass and showed her my scraped and bruised wrists. Halfway through she stopped me and said she already knew. Then she told me what had happened on her side.

Shortly after ten the night before Bret had arrived at the Falcon. Luckily, as I predicted, Arthur was there and he let Cass take bail money for me out of the till. But once at the jail Cass realized she still had an eight ball of coke on her, and so she stopped short and skipped back down to the Cellar, where she transferred the coke to Don and then took off for the jail again to try to get me out.

When she finally talked to the cops they told her I was still being "processed" and it could be hours before I was released, at which point she headed back down to the Square to meet with Don and wait for me. She knew what I had just recently discovered, that I couldn't go very far because Bret had been left with all my stuff—including my coat and money—and it was winter in Seattle and raining.

I stopped crying long enough to hear Cassady's story and then fell into her and hugged her, hard. I asked if she could take me home.

Before she could answer a long thin shadow crept up by her side. It was Lana. Even more haggard and ghostly than usual, she placed a cold hand on my arm, her fingers splayed over my pulsing aching wrist like a frozen spider. She locked onto Cassady's eyes with her own.

"You're not leaving, are you?"

She made a short motion with her head in my direction but didn't look at me.

"She'll be fine. Put her in a cab."

Her fingers tightened their freezing blue grasp as she pulled me back, away from Cassady.

"Lana—no. I'm taking Lo home. Now. She needs me."

The circle of cold left my wrist and Cassady's warm sturdy hand clapped me on the shoulder and steered me out of the bathroom. I turned and saw Lana following us with eyes that seemed to have shrunken into wrinkled black pits. She hated me. I mentioned it to Cassady.

"She doesn't hate you," Cassady sighed and sounded tired.

"She just wants to siphon more coke off me."

I turned again for one last look, and saw the wasted goblin Lana was now. I couldn't tell if it was the strobe lights, the distance, or my fevered brain, but it didn't matter. Lana was just another demon living and partying on strong in the waking nightmare of my life.

I let Cassady take me home.

Chapter 10

Somewhere toward the end of that bleak February I saw Tom for the last time. In hindsight, if I had known that was the last time I would see him ever, I probably wouldn't have been such a bitch.

He was back to doing meth multiple times a week. Flaco, that greasy little shark, was still hanging on as his "best friend." As strung out as he was, Tom still retained traces of the old loyal lion that I saw in him when we first met. But what he'd had to do in the past in order to go on in the present had changed him. Parts of him had hardened, twisting into glossy knotted shapes like lava flowing down a mountain and then freezing into place.

I knew it was partly my fault too, because Tom *was* my real friend and I had given up on him. I had lied to myself and to everyone else. Sure, I talked about Tom's "meth problem," but I didn't talk about calling in the professionals because what would they say? They would say we all had problems, we were all addicts. They would take one look at us and know that we were all lost forever and for good. Especially me and Tom.

And that I already knew.

That night at the Cellar I ran into Tom by chance. I was chatting up a guy at the end of the bar when Tom sidled over out of nowhere and started taunting the guy and calling him names and that was it. I lost it. Exploded. I let go of everything I had chewed over inside for the past three years, all the hurt I'd packed away to rot and fester just so I could spew it back upon him at this moment. I told him he'd always been weak. I told him his weakness made him whore himself, take any drug, do any *thing* for attention, for love. The truth was, I said, he had always been willing to be bought and sold for any interest, any show, fake or otherwise, of love from another. The truth was—I finished viciously—was that Tom was a nothing.

I only said the things you can never really take back. The things you always remember that somebody else said about you when you're at your lowest point. And I said these things to one of my best friends. I said these things to Tom.

Like I said, I didn't see him after that. Not ever again.

I said the word "alcoholic" to myself a lot. When I ran through the rainy streets in the mornings, and when I worked amidst the quiet dusty sunbeams of the bookstore in the afternoons. I knew I was one. I'd always known. It was easy to see the difference between me and normal people, and just as easy to see the similarities between me and the other bad drunks I knew. I never tried to hide it. It was mine, and in a way I was proud of it. Like my hair that I'd tried over and over to straighten, only to have it kink its way back into crazy springy curls, it was something I had been given. It was something that truly belonged to me.

I told most people I was an alcoholic if they asked and some if they didn't. It knocked out a lot of the confusion they might have experienced when first getting to know me. Plus, it equipped them with a rough idea of what to expect in the future. I figured everyone deserved a fair chance to cut and run at the very beginning.

I'd been intently watching people for years now and I knew that almost every person had something eating away at them inside. Most didn't talk about it, and they lived in fear of anyone else discovering it. They swam with it in their own mind because they had no choice, but they stayed carefully in the shallow end, pretending at having a life there, pretending everything was fine, pretending the deep end, separated from them by an invisible line only they could see, wasn't churning with blood.

I was in my deep end now and I knew it. But I didn't want to die there. It seemed like it would be too funny, like it was just what everyone would expect of me.

So, I considered that word: Alcoholic. Tasted it a hundred different times a day and rolled it around in my mouth, liking the way it perfectly balanced itself on my tongue, loving the way it burned brightly and steadily always just behind my eyes.

I also still watched and wondered about other people. Other people living in the year 2004. Other people living in Seattle, and in the United States. In the whole world. All the others in this one fixed spot in the Universe, fixed and moving in this time, in these lives. Most of the people I came across were in despair. Were they like that in other places? In other times? In *this* time and place I definitely wasn't the only one crying so hard I couldn't breathe in the middle of the night, puking so hard I couldn't see in the early morning, and then acting like none of it had ever happened that afternoon when I was at work, when I was engaged in my "real" life that wasn't very real at all.

If I really went to work on a person, I could usually get to the real thing inside. I was good at waiting and always had been. I waited out a person's play-acting, the various masks they cycled through. When they were exhausted with shining lights in my eyes, then they looked back at me scared and naked. They looked like I did in the mirror in the morning coming off a drunk or locked in the bathroom at work in the afternoon. Back and forth their eyes searched mine, terrified and lost. They didn't know who they were, what horrors they were capable of—only that if everyone else found out then it would be the end of everything. That was the worst part, because they needed to tell someone else, even if it were only one other person, about the scared lost feeling and their certainty that they were worse than any other human being. They needed someone to look into their deep end, to inspect their wound to see how bad it was, to tell them if they would die from it.

Everyone, at the bottom of it, wanted to know that someone else was swimming through blood too.

My word—alcoholic—was a talisman. It initiated transfiguration. The people held together with thick knots of twine, the people who breathed fear every second, and had, a long time ago, resolved never to look into their deep end, really looked back at me for the first time. Their eyes slowed and I could feel they weren't so terrified and lost anymore. Now they drew a shaky breath, catching and holding their own secret word, the one that was ever present in their mind already—their talisman. Sometimes the word was "pervert," sometimes it was "junkie," sometimes it was just a nice plain "loser" to cover all the bases. But everyone had a secret word, that was the important thing, and with almost everyone it wasn't long until I found it.

No one really knew what they wanted, that was problem number one. Of course, I didn't know what I wanted either. Every time I hit upon something that I thought I wanted, then I wanted something else. Or I just started wanting again without wanting any one thing. And the things I wanted that never changed I also believed I could never have. On top of it all, I hated myself.

It seemed to me that, really, what we all wanted was to feel like no one else could replace us, but we secretly believed anyone could. We settled for feeling important because it seemed like the same thing, but it was actually a different thing altogether. So we got confused, we gripped onto the idea of "important." If being important seemed to mean having a big house, we put all of ourselves into getting a big house. But we couldn't escape the feeling that we had never wanted that house, we had only wanted to be someone that no one else could be.

So, living in the big house we'd never really wanted, not feeling important exactly, but at least feeling like other people probably thought we were, the nagging feeling of not having what we actually wanted, not *being* what we wanted—a person like no other—that nagging feeling never left us. So we drank, or we shot up, or we cut ourselves, or we watched people shitting on themselves and having sex at the same time on the internet—we did *whatever*—to forget about it, to forget ourselves, to forget our secret word.

It wasn't surprising that nearly everyone's eyes looked so scared and so lost to me.

But, I had a key. I had a talisman. My word: Alcoholic.

I knew that the acknowledgment of my talisman was forward motion. It was me getting the fuck out of that house. The telling was the first part of moving forward.

After I spoke my word out loud like that enough times I started waking up. And that's when I started collecting the people that came to me. I took the secrets they gave and drank up their fear and stored it away in tiny, carefully labeled bottles in the back of my mind. I never showed anyone's bottle to anyone else. And as much as I hated myself I never used anyone's secret word against them. My word was a talisman, but it was also a curse, and it worked that way all around. People always threw my word back in my face when they got scared. I vowed to never dishonor the power of anyone else's secret word in that way.

Chapter 11

The rest of February was like watching someone being taken off life support. I didn't have the heart to fight anymore. My fucked up life was getting to be even too fucked up for me.

But then one day it was March. That meant spring, and I felt new life in the air even though dirty puddles dotted the streets and the tree branches still shone wet and bare. The smallest vibration of hope stirred the fine hairs on my arms, and suddenly that seemed to be all that mattered.

A week or so after getting arrested I received a court date in the mail and my biker buddies at the Cellar gave me the name of the lawyer everyone in the Square used. They told me his name was Michael Blackstone and that he was a guy who looked like Christopher Walken and was sharp about the law and cool with every biker and every drunk around the city. His secretary, a tiny girl named Annemarie with long hair almost to her knees, was a regular at the bar. Hearing his name mentioned, she hopped off her stool and skipped to the edge of our circle. In a second I had the lawyer's clean white card in my hand and Annemarie was back on the stool, ordering her next beer. I looked at the card.

Plain, with solid black lettering, it looked like the sign of someone who knew what they were doing. It also—just maybe—looked like the card of someone who wouldn't hate me for being a drunk.

The day of my appointment I was sick as a dog. Not hungover, but really sick with the flu. I walked downtown to Michael Blackstone's office anyway. I wanted to walk, if only to feel the change in the air.

When I got to his office I made my way up three softly creaking flights of stairs in the pale golden light that filtered in from outside. The building seemed to be deserted. I found no evidence of any other offices or people, although the building had multiple floors and the directory right inside the front door listed more than a dozen names. The building he worked out of was an old clock tower, and fittingly enough, not more than a block away from the Square.

On the third floor I found Michael Blackstone's office. Annemarie was sitting at the desk in the small reception area and she nodded slightly in my direction as she lazily twirled in her chair, wrapping the phone cord around an upraised index finger. She rolled her eyes at me and made a slow pinching motion with her free hand to let me know the person on the other end of the line would have her tied up for a while. She waved me toward a small stuffed armchair right inside the doorway.

I slowly sank down, careful to sit up straight and keep my legs together. When I looked over I discovered three other people already in the room. They were sitting on the small stuffed sofa that matched the armchair I was in and I hadn't realized they were there because all three of them sat frozen and silent. I peered closer and saw that I knew one of them from the Cellar. It was Lana's little sister, Carrie.

She looked like she was about to start sobbing. So did the woman sitting next to her, who looked exactly like Lana, only 20 years older. It had to be their mom—and she looked like she'd already been sobbing for the past two weeks. Deep red circles had carved themselves under both eyes and the tip of her nose was shiny and pink, the way it is when a person's been sitting in a hospital, waiting for news for a long time. The man I assumed to be Lana and Carrie's dad sat on the other side and looked too angry to move. I could hear him breathing in hard little snuffly gasps, like an ox. He sounded like he was having a heart attack and was determined to be very quiet and no-trouble-at-all polite about the whole thing. I scanned the three of them and then looked away fast.

The minutes ticked on. Annemarie got off the phone and ushered Carrie and her parents into the main office, and while I waited I thought about how I'd heard that Carrie had gotten a DUI the week before, almost immediately before I'd gotten arrested. She'd totaled her car and smashed into another one that was parked nearby. Now she had the blow tube strapped to her ignition. It was a bad place to be in. I knew I was lucky that I hadn't been caught driving.

Then it was my turn. I smoothed the front of my job interview pants and wiped my clammy hands on the back of my sweater. I couldn't think of anything worse than meeting someone new when I was sober.

But everything I'd heard was true. Michael Blackstone did look like Christopher Walken and he was sharp and cool, and strange. He had sparkling black eyes and a million little lines in his face that jumped and danced whenever he talked or laughed and then collapsed into one unbroken landscape when he was still again, listening. Best of all, I could tell he didn't think I'd be better off dead just because I was a drunk. And even if he didn't know what a true mad, stinging, snapping alcoholic I was, I knew that he understood what kind of lowlifes I hung around with. I could tell that he didn't think it was strange that a girl who was 25 but looked 17, who was smart but did dumb things—who wanted to trade all of herself for what other people had—this girl had fucked up again and needed his help. No, I could tell, he didn't think it was strange at all.

After the meeting I ducked out of the building and around the corner. I walked a few blocks down until I was in a narrow and pleasant tree-lined area, right on the edge of the Square. I sat down on a low brick wall and watched the traffic and thought about everything. I felt way better. Michael Blackstone had clapped his long hands together and laughed like an elf when I told him my story. He told me I was right, cops were assholes, and he seemed to think none of this would be very important to me in a few years. He had the confident air of a case closed and won. And his deep black eyes lit up when I told him about flipping the guy off and all of the million little lines in his face joined hands and stretched into a wide smile.

Instead of saying anything about my manners or wondering aloud how I could have come to be in such a situation in the first place, his great wide smile only stretched wider and all the million little lines jumped out at me as he opened up and laughed deep. He slapped his knee and said it was a classic case of First Amendment Rights. And even though I knew I really was a fuck-up, I also knew he could be believed.

Now, sitting and watching the early-spring, pale-evening light bleed away, I thought about how much better I felt inside my own head. But my body was still sick. I coughed raggedly and spat on the sidewalk, shuddering and wrapping my arms around myself. I thought about walking home and felt the drink-want grow warm and rise up. It was going to start burning soon.

Then I heard a honk. Short and loud it burst across the sidewalk like broken glass, dispelling the fuzzy drink-want heating up inside my skull. An old 1950s-style pickup truck idled at the curb. The driver leaned across the seat and flashed an evil toothy grin at me.

It was Ratt Stilskin.

I bolted to the curb, and then leaned in the window and smiled.

"Ratt Stilskin."

I raised my eyebrows ever so slightly. I knew his radar picked up the finest tremors, slightly was all I needed.

"Leah." he said it flatly, and swiveled his head to look down the block at the corner I had just walked around from. I could almost see his eyes, on crafty tentacle stalks, peer around that corner periscope-style and then reel and snap back into his head just as quick and crafty-like.

"Coming from Michael Blackstone's office?"

He smirked as I stared at him, unable to hide that he'd caught me off guard.

"How did you know?"

"Leah. Really. I haven't bothered with a driver's license since 1987. And I've had two DUIs in the past year alone. I know Michael Blackstone well—very well. We are...friends...of a sort."

Ratt Stilskin's eyes lingered on me greedily. He was digging for something, but I had no idea for what.

I opened the car door and jumped in.

"Let's go." I ordered.

Now I stared at him with greed licking hungry out of my eyes.

"Where to?"

"The Crow. Where else?" I snapped. "I'm sick and I need gin."

And then I softened my tone. Ratt Stilskin had something I needed. I kept my eyes on his and gently placed a hand on his steering wheel arm, closest to me.

"Let's go now—please?" When I smiled charmingly he pulled away from me.

"Well now, Leah, it's your ride isn't it? To the Crow it is."

Satisfied that someone else finally understood, I sank back against the seat and closed my eyes.

~

Whenever I was sick I drank gin. A friend of mine back in Ann Arbor told me once that gin will always break a fever—you just have to drink enough of it. So whenever I was hacking and sneezing everywhere, and burning hot to the touch, I started in on the gin martinis. Sometimes it worked. After three or four drinks I felt blessed sweat break out all over me like a realization. Then the fever was gone. But sometimes it didn't work and I only got sicker. Since I was going to drink anyway, it didn't much matter.

When I told Ratt Stilskin I was sick and needed gin and then coughed wretchedly into hands that wouldn't stop shaking he didn't give me any funny looks. And he didn't ask any questions. He just threw his truck into gear and took the next left down to the Crow.

15 minutes later we were sitting in our favorite booth, the one right next to the pool table. I had my martini and Ratt Stilskin was working on a small glass of whiskey on the rocks. He smiled mischievously at me, exposing the gap where his eyetooth should have been, and winked.

"So Leah..."

As he grinned at me I noticed, not for the first time, how he pronounced my name. Like he was drawing the whole thing out on purpose, just to let me know how masterfully he could roll the word—my personal name word—around in his mouth before deciding to let it go.

"Did you enjoy your cozy little brunch with Joey before he left you for New York?"

I choked back a gulp of gin, almost spraying it on him.

"Of course I know." he said quietly.

His eyes glittered malevolently but remained as crinkled and gleeful as a gnome's.

"I mean…"

He paused and let the knowledge hang in front of me for a moment.

"You've just been so obvious."

He stared at me and waited.

I recognized the expression on his face. I'd felt it too many times on my own not to know it on his. It came whenever I saw the world as Lo. Ratt Stilskin was fucking with me and he was doing it to get to something deeper. He was clocking my reactions and what was revealed about me by those reactions. He was stealing my experience, any part of it he could get. He wasn't worried about whether or not he got the whole thing. The whole thing didn't matter, he could use *any* thing. It was exactly what Lo did all the time. In fact, lately, it seemed to be the only thing *I* did anymore. I looked back at him squarely.

"I don't know what you're talking about Ratt." I said, keeping my eyes on his.

He raised his eyebrows, looking up at me from underneath them. He wasn't grinning anymore but his eyes hadn't lost their merriment. He looked down at his hands clasped together on the table, perfectly aligned behind the glass of whiskey, and then slowly let out a long sigh and leaned back into the booth.

"Fine," he said lightly and grinned again. "Have it your way."

My hands tore at each other under the table but I was solid as stone from the elbows up. I could do this. I could handle Ratt Stilskin. He was no match for me. No one was anymore. I shrugged with forced casualness, feigning indifference. I took a long pull from my martini and let my eyes settle on the window. Then I heard Ratt Stilskin murmur something, so softly I doubted I had heard anything. But his words had tripped the danger wire on Lo's vicious security system, and under the circling red ambulance lights I rewound the tape and listened again.

"There's time," he had said.

There's time.

And Lo had definitely heard him say it.

What did it mean? Time for what? And what did any of this have to do with Joey? Why did Ratt Stilskin even care? The whole deal was weird. But now the gin was pooling in the middle of me and I was warm and had stopped coughing. It didn't matter. Nothing mattered anymore. Lo had trained me. Nobody got in without the password and the password was pain. The thought of Ratt Stilskin with his cheerful ruddy face and gleeful winking eyes causing us pain was seriously laughable. I had nothing to fear.

We ordered another round of drinks.

As the waitress placed a fresh martini carefully in front of me, the table shook. The perfect mirror of gin trembled and broke, spilling over the edge. Irritated, I looked up and saw someone familiar sliding clumsily into our booth. It was a guy named Scott Pharr, one of the cooks at the Crow. He glanced at me without it seeming to register in his eyes, but the way he looked at me was the way you pretend you don't see the gun under someone's coat when they move a certain way to make sure you do. He saw me all right, but he ignored me, and turned instead to talk to Ratt Stilskin.

Scott Pharr was a big guy with a delicate voice. He moved with a clumsy sort of grace that gave the impression of a ruthless innocence working behind the scenes. Meaning, he usually knocked over drinks and broke shit by accident but was also always genuinely sorry about his innate tendency to destroy carefully set tableaus just begging to be set into motion. As I watched him now I observed how his face narrowed to a sharp point culminating in the tip of his nose in front, and his fine blond hair swept into a slight pompadour on top, giving his whole head the loose

appearance of a triangle. The effect overall was that of a pterodactyl's head on the body of a bear. It wasn't entirely unattractive.

I listened in even though I could only hear Ratt Stilskin's side
of the conversation. The jukebox was going and the pool room had
started to fill up. I thought about what a nightmare Scott Pharr's
soft voice would be in the Cellar. You had to learn how to scream
without screaming, and still look sexy doing it, to even have an
opening conversation there.

I took another pull on my martini and kept watching.

After a few tumblers of whiskey Scott Pharr actually looked at
me and then let himself be pulled over to my side of the booth.
When Ratt Stilskin got bored straining to hear the low currents of
conversation between us and left to play pool, I dug further
into him.

His main routine was robots. Scott Pharr said he was going to
build a huge robot that was shaped like a piano and then he was
going to live in it. In between explaining the robot piano and other
weird statements about robots in general, he sprinkled in bits
about songs he liked and the secrets behind his massive consump-
tion of whiskey, and also made flattering statements about me
delivered in the voice of some invisible third person narrator.
After a while I realized he was flirting with me, in a really bizarre
way.

After some time passed I noticed Ratt Stilskin watching us.
His game of pool had ended and now he stood, both hands fisted
around the pool cue like it was a spear. His eyes were hard and
small and weren't crinkled at all now. He was calculating—and all
of a sudden I felt like a math problem cut open, gleaming and
exposed. I pulled on Scott Pharr's arm and murmured it was time
to go.

We hit a few more bars and talked the whole time. My fasci-
nation with Scott Pharr continued to grow. He knew Rilke's
Letters to a Young Poet and recited them all, word for word. He

drank just as much as I did and he didn't try to stop me from drinking more. The way he talked reminded me of Dustin Hoffman in Rain Man. Before last call hit, I knew I had found my Prince Myshkin, but whether he was lucid enough to recognize the Nastasya Filipovna in me remained to be seen.

Chapter 12

Over the next few weeks I stopped into the Crow more frequently to see Ratt Stilskin and Scott Pharr, and soon I was with them almost every night. The trial for my "obstruction of justice" charge came and went and I got off with only having to pay a $100 fine. I went to the Crow afterwards and got drunk with Scott Pharr to celebrate. It was warm enough to open the windows around the big table in front, and so we sat and drank whiskey and chatted about robots with the strangers who walked by.

I didn't understand what Scott Pharr was saying most of the time but it was always interesting. When he was really drunk he had a tendency to crawl around under the table or pull the table-cloth right off and wear it as a cape. I didn't mind. I just had to make sure to get him under control once I saw the bouncer or bartender giving us the eye. But of course, it didn't matter if we were at the Crow, we knew everybody, and that's where we were most of the time.

Not surprisingly, if we picked a different bar that night Ratt Stilskin always knew where we would be even without us telling him. If Scott Pharr and I settled at the very last moment on going to the Copper Jug in Ballard on a Monday night—a bar that Sadie and her punk friends frequented and that I rarely did—Ratt would find us. This happened when I was alone too. Wherever I was, whoever I was with, it wasn't long before Ratt Stilskin popped into the bubble of air beside me, crinkly-eyed and smiling with a fresh new story dancing off his fingers as he painted the scene for me with his words and his hands. The person he had just run into—the ex-girlfriend who had suddenly showed up again—the guy who had vowed revenge. Every person Ratt knew was more than just a character, they had become myth. For maybe the first time ever, drinking was not the main reason I wanted to go to the bar anymore.

March turned over into April and every day was warmer than the last. I stopped into the Crow in the afternoons on my days off. Between 3:00 and 4:00pm was my favorite time there. It was peaceful, the green and gold lazy drone of an empty bar in the middle of the afternoon. It was the beginning of falling into a drunk, the golden hour. And every time I stopped in to catch these golden hours now, I met Ratt Stilskin.

Some nights—a lot of nights—it was just the two of us, me and Ratt. We went from bar to bar and Ratt Stilskin knew everyone. He introduced me to graffiti artists and punks, poets and political warriors. I saw clearly that I was in the presence of a master collector. As the nights streamed by and we grew closer he revealed the more costly gems in his showcase: A real live pirate, the fluff guy on famous porn films, a radical feminist who built bombs—good ones—in her garage. But throughout my examination of these glittering jewels—gold thrown carelessly into my lap with the promise of more—throughout all the people everywhere that we saw and used and sometimes fucked—it always, *always*, came back to just us.

When Ratt and I sat alone with nothing but a glass of whiskey between us, he told me things about myself that I knew, but had

never said out loud. Things I thought other people didn't—
shouldn't—know about me. One late night we sat at the Crow
sipping tumblers of Jameson when he told me I only had one
racket going. I started to cut him off but he shut me up with a
single upraised finger. He said he knew that *I* thought I had at
least three, but there was really only one. Comfortable from the
whiskey and curious now, I lazily traced the rim of the glass and
told him to go on. I didn't mind if what he had to say was going to
hurt. It was probably true, and anyway I loved hearing what other
people thought of me. I had my secrets, but being a narcissist
wasn't one of them.

"Well, Leah..."

I noticed, not for the first time, that he never called me Lo.
Not ever. And he never had.

"The conflict lies in a mere fact," he continued.

"You're either emotionally available to a man or sexually available. Not ever both at the same time, and never both to the same
man."

"Is that it?" I joked. "That's my only problem?"

"That—and you dress like a hooker from the 80s." His eyes
crinkled as he finished his whiskey.

"True and true," I agreed and finished my own. I glanced at
the clock above the bar, it was ten to two.

"Let's hit up the store for reserves before last call," I quickly
suggested.

He followed my eyes and slid to the end of the booth as I slid
into my coat. Like me, Ratt Stilskin was chased constantly by time
and last call always came way too soon. Harassed by the long arm
of the clock every night, we had our routine down by now.

Most mornings we woke up together in my living room, one of
us on the couch and the other on the floor, but sometimes we woke
up in Scott Pharr's living room with no Scott Pharr. Sometimes
we woke up in a strange house and the occupants we'd met the

night before were still sleeping. On those mornings we snuck out together. And sometimes we woke up in an empty house—still strange, still unrecognizable—and we had to help each other piece things together before we figured out the place belonged to one of Ratt Stilskin's many friends who seemed to be always out of town.

But even after spending the night in Scott Pharr's bed, when I woke up at dawn I ran to Ratt Stilskin just a room or two away and stayed talking with him until I came all the way down to full sober. Ratt saw the real me, the dark side of me that I couldn't blame on Lo. Every time we talked I saw the shrewd glint of the collector harden in his eyes. I felt him spreading my wings with a gentle mercilessness, not only because he loved testing limits but also because, like Nabokov, he had the eye of a connoisseur lepidopterist. He wanted nothing more than to see the beauty and agony of that span laid out on black velvet. I felt the pins going in. I knew it was necessary, that laceration was unavoidable, but looking straight at it still repulsed me. As sick as it was, whatever Ratt was doing to me, I needed it. And it was only now, during these mornings after, that I realized in a flash of total understanding how severely I'd underestimated Ratt Stilskin.

A lot of mornings Ratt left Scott Pharr and I alone because he had to go to work. I had only a vague idea of what this work was, something that had to do with collecting scrap metal and turning it into some sort of precious item that people paid a lot of money for. On these mornings Scott Pharr and I went to the casinos, the ones on Aurora. We drank whiskey over damp pine-scented tables that glowed under the dim throbbing casino lights, and then I took off for the bookstore to work my shift.

On my days off we would go instead to one of Scott Pharr's many regular haunts, bars on Capitol Hill that were packed to the gills with too-cool-for-school punks, safety pins sparkling through eyebrows and earlobes. They sniffed us once as we passed, high and shallow-sounding like the wind swirling cold bright snow out in the mountains in January. Scott Pharr could pass—but they blipped me from a mile away. I was no punk.

Nights and mornings...mornings and nights...I probably could have swung back and forth forever on the pendulum that arced between Scott Pharr and Ratt Stilskin. But then Scott Pharr got too drunk one evening and almost broke something that couldn't be put back together again.

The year before Sadie had started keeping a loaded shotgun propped beside her bed. She said she wanted protection against anyone who broke into the apartment, but I wasn't confident we'd be protected. The gun was almost as big as Sadie. It seemed like if she actually shot the thing it would probably blow off her whole shoulder. When I mentioned it to her she only shrugged and said, "I'd rather maim myself than be raped by some dirty dick." The gun stayed by the bed.

That night we had all come home drunk from the bar. Me and Scott Pharr from the Crow, and Sadie and her guy, and our friend Lettie, from the Copper Jug. Sadie's guy was named Deuce and we all liked him. He was a scrawny kid with coke bottle glasses and an emo haircut and he was always having a good time. At least he looked like he was always having a good time, he didn't say much but he smiled a lot.

Lettie fell asleep on the couch as I squatted on my haunches on the floor pouring shots of whiskey for all of us. Deuce sat on his knees in the middle of the room and Sadie, drunk and belligerent, carefully stalked her way around him and inspected him from all angles. Every few seconds she yelled at him to shut up even though he wasn't saying anything. Not one to argue, Deuce remained silent, but smiled at any one of us that caught his eye. I was drunk but better off than Sadie. I kept pouring as I swore under my breath. Deuce was a nice guy and it already looked like he was getting thrown out tonight.

Suddenly Sadie's bedroom door banged open and Lettie woke up with a start. It sounded like someone had taken a sizable chunk out of the wall with the doorknob. Realizing I hadn't seen Scott Pharr in more than a few minutes, I jumped to my feet, but it was already too late.

Rounding the corner, wobbling crazily to and fro like a drunk toddler and crashing into both walls, was Scott Pharr. His face had turned into a patchwork of bright white and angry red splotches, like he was coming down with some weird disease that would eventually choke the life out of him. His eyes were gone—just plain *not there*—and he smiled lopsidedly, like the smile had been pinned up there on his face, but whoever had pinned it had done a half-assed job, and now it hung off to one side and fluttered like a broken streamer. His sweat-slicked fumbling hands grasped and then slipped and then barely—just *barely*—caught the awful thing he held.

Sadie's gun.

Lettie and Sadie and I all saw it at the same moment. We moved back and flattened instantly, like a terrified crop circle. Glued against the walls, we stared with horror at the target left in the middle.

Deuce.

Scott Pharr doggedly kept his course. It looked like he hadn't noticed Sadie and me and Lettie because we'd moved so fast. Too drunk to use his peripheral vision, it was like we didn't exist. But Deuce seemed not to have noticed what had happened. He maintained his goofy, happy-go-lucky smile and good-naturedly swiveled his head from left to right. Scott Pharr stumbled toward him.

Just before he got to Deuce he lost his balance. His left foot went out from under him and he plunged forward. The shotgun hooked Deuce under the chin and took him down by the throat.

I saw the three of them go down, Deuce tipping over like a bowling pin, Scott Pharr a mad pale pterodactyl bear roaring above him and then sucked down underneath—and the gun in the middle of it all.

I couldn't move. And I couldn't stop watching.

But then Sadie tricked time, with her old habit of being in two places at once. One second she was a flattened shadow against the wall directly behind Scott Pharr and the next she was in the middle of everything and had the gun. She pushed Deuce all the way to the ground and then flipped the shotgun to her other hand and turned and shoved Scott Pharr to the far wall, where he crashed and trickled to the floor. Deuce held his ear and looked around dazedly. Sadie stood triumphant in the middle, holding the gun over her head. Her eyes were cold and angry, spinning.

"You Goddamned pissant motherfucking COCKSUCKER!!!"

She turned to Scott Pharr, still slumped in a heap on the floor. She kicked him once in the side, hard, and leaned down close to his ear.

"I hope that was your spleen you piece of shit."

She turned to Deuce.

"Go. Get to my room. NOW."

He went.

Scott Pharr moaned and tried to turn over. Sadie leaned down again and jutted the shotgun under his chin. She forced his head up, his eyelids fluttered as he tried to look at her. She bared her teeth.

"If you ever go into my room again I will rape you with this gun and make you drink the ass blood."

She dropped his head and there was a sharp crack as it hit the floor. She walked into her room where Deuce was already hiding and slammed the door. I surveyed the wreckage from the wall I was still flattened against. I looked down at Scott Pharr as he lay half conscious and moaning. He had never looked less like Prince Myshkin.

I broke up with him the next day.

Chapter 13

Joey had been in New York for over three months. After ending things with Scott Pharr, I heard through Ratt Stilskin that Joey had finally run out of money. It looked like he would be back in Seattle in a matter of days.

I wanted to sleep with Joey but I also had love feelings for him, and that was astronomically different from the way I felt about the other guys I fucked. I didn't have feelings one way or the other about Scott Pharr anymore, whatever interest I'd had in him had totally dissolved. But my fucking or not fucking other people, and my love for Joey and indifference toward Scott Pharr, were not the problem. The problem was that Scott Pharr and Joey were friends, and now I began to see how stupidly I'd trapped myself.

Now, when it was too late, when May suddenly dawned bright and yellow and fresh, like a Godzilla-size dandelion monster come to ruin my great cities and then trash the remains, I began to see really how much the whiskey had set me back, and really just how off my game I'd been. I saw how careless I'd been all along, and how I'd made such an irrevocable error in wondering if Ratt Stilskin was setting me up for a fall with Joey when the real plan for sabotage had never stopped silently and efficiently ticking away behind the scenes. I saw how the person who had been behind that real plan all along had been me.

So why did I do it? Why did I fuck Scott Pharr? There were dozens of guys to choose from, there were a few different guys I already had something going on with, so why Scott Pharr? Why—if I felt the way about Joey that I claimed to feel inside my own head—did I sleep with one of his friends? And after he'd only been gone a few short weeks?

I fucked Scott Pharr for a million different reasons. I did it so Joey wouldn't ever be real to me. I did it to drive him from me, because I only loved him when he was gone and the people I loved who were right here—right in front of me—I always ended up hating. I did it because Lo and I were still fighting it out in the same little body and I was getting weaker every day. I did it because most of the time now I honestly didn't care anymore, not about anything, and if it hurt less to toss everything I had over the edge—borrowed or owned, crazy bits of love and trash—then Joey was going first. But most of all I did it because I knew that out of all the people I met and talked to and fucked, out of all the people I watched and had been watching for so many years, out of all those shitty people I hated—I was the shittiest, and the one I hated the most was Leah, and after that, Lo.

I had, after all, been the one who was so weak as to let her in.

Joey came back in the middle of May. I found out—as I found out everything these days—from Ratt Stilskin. One night, after walking in the door from work, I answered the phone.

"Hello Leah."

It was Ratt Stilskin. My stomach clenched and I waited for the familiar punch. I stayed silent.

"Thought I'd let you know that he'll be back in Seattle tomorrow. Just exactly how does that make you feel?" The punch was a dead click in my ear.

One week passed and then two. May started thinking seriously about turning into June. There was nothing from Joey. No phone call and no message sent through Ratt Stilskin. Not one word.

I refused to talk about it.

I still saw Ratt Stilskin. It was impossible not to see Ratt Stilskin. One night as we sat in my car underneath the Viaduct, I realized that I was just too goddamn drunk, my head and my hands too heavy. I raised one hand and then watched it falter and die on the seat next to me like a broken bird. But then Ratt Stilskin picked up the dead hand and it wasn't dead after all. With the precision of a surgeon he guided my hand to the ignition and held on, turning the key with me, with my dead hand that had come alive again, staring into my eyes the entire time. His eyes burned bright with whiskey.

"Nothing is over, Leah."

The ignition caught under my hand. I realized I was powerless, Lo was nowhere. The veil was full of holes. The bottle of tequila under the driver's seat was finally empty.

"You're not the one to say when it's finished—or *what's* finished—anymore." He grinned at me.

Ratt Stilskin dropped my hand and gently put the car into drive. The fatigue I'd felt only moments ago vanished. It wasn't yet two o'clock and there was another bar to go to. No, it wasn't finished—Ratt Stilskin was right—it wasn't finished by a long shot.

When we got there I turned to smile at Ratt but he was gone. I put my hand out to feel the leather of the seat. It was cold. I got out of the car and looked up and down the deserted street. It was late and no one was around but I could see the winking neon of the bar just a block away. I shrugged and wrapped my coat tighter around myself. There was still time to get another shot of whiskey. I started humming to myself and began to walk faster.

At the beginning of June my car caught fire. Sadie and I were on the way home from the bookstore when something under the hood bucked wildly and then—KA-CHUNK—fell out from under the car. All power gone, I coasted to the side and parked. Sadie jumped out and popped the hood.

"Oooohhhhh...FUCK. Run! Run now! FUCKING RUN!!!"

I ran from the car and toward Sadie, her small black shadow disappearing fast into the darkness ahead. Focusing on the tiny determined shape, I caught up with her and then turned around. Panting hard, I looked back at the car.

It was engulfed in flames.

Orange streamers of fire exploded into the sky. I heard cozy popping and crackling noises like we were in front of a fireplace at Christmas. I turned back toward Sadie and saw the small pale oval of her face outlined in flame and shadows.

That night, after the cops drove us home, I lay in bed and stared at the same ceiling I'd been staring at for almost two years now. I knew my soul was dying. I could feel it. But I didn't want to die. Right now I didn't really want to live either, but I wasn't sure exactly what I wanted to do. If I stayed in Seattle the choice would be made for me. If I stayed in Seattle I would die.

It was time to go. I saw now that all of my ideas about New Orleans and San Diego had come to nothing because neither city was what I needed it to be. I needed another life and another chance. The name of one city flickered in the back of my mind as I stared at that ceiling and then the vision came. I saw neon on red brick walls and Joan Rawshanks in the fog. I knew now, and all at once, that there was nowhere else to go. Settled on a decision, I rolled over and fell asleep.

I was going to San Francisco.

Chapter 14

I had never been to San Francisco before. I had never even visited California. But I had never been to Seattle before either when I moved to find Jared and I'd figured it out. I assumed I would figure out San Francisco too. I just had to get there. I made immediate plans to cash in the insurance policy on my car and started packing.

As I sorted everything into boxes from my room and the little kitchen I shared with Sadie, I started sorting through the boxes I kept hidden away inside my mind too. It hurt to look at those boxes. It hurt to even think about them. When I brushed up against them pain throbbed through every inch of my brain and when I tripped over them in the dark I felt sharp and glowing teeth sink into my ankles. In the dim light of my thoughts I could just barely make out the script that crawled across the labels —*Jared*, *Tom*, and other faded names, all of them male. Behind these boxes there was another whole stack and for some reason this pile terrified me the most. Whenever I glanced at the sign hanging over it—a small plain card that read simply *First Life/ Family*—my nerves screamed in agony.

Shortly after I had announced I was moving, Sadie had

decided she was done with Seattle too. She was scheduled to take off for Chicago the first week of August. But we still had to make it through the middle of the Seattle summer, and the sneak attack heat waves that came with it.

The bookstore didn't have air-conditioning and in the thick of July Sadie and I felt like pigeons cooking in a clay pot. We kept bottles of water with us at all times and strategically aimed the electric fans at ourselves while we shelved, but we still succumbed to the heat. Sweat streamed down our backs and in between our breasts, staining our shirts with wet black hourglasses. Our cheeks were always warm as if we were running fevers and our hands always smelled funny, sort of like hamsters, and sort of like we had just pulled them out of someone's crotch.

The heat wanted to destroy us. Without mercy it followed us around the store and sucked our energy until we were exhausted by the end of the night, flickering like sick light bulbs.

The books still held the same soothing power for me that they had three years earlier when Jared left me and something in my mind broke and then never healed quite right again. Sadie and I were the only ones who worked the store at night. I wandered through the thick hot air and trailed my hand over the rows of familiar titles. Fixed at key points, they made the only path I'd ever known.

I sat in the children's section and read poetry. I hid in the business section from the few evening customers who trickled in (no one ever shopped the business section at night) and read the autobiography of a fat girl who wanted to be skinny. I lay on my stomach amongst the paperbacks and paged through murder mysteries, memorizing the formulas. Sometimes I just sat in the back room up on the book buying table, swinging my legs and kicking it with my heels, and talked to Sadie about the end of summer coming and how sad I was that we were moving away from each other.

At night, after getting home from work, I lay in bed and twisted from side to side, buckling into a half circle when a particularly bad spasm of pain hit. My mind turned around itself relentlessly, swinging between Ratt Stilskin and Joey, and then between Joey and Jared, and then between Jared and everything that had come before, in that (First Life) time before Seattle, and then back between Joey and Ratt Stilskin again. My brain spun until it was so dizzy and sick that it left long ropes of foamy drool hanging between all the thoughts, binding them together in a hot sticky spider web. Sometimes the brain vomited uncontrollably all over me. I whisper-groaned in the dark so that Sadie wouldn't hear me. I never cried anymore, or maybe, I never remembered crying anymore. I couldn't be sure.

Lo had finally gotten what she wanted. I stood in a cold lost place totally alone and looked out into nothing. The nothing looked like the sky in Seattle, and like every sky I'd ever stared at while lying alone in the fields around the farm where I grew up as a kid. I didn't have the luxury of tricking myself anymore. This wasn't about Joey. I wasn't lying awake at night in pain thinking about him. The thought of him didn't make me cringe. Nothing made me cringe. It wasn't about something else either. Just like before, when Jared had left me, it didn't seem to be about anything at all.

～

Ratt Stilskin still called sometimes, but I never returned his calls. When I ran into Scott Pharr I hardly remembered meeting him. My life two months before seemed like a movie I'd watched five years ago.

But then one night around 3:00am the phone rang and, without opening my eyes, I picked it up and croaked a rusty hello. It was Scott Pharr.

"...And in the bushes there's a man...there's a MAN! He's bleeding...maybe a broken arm...he's a MAN! Not a broken robot, he's bleeding and we have to help...he's THERE!"

I cracked one eye open. Then I hung up. I rolled over and went back to sleep.

The phone rang again.

The same nightmare. I opened my eyes and then squinched them shut again and clenched my teeth. Poising my thumb directly over the OFF button, I mentally gave Scott Pharr the finger as I prepared to hang up on him again.

"Wait! Leah. Please don't hang up. I need you and it's really important."

It was the first fully intelligible sentence I'd ever heard out of Scott Pharr.

Ratt Stilskin was the man in the bushes he'd been talking about the first time he called. And he was still in the bushes. He was hiding in the bushes, from the cops.

Earlier that evening Ratt had been driving the car of one of his many lady friends. He'd gotten into a fender bender with another car and switched seats with the chick, who had been in the passenger seat when the accident happened. But the other driver saw the switch and yelled that he was calling the cops. Ratt was already on probation for three DUIs and he'd get certain jail time if he was caught and breathalized. He took off running and dove into the thick brush at the edge of the park next to the street.

Somewhere along the way he got lost. Somewhere in the dark he ran up a hill without knowing he had reached the top and catapulted full speed down the other side. And some time later, after taking cover in the bushes and listening to the cops and dogs come after him, he realized his whole left side was throbbing because he'd broken his arm.

Ratt stayed in the bushes for a long time, maybe for hours (Scott Pharr wasn't sure), experimenting with the injured arm in different positions and calling his most loyal contacts from his cell phone. Joey was unreachable, and so Ratt had called Scott Pharr and Scott Pharr didn't know who to call so he called me. And here we were...he finished in between ragged gulping breaths.

I lay on my back and stared at the shapes moving on the dark ceiling above me. Was it possible that even the most ephemeral of shadows could take on life? I asked Scott Pharr why Ratt Stilskin didn't simply extricate himself from the bushes and grab a cab home.

"COPS!" Scott Pharr exclaimed furiously. "And he's only a man! A MAN in the bushes!" Ratt wasn't only hiding in the bushes from the cops, he reminded me. He was also hiding from the German Shepherds they'd set loose and the helicopters flying overhead searching for him with wide slashing searchlights, cutting up the dense greenery of the park like flimsy black construction paper.

I yawned and scratched the sleep out of my eyes.

"Scott Pharr—" I broke through the gibberish. "What do you want me to do? Go in there and get him? Root around in the bushes until I find him and drag him out? Or maybe I should go down there with a bucket of water and wash away the blood trail before the cops follow it to his body? You know—"

"Leah—" Scott Pharr interrupted me.

"Jesus! What!" I snapped, squeezing my eyes shut.

"I just need help," he said in a small scared voice.

I squeezed my eyes tighter. I really was an asshole.

"I'm sorry Scott Pharr," I let out a long breath. "But there's nothing I can do." Hoping the disconnection wouldn't shatter his fragile belief in humanity at this too-late hour, I softly pressed the OFF button and hung up the phone.

This time he didn't call back.

The next day Ratt Stilskin called around noon. He'd just gotten out of jail and wanted to see me as soon as possible. I suggested a bar but he cut me off and said no. Irritated, I suggested the pizza place two blocks away from my apartment. If we weren't going to a bar then I wasn't going out of my way. We agreed to meet in half an hour.

I spotted him when I walked in. Sitting at one of the tables in back, Ratt hunched in on himself and looked around nervously like an old Nazi coasting into senility in Argentina who knows he's still hunted. He didn't look like death, not yet at least, but he looked like shit. That's how everyone looks the morning they get out of jail, like they've just been put through a dishwasher.

When he saw me he patted the chair next to him with his good arm. I saw that his other arm—the left—was in a very clean-looking sling. I noted the contrast between the crisp white cast and the rest of him, and pulled the chair he offered away and across the table. I saw the dim resignation in his face as I sat down. We weren't friends anymore. We were only fellow drunks.

I sat there for the next 20 minutes while Ratt Stilskin stared down at the small round circle of table between us and quietly laid out what exactly he was going to do. I listened without caring. I knew he just needed to get it out—the story, the craziness, the sound of the German Shepherds triumphantly barking his location in the bushes to the police. Like most drunks who want to know the worst of what they did before they hear it from the wrong person, he had to tell the story over again because he hadn't really been there when it was going on, when it was happening to him. The person who had hit the other car, run from the cops, and broken his arm had only filled him in on half the details. He was working out the rest the next day right here with me. It was something I had done countless times.

When he came to the end he dovetailed seamlessly into plans for the future. Getting an appointment with Michael Blackstone, getting the signatures from AA, getting his hands on cash quickly.

Unlike his normally cheerful evil self, Ratt Stilskin spoke in a monotone. He stared at the table the entire time.

When he was done he finally looked up at me. We locked eyes for a second before giving a curt nod. We pushed back our chairs at the same time and stood facing each other. I felt like maybe we were going to shake hands, but knew we wouldn't. We never touched each other when we were sober.

"Well...see ya around." I started toward the door.

"Yeah," Ratt replied. He stared out the window as I left him. And walking home, I still felt nothing. Ratt Stilskin had broken his fucking arm and I wasn't even happy about it.

Like everything else lately, I didn't feel much about it at all.

Chapter 15

Sometimes at night at the bookstore I stayed in the backroom, buying books from customers that brought them in late and packing and unpacking boxes, but mostly just listening to Sadie's music and thinking. One night I put on one of Sadie's albums, something by the Cure that was her favorite. It was called Disintegration. I didn't know anything about it but I liked the name. It filled out and defined the edges of what I was feeling, what was going on in the spaces in between.

I cleaned as I listened. I stacked all the boxes neatly, wiped down the counters, and then began sweeping. The back door stood open and my eyes were drawn again and again to the deep soft blackness outside. I could hear crickets chirping.

The parking lot was empty. I stopped and held the broom handle to my chest. I felt the stillness all around me. It swelled with the music and then something in me let go. The only thing that had really happened to me—the only thing that was still real—was that my family had died one by one. First my little brother when I was 8 years old, then my mother when I was 11, and then my grandmother who raised me, right after I'd turned 17. And even though it took almost nine years for me to lose all three, the cancer working its deadly magic slowly in all of them, it seemed like a few short months. Like I had woken up one morning to see that it was all of a sudden the end of autumn and everything was dead all around me.

The night and the music, the ugly parking lot and the slick handle of the broom under my fingers, the feeling of slowly crumbling to death inside my heart...disintegration was a good word for it, I thought.

~

I headed to 6 Points one morning at the end of that summer with the intention of having breakfast, but when I got there I ordered a double Bloody Mary instead, and when I finished it I was in no mood to go back home. I was getting that distinct early-morning buzz that had me convinced the world was my oyster and there was no going back now.

But an hour later—after ordering a Mai Thai and sucking on it for a few minutes—I was bored again. I was high off the drunk I had going, it was 9:00am and I hadn't run into anyone I knew. If I didn't figure out a strategy the boredom was going to plant itself on me permanently after my next drink. By noon I'd be in a blackout. I had no choice but to leave the booth and prowl around the small dark bar until I either found or made a friend.

Because 6 Points was so small I was able to see the entire contents of the room I was in. The contents were not promising. Behind me was a heavyset slag of a woman with greasy gray-blonde hair and some old guy who was loud and pounded his fists on the table every few seconds. There were a couple of chicks sitting up at the bar who were obviously continuing the party from the night before. But they seemed to be more interested in making out with each other than drinking.

There were a lot more people on the other side of the bar, but no one I knew. Everyone looked like they were with someone already or having fun in small groups, probably with old friends they'd known for at least ten years. No one looked alone or crazy or even high voltage. And then I saw someone, someone I thought I knew.

Yes, I definitely recognized the guy. I'd seen him around the Square, but I'd also run into him the night before.

I'd been standing at the end of the Cellar's long bar when I'd run into him. He'd said hello and then told me his name was James when I flashed him a quick polite smile. I hadn't been drunk yet and I wasn't interested. If I stayed cold from the first he'd get the picture and move off. And after a few more minutes of cordial conversation he did.

But now, at 6 Points, when it was 9:00am and I had no one else, well, now I was interested.

The guy—James I reminded myself—was standing at the bar taking shots. He was small like me, but he looked tough. Really tough. It wasn't just the tattoos that covered his arms and neck or the nose ring, it was the dark circles under his eyes, black rings that made him look like he'd died and come back. Even though he looked friendly enough—I saw him trading jokes with the bartender, and shaking hands and slapping palms with almost everyone that came in—those circles under his eyes showed me that whatever darkness was in him was never very far beneath the surface.

And he did seem to know just about everyone who came in, a point that piqued me. I didn't know anyone and I needed someone now. In fact, I didn't know anybody but that guy—James, I reminded myself again. Curious, I walked toward him.

When he saw me he smiled but his face didn't light up. He remembered me from around and my name from the night before but he shook my hand just like everyone else instead of giving me a hug and rubbing my back or feeling me up in the process. I wondered if my hungover bloated cheeks or my hair that I hadn't bothered to wash had finally become too much. Was it that bad? But I had just checked myself in the restroom mirror and nothing had looked awry. I shrugged uneasily inside. There was time and it was only the first few moments. I promised myself that within an hour he'd be under my control and smiled widely at him. I suggested we get more shots and go back to my booth and he agreed. Soon we were back in the near dark, just where I felt the most comfortable.

The shots came and we drank them without the nuisance of a toast. I immediately ordered more. He didn't flinch. When they came he drank his down like it was water.

Talking with James was one of the weirdest experiences I had ever had. For maybe the first time ever, I felt like I was talking to someone normal. James didn't ask me what I did for a living or what I liked to do "for fun," a question that always made my gorge rise. He didn't look away when I peppered him with questions. He just answered them, simply and honestly. Suddenly, I didn't care anymore about getting him under my control. I was having a good time, for the first time in a long time. Oddly, I wanted to be exactly where I was and I was okay with everything around me. It was surreal.

What was even weirder was that James didn't seem to be getting any drunker. He'd been there since the wee hours of the morning when he'd gotten off work from one of the nightclubs in the Square. He'd been drinking the whole morning and now it was almost noon but the rims of his eyes were only slightly red. Other than that, he seemed perfectly sober.

As the afternoon wore on we continued our funny, strange, and, by turns, curious conversation. We talked about sex and what worms people were and how it had become too hard to get a quality piece of ass these days. James didn't use our sex talk against me, he didn't take it as an opening and he didn't try to make it one either. In fact, he didn't do much at all but sit across from me and let me talk, and talk himself sometimes. It seemed like what a lot of other people had done with me in the past few years, but I always ended up wanting to leap across the table and choke the shit out of them. Somehow James was doing it in a different way.

I switched to wine to stave off the blackout. I was pretty sure that the 6 Points wine was really cooking sherry from the kitchen, but I didn't care—it would do. My head got heavier anyway and I suggested we break out of the bar and go to the beach.

When we got to the waterfront park just minutes away I bounded toward the water like a drunk Golden Retriever and promptly lost my balance at the edge. I fell over and landed on my ass, then skidded down the rocks toward the water on my palms. With my feet in the surf I raised my hands and saw thin red rivulets of blood coursing to my wrists. I couldn't feel a thing. But the blood was kind of gross. I looked around for a makeshift bandage and lunged for a slimy green hank of seaweed floating around my ankles. I slapped it on and raised both arms to James triumphantly, still reclined on my ass and lost in the rocks, and waved.

James stood on the grass a little ways up the hill, before the rocks began, and intently puffed on a cigarette. He squinted into the sun but didn't try to shade his eyes, and I realized now that when I had run, slipping and falling down the rocks to the water's edge, he hadn't tried to stop me. I had the same feeling I had around Bret and Sadie and Cass. I felt like he would leave me alone. There was something in James that blocked me from seeing into him, and instinctively I knew this thing was stronger than me, faster than my tactics. It might be called integrity or grit, but what it felt like was steel woven through his character. He wouldn't interfere with me because he didn't need me. He didn't *need* anybody. He already had himself.

And there was something else. James could see into people like I could. I didn't know how I knew that, but I did. I had watched him closely at 6 Points when he talked to people, and whatever it was I had, that receiving ability that I couldn't turn off, he had it too, and he used it just like I did.

I had never met anyone else like me. Considering the possibilities, a bright happy bubble formed in my mind and I watched it float and shine as I lay back on my elbows and let the ice-cold water of the Sound wash over me. I looked back up the beach and saw James still standing there, smoking his cigarette determinedly in the glare of the sun. I waved again and then looked back out over the Sound. It was going to be a good day.

Chapter 16

Right before I left for San Francisco, Cassady and I flew to New York to visit my father. We stopped at the Cellar on our way to the airport and Cassady got wasted. Our flight was a red eye and my dad was scheduled to pick us up at La Guardia the next morning. I didn't drink anything because I didn't want to be coming off a drunk when we met my dad, who I hadn't seen in almost two years.

Cassady got drunker at the airport and then progressed into a full scale pain-in-the-ass by the time the plane took off, knocking her drink down the front of herself and some of it into my lap as the engines picked up speed. She passed out a few minutes later and spent the rest of the flight snoring peacefully next to me with her mouth open. From my aisle seat I pushed her to the other side until I heard the soft thunk of her head hitting the window. The flight attendants turned out the lights and passed out blankets, but I sat wide-eyed and strung out sober in the dark until we covered enough distance to fly into the sunrise yawning and stretching itself over New York.

My dad was the same as I remembered him. Feet planted shoulder-width apart, settled into his hips, his arms crossed in front of him like a small, strong fort, eyes always crinkled up and smiling. But whenever I spoke his eyes went empty, and then it seemed like he looked right through my skull and the wall behind me. That summer, I still believed he could see through things like that—that he could especially see through me. I couldn't remember a time when he didn't use that laser-like vacant glance. I figured he had looked through me so many times by now that he didn't really see me at all anymore.

My dad grabbed our baggage off the conveyor belt as Cassady rubbed crumbling black mascara out of her eyes and I sniffed my armpits. He ushered us outside to a long black car that wasn't exactly a limo but still got the same idea across. We slid into the air-conditioned interior and my dad gave the driver his address. The inside of the car was dark and the seats felt smooth and dry, like the hands of a capable doctor as he feels for the lump in your breast. We glided over the bridge in our air-conditioned shell and my dad and I smiled at each other as he asked me about Seattle and I asked him about New York and Cassady continued to dig bits of sleep and make-up out of her eyes.

My dad's apartment was a spacious one-bedroom in the heart of Greenwich Village. The inside was almost bare. But of course, there was an aquarium. It had always been the one thing he cared for meticulously. The walls were covered with art, a small Picasso winking out from a corner, a Matisse positioned elegantly in the hall, and a Rembrandt sketch he had purchased for my grandfather before he died hung with sophisticated understatement front and center in the living room.

No sign of my stepmother. They were still married but she lived in another state. His job in New York was the other woman.

That night my dad and Cassady and I went out to Times Square. After a short nap that afternoon I woke up with the drink thirst burning in my throat. I had that familiar feeling I always got when I went without drinking, the feeling of not being able to get enough oxygen. Like I was trapped under a blanket and breathing recycled air.

My dad was itchy to drink too. In spite of the drunk she had been on the night before, the six-hour plane ride, and the jet lag, Cassady splashed some water on her face—finally vanquishing the last of the tar-like mascara—changed into a sundress, and looked fresh as a daisy. I wasn't hungover but I was still tired. Way more tired than usual, and lately I couldn't seem to pull out of it. I battled the fatigue uphill every day now, feeling like I was in one of those dreams where I had to get to some urgent emergency but I was stuck swimming through mud. But I was also my father's daughter, and while I didn't care so much about seeing Times Square, he'd mentioned gin martinis and I knew they would be dry.

We had planned on bar-hopping, but ended up staying at one bar all night. It was an Irish pub, a lot like the Emerald Crow, but I couldn't remember the name even when I was sitting in the middle of it. O'Flunnery's? O'Leander's? O'Lunney's? The name flitted past like a fish. When I tried to seize it, it slipped through my fingers and darted away. After my third martini they all seemed to be the same name and it didn't matter anymore. Halfway through my fourth, nothing mattered anymore.

It was at this stage that I tried actually talking to my dad.

I chewed on half of my olive while searching for words. None came. I wanted to talk about my mom, and about my brother. My dad never talked about either of them. I willed myself to speak, to say anything at all in the hopes of starting somewhere. But nothing happened. My mouth locked shut. I was too drunk to see my dad clearly, but I knew he was giving me that same vacant see-through-you look. I would have known it if I had just given up and shut my eyes. And a few minutes later it was like I had done just that.

I was in a blackout when we left the bar and when the three of us walked through Times Square with arms linked, singing silly songs. I was in a blackout when Cassady twisted her knee and fell, bringing me and my dad down with her. I was in a blackout when we got back to the apartment and my dad hauled out his old record player. I was in a blackout the whole time, the veil came down right around the end of the fifth martini, right after I tried to tell my father something—maybe something urgent, maybe even something that constituted an emergency—but as always, I was still swimming in mud.

I was in a blackout. I ended up telling him nothing at all.

The next afternoon Cass and I sat on my dad's balcony, which overlooked another Irish bar, and lazily sipped Coronas. We tried to move as little as possible in the heat. The air of August in New York City felt baked. The brick buildings across from us shimmered. In between cursing the heat and working on the Coronas, we eyed the bar below and discussed the possibilities. When darkness fell like a cool black net over the city, we changed clothes and made our way across the street.

After finishing our first shots of whiskey, we took our beers outside and sat at a little wrought-iron table that was identical to the tables at the Cellar, a whole country away. It struck me that all bars probably used the same wrought iron table and chair setup. There was probably a catalog called BarMart that everyone ordered from.

Cass and I started a conversation with the guys at the table next to us, and a couple hours later we all went to another bar, the same place we'd been the night before—O'Flunnery's or O'Leander's or O'Lunney's—I still couldn't get the name right. But when I looked around I saw it was actually the Crow, and it was the bar across the street from my dad's, and it also might have been called 6 Points. From the gleaming mirrors advertising different liquors, to the shink-shink-shink sound of the bartender cocking his elbow back and forth to shake that next martini, to the low click of the pool balls in the back, it was the exact same bar I'd been sitting in for four years now.

I sat with my martini and watched Cassady and our new friends play darts. I noticed how much these guys looked like people we already knew. A hot wave of nausea rose in me and I covered my mouth. I took a long drink from my martini to force it down.

On the way home I played unconscious, covering the upper half of my body with my coat, and gave one of the guys a blow job in the backseat. Afterward, watching the sun rise on the balcony with Cassady, I felt much better.

Our last day in New York my dad threw a party for us. He invited Gogo Rezzi, a guy whose father I'd heard about all my life —he had been my grandfather's medical partner. My grandfather had been a brilliant surgeon, just like my father had become after him, and his partner was a man everyone in my family had spoken of with high admiration and esteem.

I'd never met Gogo Rezzi or his dad, but the moment Gogo walked in I knew it was him. He looked about 30 but I knew he was closer to 60. He had dreadlocks down to his knees and was wearing a plain thin white t-shirt that said "Fuck Bush" on it in block letters on the front. His boyish face broke into a grin as soon as we were introduced. A few minutes later he and Cassady and I were seated around the kitchen table with glasses of wine, talking and laughing like we'd known each other forever.

Gogo started telling us all about his past overdoses as soon as we sat down. He said he had OD'ed on heroin, but the really bad one was when he did it on PCP. He gulped the last of his wine fast and poured another glass as he told us how he woke up from the PCP binge in the hospital with his dad, who he thought was a giant man-size beetle, sitting on the bed and staring at him. The beetle started talking and even though it looked like a beetle he recognized the voice of his father. His dad's voice coming out of the beetle told him he had to make a choice: life or death. If he wanted to choose death, fine, but playing around with it using powders and pills was something a child would do and not a man. Then the-beetle-who-was-really-his-dad told him over and over again that he loved him. He quit the drugs after that.

But he still drank. A lot, judging from the quantity of wine he'd already taken down in our half hour conversation.

I swirled my own wine and thought about Gogo Rezzi's dad. I always pictured him like my grandfather—intellectual and sophisticated, and above all, respectable. Someone who didn't swear around women and always stopped after his second Manhattan. I tried to picture my grandfather sitting at his child's hospital bedside after an overdose on PCP. I tried to hear him telling me that I had to make a choice—the choice was now—and if I couldn't make it I really was still a child. But listening for that voice was like everything else...I didn't hear anything at all.

Then another of my dad's friends showed up—a music producer big shot who brought his hip pretty girlfriend—and our small party was complete. The music guy had met Allen Ginsberg and lived next door to Gregory Corso. I kept swirling my wine— the only thing I could think to do with it if I wasn't going to slam it —and smiled politely at him. I wondered if he would look at me so friendly and nice if I told him I had spoken to Jack Kerouac just last night in my dreams, that he had sat me on his knee, in fact, and looked at me sadly and told me my body was dying. I had a feeling the music guy, a nice man with the innocuous name of Dale, would give me that look I'd seen so many times before. The look that said I was crazy, and that I couldn't be believed.

But I kept my weird thoughts to myself and that look never crossed music producer Dale's face. I swirled my wine and he talked about all the people he knew and I assumed this must be what normal life was like.

At the end of the night, after wine and dinner, dessert and

more wine, Gogo Rezzi pulled out a collection of what looked like postcards. But as he fanned them out and passed them around I saw they were something different. Cassady paused and held one up to the light as we examined it. It was a small piece of card stock, brilliantly white with a circular colored design in the center. The blue of oceans and sapphires, red fire, and the dazzling green of parrot feathers flashed and jumped between us as we passed the cards around. After Cassady and I studied the first, I slowed down and took in each one carefully. They were exquisite—alive and beautiful and perfect.

Gogo explained that he didn't sleep much. He'd been touring with a dance company for a while and last year when they were in Tokyo he stayed up and roamed the streets for hours after the show ended and everyone else was in bed. During these nocturnal wanderings he noticed the manholes in Tokyo, or rather the manhole covers, each of which had engraved designs. As he bent over again and again all over the city, all that night and through the dawn, he found that the design on each manhole cover was unique. The next night he went out and made rubbings of every manhole cover he came across. When he came home he copied the rubbings exactly and colored them in. These were the cards we were looking at now.

I turned the last one passed to me over in my hands. For some reason it made me feel like I might start crying. I saw Gogo Rezzi in my mind, squatting down on 59-year-old knees, dreadlocks swaying rhythmically as he repeated his process, rubbing a manhole cover—the entrance to the sewer and the gate to all of our shit in one form or another—stooping there I saw him, rubbing and rubbing so vigorously, getting everything that he could, making what is beautiful—willing that beauty—out of something everyone else just stepped over.

Clutching the card to my chest, my heart beat fast. For the first time maybe ever I lost interest in my glass of wine and it actually sat untouched beside me. Seeing the odd expression on my face, Gogo Rezzi leaned over and asked me if I wanted to keep the card. I nodded mutely, feeling like I really would start crying soon if I didn't watch it, and he folded my hand in his hand over the card and smiled at me.

And finally, I felt something. Although I didn't know at all what that meant.

On the plane ride back, I thought about choosing between life and death, and I tried to remember what my grandfather's voice had sounded like.

Chapter 17

By the end of that summer James and I were together. Although neither of us could explain exactly what that meant in words, we knew without having to talk about it. And I knew I loved James in that same way, without talking about it, without even having to ask myself.

When I woke up at the crack of dawn after a bad drunk, James was on his back beside me, eyes wide and dry, his chest hitching upward in short little gasps, silently fighting the panic written in his dark-circled eyes. When he saw I was awake, he moved closer to the window and cracked it open, lighting a cigarette without saying anything. Smoking half of it furiously, he violently stabbed it out on the windowsill before settling his large tortured eyes on mine.

"I have to go," he said. And then he went.

I hadn't been wrong. James was just like me.

James had grown up on an island about two hours north of Seattle. A few days after I got back from New York he took me there. We went in his car, a black mud-spattered machine with tinted windows and an overflowing ashtray inside, and drove around the whole island, which seemed even bigger than James had promised.

On one long stretch tree branches and thorny tendrils reached out to brush the car windows, the only other sign of life a few cows in the field next to the road. It was eerily similar to the Midwest countryside I'd grown up in. It was like being back there again, only I wasn't. I was still living in Seattle. My family was still dead.

My mind looped back for a second, started to skip, and then righted itself with the slippery footing of a ship in a storm.

I looked over at James. He smiled in his constrained way and passed me the joint we were smoking. I fielded it neatly and took a long drag. The black car emerged from the trees and into the sunlight of the fading day. Lo, the veil, the thirsting drink-want, the broken pieces of my life—all of it seemed far away, like it had happened a long time ago.

And Lo was quiet, like she was asleep, or comatose...

Or (*maybe*) gone.

Maybe for good.

But I couldn't think about that too much, because the thought of her name—the saying of it to myself—was a way to rouse her, a ritual of sorts. Her name was an incantation, a chant to wake the dead. And although I missed her strangely and achingly, if she *was* gone, if she was sleeping, I didn't want to wake her up.

I watched the trees stream by and smiled at James when he passed me the joint again.

Two days before I left for San Francisco I stood with James in the parking lot of a sushi restaurant as we decided how many bottles of sake to order before the food came. He took my hands and faced me. Straight-faced, almost angry, he looked at me hard and said he loved me. Then he looked down at our hands together and dropped mine. I wiped them on my pants and looked back at him. He looked over my shoulder, off and away, and told me he was coming to San Francisco. He would meet me there in two months after he tied up the loose strings of his life in Seattle. Then he looked back at me and set his face. He was going to stand his ground.

"Well, okay." I said. I started walking toward the entrance of the restaurant.

"Okay," he agreed, and he fell into step beside me.

Sadie had taken off the week before, waving out the passenger-side window of the car driving her to Chicago, taking a picture of me waving goodbye and taking her picture at the same time she took mine.

Without Sadie, the apartment felt totally empty. Bret helped me pack my important stuff (books) and I gave away the stuff that didn't matter (everything else). Now, the boxes I was taking with me sat stacked in one of the empty corners of my bedroom, waiting to be moved into the room I still couldn't picture, the room I'd found through an ad online, waiting for me in San Francisco.

It was like I was watching someone else's life. All of a sudden there was James, and all of a sudden Sadie was gone, and all of these things were happening at once, but I couldn't look at them. I couldn't be with them as they were happening. My eyes were frozen, but the rest of me was moving at top speed. I leaned into the future, and the rapid fire of my eyelids beat time to invisible wings behind me. I leaned forward so far and the time beat so fast those wings looked like sails streaming out from the back of me— like a hummingbird's wings in mid flight, only visible through their movement, never through their form.

The days ticked down to the last day, and then it was the last hour.

My room was empty. All the boxes had been loaded into the truck I would drive to San Francisco. James and I sat together on the few blankets we had fashioned into a makeshift bed. It would be two months before I'd see him again and now it suddenly seemed important that I'd never been to San Francisco before, suddenly it seemed crucial.

After gathering the last few things around 5:00am that morning, it was time. James kissed me hurriedly on the cheek and then left with as few words as he normally did. Cassady and Bret gathered around to see me off. We walked out into the cold early morning dark and Cass took one last picture of me in Seattle, standing in front of the truck with a big scared smile on my face. A few minutes later I jumped behind the wheel and headed for the freeway, leaving Seattle behind.

I tried to see the ending of the story, I really did. I thought about all the books I'd read and how their stories were still unfolding inside of me. One of my college professors had told me that Anna Karenina never stopped jumping in front of that train, because she was caught in the pages of a book, and so she would never stop living the moments of her death. It wasn't preservation, it was immortality. I thought about all of these things and tried to have courage, but I didn't feel immortal or even very brave. I just felt like a page was turning and I couldn't see what was on the other side.

So I did the best I could. I drove.

West Coast Trilogy
by Lauren Sapala

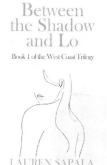  

Book 1: Between the Shadow and Lo – Leah is an alcoholic who is also battling a voice in her head she calls Lo. As Leah spirals deeper into addiction, Lo steadily tightens her hold. As Leah prepares to make one last bid for survival, she knows her only chance is to transcend Lo's terrifying drive toward death.

Book 2: West Is San Francisco – Leah lands in San Francisco, quits drinking, and resolves to live a new life. Then she meets successful writer Scarlet Monroe. When Leah joins Scarlet's cult-like company, she begins to see behind the mask Scarlet has so carefully cultivated, and the demons from her past come alive again.

Book 3: Enormous Forces – After four years in San Francisco, Leah joins another startup in Seattle. Meanwhile, in a parallel universe, the Informant is sent to an alternate Seattle to neutralize the threat of an unnamed assassin. What neither Leah nor the Informant knows is that whatever happens in one world affects the other, and there is no escape until the two—somehow—come together.

About the Author

Lauren Sapala is the author of the West Coast Trilogy: *Between the Shadow and Lo* (Book One), *West Is San Francisco* (Book Two), and *Enormous Forces* (Book Three). She also writes nonfiction books for writers and other creatives. To find out more visit laurensapala.com.

Made in United States
North Haven, CT
03 November 2024

59792608R00176